ON THE BACK OF THE TIGER

Also by Zülfü Livaneli

The Fisherman and His Son
The Last Island
Disquiet
Serenade for Nadia
Bliss

ON THE BACK OF
THE TIGER

Zülfü Livaneli

Translated from the Turkish by
Brendan Freely

OTHER PRESS
NEW YORK

Art on pages iii, 3, 223 from "The sandals (na'layn) of the
Prophet" (Tahlîl al-Qur'ân wa-al-adiyah), Ottoman Empire, 1874.
Manuscripts and Archives Division, New York Public Library
Digital Collections. https://digitalcollections.nypl.org/items/
f9f73930-0759-0131-221c-58d385a7bbd0

Production editor: Yvonne E. Cárdenas
Text designer: Patrice Sheridan
This book was set in Palatino by
Alpha Design & Composition of Pittsfield, NH

1 3 5 7 9 10 8 6 4 2

Library of Congress Cataloging-in-Publication Data
Names: Livaneli, Zülfü, 1946- author. | Freely, Brendan, 1959- translator.
Title: On the back of the tiger : a novel / Zülfü Livaneli ;
translated from the Turkish by Brendan Freely.
Other titles: Kaplanın sırtında. English
Description: New York : Other Press, 2024. |
Includes bibliographical references.
Identifiers: LCCN 2023035504 (print) | LCCN 2023035505 (ebook) |
ISBN 9781635423914 (paperback) | ISBN 9781635423921 (ebook)
Subjects: LCSH: Abdülhamid II, Sultan of the Turks, 1842-1918—Fiction. |
Turkey—History—1878-1909—Fiction. | LCGFT: Biographical fiction. |
Historical fiction. | Novels.
Classification: LCC PL248.L58 K3713 2024 (print) | LCC PL248.L58 (ebook)
| DDC 894/.3533—dc23/eng/20240220
LC record available at https://lccn.loc.gov/2023035504
LC ebook record available at https://lccn.loc.gov/2023035505

Even though, naturally, I dislike the phrase "imperial paranoia," I am unfortunately obliged to accept it because I don't expect that historians will write poems of praise about my father.

—PRINCE ABID EFENDI, SON OF ABDÜLHAMID II

THE MOMENT I WAS born, he thinks, they placed me on the back of a tiger, this is the fate of princes, to grow up on the back of a tiger; a show of strength sufficient to dazzle everyone, the sense of dominating a creature as magnificent as a tiger, feeling the tense spasms of the predator's steely back muscles between your legs, the satisfaction of mastering a cruel-eyed killing machine that everyone fears, privilege, superiority, being seen as a god, but also fear. Yes, fear. From time to time, a cold shudder like a wet snake slithering down my back makes me tremble from head to toe.

Most princes are born doomed to be killed, he thinks. In our family, have babies not been strangled with eighteen of their older brothers while their mother's milk was still wet on their lips, have silk cords not been wrapped around the necks of hundreds of princes who could not become sultan? He wonders if most of those who were allowed to live went mad after being imprisoned for years in boxwood cells, fearing that each approaching footstep was that of the executioner. He tries, meanwhile, not to think of the brothers he has kept in prison for years.

In this world, you are either the head of state or a raven's carcass. When you're on the tiger's back, you control a great power that obeys your every command, you're mighty, and happy; however, the moment you dismount, the tiger will shred you with its claws like a poor gazelle, it will never hesitate. The only way to live with the tiger is to be its master; you are either its master or its prey.

I didn't choose this, he thinks, no one gets to choose the family they're born into, we all come into the world with our own destinies; in a sense, our fate is to be born on the back of a tiger. You can't change your destiny.

PART
ONE

April 28, 1909

The first night of exile in Thessaloniki—

Ice cream at midnight—Imperial paranoia—

La Traviata

ON THAT DARK NIGHT, Abdülhamid II, the thirty-fourth Ottoman sultan and caliph of the Islamic ummah, pushed himself up off the floor with his right hand, and as his left hand searched for something to hold on to, he touched something soft. He attempted to stand by leaning on it. His arm, his leg, and his hip were hurting. When he was on his feet, he took the lighter he always kept in his caftan pocket and lit it; the flame partly illuminated the dark room, but what he saw in that faint light made his heart tremble even more. First he looked at the object he'd leaned against. A large, dark armchair, he couldn't make out the color, it seemed to be upholstered in velvet, another matching armchair was pushed up against it. Not back to back, but with the seats facing each other. At that moment the sultan remembered everything, it was as if a sudden bolt of lightning had struck his aging body. He was not in the palace in Istanbul, the city in which he'd woken every morning for thirty-three years, he was far away. He was imprisoned in a room in a mansion in Thessaloniki. He held up the lighter and looked around; as his arm moved, the faint light flickered across the decorations on the high ceiling, the shuttered windows, the brown floorboards, and the two armchairs.

The sultan felt an indescribable sense of strangeness. He found himself in this strange room, hungry, deprived, and alone. His children, wives, and servants must have been lying on the floor in various rooms of that empty mansion. After they'd been brought to the mansion and the soldiers had locked the wooden double door, they'd found themselves in a large, empty hall that contained nothing but a dining table. They sat on the floor and hung their heads as if they were embarrassed to even look at one another. Sometime later his eldest daughter had seen the two armchairs that had been forgotten in a corner. Cumbersome armchairs upholstered in dark green velvet. With his daughters' help, the servants carried the armchairs to the room on the left, pushed them together, and said, "My sultan, rest here for tonight and we'll work everything out tomorrow. Your own soldiers would never leave you in these conditions, they must not have had time to get everything ready." Just then he heard the mansion's gigantic door open and saw a commander enter, accompanied by soldiers carrying lamps. It was a stern, soldierly entrance, and the aging sultan, who all his life had feared assassination, felt his nerves on edge. The sound of their boots echoed through the empty mansion, the lamps lengthened the shadows, the severe looks the soldiers gave him and his family and the commander's relatively civilized expression announced that their last hour had arrived. Perhaps they would be lined up right there and shot, perhaps, like everything else, the custom of not shedding dynastic blood was a thing of the past. He noticed that his children stepped in front of him as if to protect him. His wives, his three daughters, and his eldest son were shielding him. The commander, who must have understood what they were thinking, said, "Sir, we've brought you food and water."

The soldiers behind him carried in a large round tray and placed it on the table that stood in the middle of the hall like a statue of loneliness. The commander said, "Please excuse us, your arrival was so sudden we didn't have time to get the mansion ready. Robillon Pasha was living here, he was ordered to move so he took his furniture and left. Hopefully tomorrow we can procure some beds and things from the hotels." The commander seemed sympathetic to the royal family's plight, but the others continued to regard them with hostility.

"Thank you, officer," said the sultan. "Bless you. What's your name?"

"Ali Fethi, sir. I came from Istanbul. I am responsible for you. They said they had this food prepared at Pastacıyan, the best restaurant in Thessaloniki," said the commander. If only he hadn't, because as soon as the sultan heard about food having been prepared, his legendary "imperial paranoia" reared its head and his fears returned. It occurred to him that they were going to be poisoned. He could not eat this food, but he could not refuse it either. He had to find a solution at once. "Commander, my stomach is upset," he said. "I can't eat this. If it's possible, I would like some yogurt and some mineral water." Surprise registered on the commander's swarthy face, but still he agreed to the sultan's request and ordered one of his men to bring yogurt and mineral water.

The soldier rushed out the front door and returned almost immediately. The sultan looked suspiciously at the bowl of yogurt and the unopened bottle of mineral water, but supposed they wouldn't have had time to mix in the poison. Besides, the commander was winning his confidence. He thanked him. As the commander was leaving, he patted the sultan's youngest son on the head and murmured something. Later Zülfet, the overseer of the servants, who'd been closest, reported that he'd said, "Poor little boy," and this led him to begin liking and trusting the commander.

As soon as the front door was locked, the hungry children rushed over to the tray and began lifting all the lids. Unfortunately they were disappointed by what they saw. Most of the plates were empty; there was some yogurt and a few slices of bread but—strangely—there was lots of ice cream. The sultan's family had been taken from the palace and put on a train the day before, they'd been hungry for hours, whose crazy idea had it been to offer them ice cream at that hour? It was clear that the honest-looking commander had no idea about this. He'd responded to the sultan's thanks by bowing respectfully, but not everyone in the army was his friend. The revolutionaries, the guerillas, and the pro-French officers hated the sultan and blamed him for all that was wrong. Perhaps he had more enemies than friends in his own army. Otherwise, when they entered the city to put down an insurrection, would they have taken him from his palace and packed him off to Thessaloniki?

The children ate a bit of yogurt and bread and then, as they were about to turn their attention to the ice cream, the sultan shouted, "Stop! Do not eat that ice cream!" It was clear that the poison was in that ice cream. Why else would they send something so meaningless? The family, gathered around the table, stopped in surprise and pulled back their hands, but he saw that his eldest son already had some ice cream on his mouth. Oh no, he said to himself, my son is gone, my prince is gone. There was no silverware on the tray. There was nothing to eat with. So the prince had stuck his finger into the ice cream. They thought this was why their father had shouted, "Stop!" They were civilized children who had grown up in the palace, they knew all the rules of etiquette and politeness, they'd had private tutors teach them piano, singing, French, and Italian. Surely they would know better than to eat ice cream with their hands.

The sultan realized this, and decided not to say anything. In any event, his son had already eaten the ice cream, it was too late. There was no point in frightening the boy, and perhaps he was being paranoid for nothing. He quietly withdrew to the room that had been prepared for him, holding a bowl of yogurt and an unopened bottle of mineral water. He stopped in the doorway and addressed his family and the servants. "May God grant you peace. Our Lord knows what's best for us. He protects us and watches over us. We will see what tomorrow brings." More than thirty people politely wished him good night, then after he had closed the door, the family began eating the ice cream with their fingers. When they'd had their fill, the servants gathered to finish the rest.

The sultan took out the pocketknife he always carried, ate some yogurt with it, used it to open the bottle of mineral water, then after quenching his thirst he curled up on the armchairs. Indeed at the palace—especially during the day after eating—he would lie down on lounge chairs in various rooms, he found beds uncomfortable and occasionally slept under the bed. It had astounded him to see the children eat ice cream with their fingers despite their rigorous upbringing. Even the snow-white Angora cat that seldom left his lap at the palace wouldn't eat anything that was not offered on a fork. She was such a well-behaved, noble creature. Still, he'd seen enough of life to know that hunger could make a person do anything. During the endless wars, people even ate their sandals. But he had taken good care of his army, making sure never to leave them without rations. "May God not punish anyone with hunger," he murmured.

He hated war, but despite this, he'd found himself in the terrible Russian War as soon as he ascended to the throne. Although the sultan didn't admit this to anyone, there had been times after the Russian War, which had devastated the nation and the army, when he'd thought the empire would fall apart, that it would soon be drawing its last breath. His political maneuvers had delayed this end. *I'm a politician*, he thought, *I'm not a soldier. What need was there for war? If only we hadn't entered that war. They convinced me that the army was in good shape, but it seems it wasn't. If only I'd met the tsar, if we hadn't gone to war, everything could have been solved through politics.*

There were many things he praised himself for, but this was the quality that pleased him most. He'd always dealt with the Russians, the English, the French, and the Austrians on the principle of peace, and he'd solved the problems. There had been some confusion along the way, but was it easy to manage so many different nations? He thought of his noble cat, who would starve rather than eat food not offered to it on a fork. He missed the cat, and his clever parrot, and the dog that had managed to get him to love it. He was proud of how these three creatures coexisted under his supervision, and he used this as an example. "Look," he would say, "if these three creatures that nature dictates should tear each other apart can live together,

why can't people?" If they could overcome their in-
stincts and not attack each other, there were many les-
sons to be learned. To do this, one had to establish a
balance of power. In any event, the sovereign was the
father, and the many peoples were his children. Just as
a good father treats his children fairly and justly, for
thirty-three years he had maintained balance among
Muslims, Orthodox, Jews, and Catholics.

The sultan liked to contemplate his virtues—
perhaps because there were few others who remembered them—and to feel pride in them. But at the
moment there was an unconscious thought buzzing
like a fly in the back of his head, making him uneasy,
and undermining his sense of self-satisfaction. What
was it? He went back over everything that had passed
through his mind, and when he remembered thinking
about fathers and children, suddenly it came to him:
What had happened to those who'd eaten ice cream?
There'd been no sounds of distress, so it seemed everything was fine. He felt a sense of relief. Once again
he curled up on the armchairs. The shutters had been
closed from outside, and this gave him a sense of
security. He was a skilled carpenter and wished he
could have brought his tools from the palace. He used
to make closets, desks, and bookcases that contained
secret drawers and safes that no one could open, he
would have had no trouble closing those gigantic
shutters from inside. Those who had deposed him had
promised his life would be spared, but could he trust
those liars? Perhaps the reason they'd brought him as

far as Thessaloniki was their fear of the public reaction if he was killed in Istanbul. No one would rise up over a sultan being killed in an isolated mansion in Thessaloniki—especially if it was kept secret—even those who heard about it would pass it off as gossip. The more he thought about it, the more this ominous logic took hold in his mind. Would it not have been easier to house him in Çirağan Palace, so close to his own palace, by the glistening waters of the Bosphorus? Hadn't he kept his older brother Murad, whom he had deposed, in that palace for so many years? Murad had been forbidden to leave the palace, and he himself would have been willing to accept that condition. In any event, he hadn't left his own palace for years. What could have been wiser than to have a magnificent and elegant prison built for himself during that time of turmoil and assassinations? He could have lived in Çirağan Palace in the same manner. But instead they'd bundled him and his family onto a special train to Thessaloniki. This city also belonged to him, to his dynasty. But of course, it wasn't Istanbul.

As Sultan Hamid thought about this, his imperial paranoia once again raised its head. He no longer had any doubt that he'd been brought there to be killed. At any moment they were going to enter the room and put a silk cord around his neck. He trembled with fear and his mouth had dried out. He got up, felt for the bottle he'd placed next to the armchairs, took a few sips of mineral water, then lit his lighter and looked around the room. He went to the door and listened, but he heard nothing. Would they kill him before they killed his family? He went to the window to listen. There were faint sounds of soldiers walking and talking. These must have been the sentries patrolling the garden, but what if they weren't? With his heart pounding, he thought of the door, any danger he faced would come through the door. He dragged one of the armchairs toward the door. He needed two hands to do this, so he extinguished the lighter. In the dark, taking care not to make any noise, he managed to drag the heavy armchair and push it against the door. Then he dragged the second armchair and pushed it against the other one.

He was out of breath, he would have liked some tincture but he didn't have his medicine bag, he had nothing, not even the Atkinson cologne he always kept within reach. All he had was the yellow bag his daughter had brought out of the palace at the last minute. She'd handed it to him and said, "Father, this is your water bag," though she hadn't known what it contained. In fact what it contained was much more valuable than water, though none of it was of any use to him now. The gold, rubies, and gemstones, the dazzling diamonds from India and Africa, could not help him now. It was a miracle that the poor girl had managed to save this bag from the bandits who had invaded his palace.

When his daughter handed him the yellow bag he'd wanted to kiss her on the forehead, but such a display of affection in the presence of strangers would not have been appropriate. They might have wanted to see what was in the bag—God forbid. Despite the haste with which they were expelled from the palace, he'd managed to put together a small fortune to support his family. At the last moment he'd taken another bag full of gold, jewelry, and cash, but as he was getting into the carriage, one of his men had taken the bag as if to help him and then disappeared. This incident had hurt the sultan deeply, and also proved that he'd been right to suspect he was surrounded by traitors, that what they called his imperial paranoia was in fact founded in reality. No one found it strange that the water bag was locked. Everyone knew that because of his fear of being poisoned, the sultan drank water from sealed bottles that came from a locked bag, he would never drink from an open bottle. In foreign newspapers he frequently encountered mention of imperial paranoia, and he'd even heard it whispered in the palace, but this didn't anger him. If they'd just said paranoia they would have been wrong, but imperial paranoia was correct. In this age, what could be more natural than an emperor fearing for his life? The French newspapers called it *paranoïa impériale*. Look at that, he thought, *paranoïa impériale*. In fact he would have liked to ask each of them: *Have any of your grandfathers been killed while they were on the throne, did your brother lose his mind, did you survive being assassinated by a bomb because you were a minute late getting into your carriage, do you receive daily reports of planned assassinations, did they cut your uncle's wrists to make it*

*look as if he'd committed suicide? These are the realities of
my life. Just look around and see what happens to kings and
shahs. They shot the Russian tsar Alexander. What kind of
paranoïa impériale is it if it always turns out to be true?
In this age, no monarch can keep his head on his shoulders.*

This was why he left those magical palaces on the
shores of the Bosphorus, where the water changed color
from moment to moment, from blue to green, from
purple to lavender, where shearwaters swept past and
seagulls perched on the columns by the quay, and built
himself a kind of high-walled prison on a hill. He collected all kinds of animals and rare plants, had ponds,
mansions, and even an opera house constructed, had
Italian artists on the palace staff, and lived for many
years without leaving the palace grounds except for
the short trip to the mosque for Friday prayers; he appointed one of his most trusted men to run the coffeehouse at which he was the only customer, but he
was still never at ease. Just in case, he sipped his coffee
from two separate cups, only drank water from sealed
bottles, he once even pulled out his own aching tooth
to avoid letting anyone touch his mouth, and brought
in doctors from Europe to check his own doctors' conclusions. He kept track of the changes in Istanbul and
other cities of the empire by studying photographs. He
rode pedal boats in his ponds, spent time with the pea-
cocks, parrots, goldfinches, and gazelles in his park,
with his wives, most of whom hailed from the Caucasus, and his children, and conducted world politics as
if he were playing chess.

This was how he had survived coup attempts, assassination attempts, and bloody uprisings. He also had a network of spies who reported regularly from every corner of an empire that stretched from the Adriatic to the Persian Gulf and from the Caucasus to Africa.

Yes, yes, they'd brought him and his family to Thessaloniki in order to kill them discreetly. He was now certain of this. Opposition to his reign was strong in Thessaloniki, it was swarming with dissident officers, and anarchist ideas had been spreading since the French Revolution. Hadn't the Movement Army that had deposed him come from Thessaloniki? What a twist of luck; the rebels had left this city for Istanbul, where they'd settled, and they'd sent him off to this city that smelled of revolution. What a strange fate this was. Even the city's name was inauspicious. What did Alexander the Great's unfortunate sister have to do with the Ottoman Empire? If only they'd changed the name centuries ago when they conquered the city, but during his time in power it had never occurred to him to do so. The princess after whom the city had been named, Philip's daughter, had become queen but then had been killed like her two sisters. She was an unfortunate child who lost her mother at an early age and remained under the control of her stepmother. He remembered the history books he'd read in the palace library, and began to think that he and poor Thessalonica shared a common destiny. She was born on the day her father, Philip of Macedonia, defeated Thessaly, so he'd named her Victory over Thessaly. Had Thessaly not belonged to him until recently? It was all so similar, and Thessaloniki smelled of death, and its history would now include the murder of an Ottoman emperor.

He listened to what was happening outside, afraid to even breathe. There was no one outside the door to his room. It seemed that everyone had withdrawn to different rooms. The poor princes and princesses were lying on the bare floorboards. There was no sound.

Then a miracle occurred. First he heard a melody being played timidly on an out-of-tune piano, then a young, bright, crystalline voice began to sing an aria. It was his daughter Ayşe Sultan, singing her favorite aria from *La Traviata* so her father could hear, her voice was like a silk shawl fluttering in that dark and isolated mansion.

Discover the new, discover the new day...

As he was to learn the following day, when she found the piano that had been left upstairs temporarily, she decided to play it as a way to say, *Father dear, I'm with you, there's nothing to worry about.*

The sultan couldn't hold back his tears as he listened to this aria being sung in such strange circumstances, and for a brief time the imperial paranoia lifted like a Bosphorus fog dissipating as the sun rose. Weary from the journey, he drifted into a restless sleep to his daughter's lullaby.

Night is the mother of delusion—The former
sultan's confusion—Sheikh Zafir—Queen
Victoria—Sherlock Efendi—Diamond
earrings—A silk cord around the neck

HE DIDN'T KNOW HOW long he'd slept. He woke with a
deep sense of disorientation, and almost at once heard
a loud noise. As he felt his head hit the wood, he wondered if he was dead. He remembered how the soft,
white-bearded Greek Orthodox patriarch, whom he
invited to the palace occasionally because he enjoyed
his conversation, said that people don't realize it when
they die, it's only after their funeral, when they try
to stand and hit their heads on the coffin, that they
realize they're dead. If the patriarch was right, he'd
just hit his head on the coffin. However, thank God,
he was a Muslim, indeed he was the Caliph of Islam,
the successor of the Messenger of God, he could not
be buried in a coffin, he would be buried in a shroud,
and part of that shroud would be opened so his skin
would touch the earth.

As he stood up slowly in the dark room, he remembered his sheikh. When he was young he joined the Shazeli sect, and one day the saintly Sheikh Zafir had said to him, "Look, Hamid, my boy, everyone's destiny is written. Everything is written here." When Sheikh Zafir said this he put his hand on the young disciple's forehead. "However, my boy, you weren't born with one destiny like everyone else, you were born with three destinies. Three destinies were written on your forehead, I don't know which one is valid. You will either rot in prison, become an emperor, or be killed. It seems to me as if you will experience all three of these, very few people in the world experience this."

Hamid looked at his sheikh and said, "Of course I will accept my destiny, what choice do I have, but one of the possibilities seems very remote to me."

"Which one, my boy?" asked the sheikh.

"The sultanate," he replied. "The other two, that is, prison or being killed, seem quite likely, this was the fate of many of my ancestors, but unfortunately the sultanate seems remote, I'm ninth in line for the throne. There's no throne in my destiny, that's why I've decided to go into commerce; I'll buy sheep and raise them, sell wool, milk, buy and sell stocks and bonds, grow wheat. I'll spend very little of the allowance I get from the palace every three months, I'll save money and invest it."

The sheikh said, "I know, my son. God will dictate what happens, you can't know whether or not you'll ascend to the throne."

Things didn't happen the way he thought they would, he ascended to the glorious Ottoman throne, and for thirty-three years ruled an empire that stretched over three continents.

It seemed it was now time for his third destiny. How many thousands of times during his thirty-three years of rule had he woken in panic, his sheets soaked through with cold sweat. His entire life he had suffered in anticipation of this cruel destiny that had been written on his forehead, he had done his utmost to escape it, but now it had finally caught up to him in this strange, dark room. Nothing helped, not camphor baths, nor hot plasters, nor senna tea, nor elixirs prepared by private Jewish doctors, nor the leaches that reminded him of his opponents. Death arrived with the executioners who carried silk cords in their rough, hairy hands. The only privilege granted to the Ottoman family, which had ruled for six hundred years and had given many of its rulers and princes to the executioners, was to not be beheaded by a sharp ax, because dynastic blood could not be spilled, or to be hung with a coarse rope, but to be strangled with a silk cord. But no matter what a person was strangled with, the result was the same. Indeed those dishonorable executioners could even have used their bare hands. All his life, he'd wondered how those of his ancestors who had been strangled with a silk cord had felt in their last moments. His ancestor Young Osman, who hadn't realized how close the throne was to the grave, had been overthrown in a day and strangled in the dungeons of Yediküle... How could the caliph of the earth, the shadow of God, the representative of the Prophet, the ruler of three continents, at whose face no one could gaze, who only the noblest could approach on their hands and knees to kiss the hem of his robe, so suddenly be handed over to the coarse, ruthless executioners? It was said that before he was executed, his unfortunate ancestor had been subjected to an unspeakable evil that would tarnish the Ottoman dynasty forever, but, God forbid, this could not possibly be true. It couldn't be true.

Something strange was happening to him, even with the silk cord around his neck he could speak and hear his own voice. Was this a miracle? What could it be but the intercession of the two masters of the world, to one of whom he was the successor, the beautifully named Muhammed, who left behind a scent of roses that made everyone faint?

He struggled and moaned. "Look!" he exclaimed once again. "Even if you are executioners, you're still my children, my servants, you swore to serve the Ottoman dynasty, God above can see what you're doing now. He's saying that these unbelievers deserve to go to hell, they're killing my caliph. Listen, my children, they've taken me, they've betrayed me, do not be fooled by them, let me tell you the truth: When Kaiser Wilhelm, who visited me twice and had the magnificent German fountain built in front of Topkapı Palace, was accused of stealing Queen Victoria's jewels just because he was my friend, I objected to this and vouched for him. I said that this crime could only have been committed by Tsar Alexander, or Emperor Napoleon, to whom my uncle was so close. Even though I risked angering the great powers, God knows that I did not stray from the path of righteousness. I ordered my thousands of spies across the world to work on solving this mystery, and even offered ten bags of Ottoman gold to Sherlock Efendi, who was clever enough to herd them all like a flock of sheep.

"You might think it was his assistant Doctor Watson who facilitated my contact with the famous detective. But no, I swear it wasn't. I contacted Holmes's creator Conan Doyle. I invited the author to Istanbul and explained what I wanted, and when he promised to help me I awarded him the Order of the Mecidiye and his wife, who revealed too much décolletage, the Order of Compassion. These English are clever, the cleverest people in the world, I've never trusted them. When I was young my uncle Sultan Aziz, may he rest in peace, brought me to London. In London they greeted my uncle with great fanfare. Queen Victoria showed him unparalleled respect and bestowed the Order of the Garter on him, but then they asked my brother Murad to overthrow him. Because they made my brother a Mason. My uncle wasn't useful to them, but my brother was a Mason and he was close to them. He even had the English anthem played at his coronation, can you imagine that, as if this were England. But then my brother lost his mind, he used to stare at the walls and laugh and mutter nonsense, and he was useless to the English. As my sheikh had foreseen, the throne was left to me, no one else wanted it, and since that day they've been after me, for thirty-three years they've done everything they could to get rid of me. Look, I'm telling you the real story, listen to me. The detective Sherlock Efendi, the cleverest of the clever English, discovered clues concerning the stolen diamond. My late father, Sultan Mecid, sent Queen Victoria a brooch inlaid with precious stones. The queen, though, removed the stones from the brooch and had diamond earrings made. The palace jeweler, a corrupt and immoral man, replaced the diamonds with counterfeits. Then, when he tried to sell them in Prussia he was caught. This is how Kaiser Wilhelm's name became associated with the crime. The poor man had done nothing wrong. In any event, the Germans are honorable people. If Victoria had opened her eyes, if she'd had her spies watching the palace staff, none of this would have happened. I wasn't that naïve, I was always aware of everything that was going on in my palace, but still, in the end I was caught by surprise. So, my sheikh, it seems there's no escaping destiny. Everything you said came to pass: I ruled, I was imprisoned, and now I am to die at the hands of these brutes."

As he struggled, he was stunned to realize that there was no one in the room, that he was not being strangled. He'd rolled onto the floor and bumped his head, but what he didn't understand was where he was. *Where am I? I'm not in my apartments in Yıldız*

Palace, I'm not in another palace. So where am I, and what is this dark room? What am I doing here? What would a sultan be doing in a room like this?

Just when his distress was at its deepest, he felt Sheikh Zafir's peaceful, blessed hand on his forehead; this calmed him, eased the fears that had tormented him all his life. He heard him say, *Don't worry, my boy, in the blessed light of morning, none of this will remain. Night is the mother of delusion. The cruelty of the night drives you to despair. Everything will be fine in the morning.* As he felt himself being drawn down into the dark waters of sleep, he heard his sheikh reciting the Surah Inshirah.

> *Have We not expanded for you your breast,*
> *And taken off from you your burden,*
> *Which pressed heavily upon your back,*
> *And exalted for you your esteem?*
> *Surely with difficulty is ease.*
> *With difficulty is surely ease.*
> *So when you are free, nominate.*
> *And make your Lord your exclusive object.*

Greathearted Thessaloniki—Dr. Hüseyin Bey— The end of the tyrant—Love letter

THREE AND A HALF years later, Thessaloniki, sunk in indolence and lethargy, would surrender to the Greek army without firing a shot, but on that warm spring evening in 1909 it was bustling and lively. No one could even imagine the possibility of the city changing hands after so many centuries. The empire's most European city smelled of the sea, fish, raki, ouzo, and sometimes revolution and gunpowder. This was a city of fear, known to some as "greathearted Thessaloniki" because officers sent from Istanbul were assassinated one after another.

The population of the freest and most cosmopolitan city of the empire consisted of Jews, Turks, Bulgarians, Avdeti, Greeks, Macedonians, French, and Italians; here the smell of anise mixed with the sea breeze and everyone devoted themselves to enjoyment. In the Muslim neighborhoods, a devout and dignified silence reigned, no sound was heard but the call to prayer and the sound of the night watchman banging his staff on the ground and calling out, "All is well."

Officers serving in the empire's Third Army would occasionally meet to talk at the café behind the White Tower on the Cordon, or at one of the nightclubs where lively Greek girls sang; they would exchange gossip about Istanbul, the palace, and Thessaloniki, but generally avoided discussing the growing unrest in the Balkans. One of these officers was Captain Atıf Hüseyin Bey, who was serving as a doctor at the Third Army Hospital. As he was single, he occasionally spent time with his unmarried officer friends, and he was particularly fond of the Olympos nightclub, where his heart would be quickened by the scorching voices of the Greek singers he loved so much. He was kept very busy at the hospital, he worked hard and was left exhausted. It seemed as if the evenings he spent with his friends were his only reward. Because he was a disciplined, well-balanced officer who took good care of himself, he contented himself with a single glass of beer; he seldom touched spirits such as raki and ouzo that his friends drank until late. Though once in a while, when he was feeling down, he would have some of the tsipouro he liked so much. Sometimes they would go to Dimitris Sarayıotis's coffeehouse in the Sindrivani district, the Tumba, to drink frothy coffee. They would also play billiards at the Parthenon on Hamidiye Avenue. It was said that Captain Mustafa Kemal Bey was the best billiards player. He'd met this fair-haired captain at the Greek

Cultural Dance Society, which began operating in the period of freedom and openness after the proclamation of the Second Constitutional Monarchy in 1908. The young officers burned with the fire of rebellion, they dreamed of something like the French Revolution, of breathing freedom, of overthrowing Abdülhamid, "the vomiter of blood, the cruel, bloodthirsty tyrant who won't allow anyone to breathe." They hated him with a burning passion, referring to him as the Red Sultan, or sometimes in French as Le Sultan Rouge. They recited a famous poet's secret poem that described him as resembling an owl, and wished that the Armenians had succeeded in blowing up his carriage. They memorized Tevfik Fikret's poem "A Moment of Remembrance," in which the would-be assassin, Edward Joris, is described as a glorious hunter.

Oh glorious hunter, you did not set your trap in vain
You threw, but alas you missed

The poet Mehmet Akif went even further, referring to the sultan as the Crimson Unbeliever and "the owl of Yıldız," and "the spirit of the demon":

Oh, if the owl of Yıldız does not die
the end will be terrible.

For them, this large-nosed, black-bearded hunchback was the cause of all the evil in the empire; he was like a black sheet covering the nation, and no one could breathe. It was as if the sun would shine brighter without him, the stars would be more enchanting, the smell of the night jasmine would be deeper and the breezes more refreshing. The young officers were so obsessed with Abdülhamid that they rarely spoke of anything else. He was a bloody murderer who sat up all night in his high-walled palace making evil plans; he inflicted pain not only on Muslims but on Armenians, Greeks, and Jews as well. He didn't hesitate to scrap the Ottoman constitution. Even though the most important promise he made to those who put him in power was to uphold this constitution. He betrayed them. The newspapers were so heavily censored that they reported that foreign leaders who had been assassinated had died of the flu or whooping cough. So that the people wouldn't get ideas. In the foreign newspapers and magazines that reached Thessaloniki, he was depicted as a butcher or the angel of death, rolling up his sleeves with a bloody knife between his teeth. European magazines got so carried away with this propaganda that they depicted Le Sultan Rouge as a mad and lascivious rapist. They reported as fact that he had his opponents weighted with rocks and thrown into the sea. Europeans reported that the sultan liked to eat rooster brains, that three hundred roosters were decapitated every day in the palace kitchen and that their brains were made into a salad.

The young officers, to whom the waiter was attentive because they were regular customers at Olympos, engaged in heated discussions every evening, but this evening they seemed even more excited than usual. They didn't sing along and sway to the intoxicating songs, their manner was serious and they spoke in whispers. There was a sign in Turkish, French, Ladino, and Bulgarian stating that it was forbidden to sing along with the performers, but the officers usually didn't pay attention to this. They were all young and serious, with curled mustaches in the fashion of Kaiser Wilhelm. Even though they hated Abdülhamid, they admired the kaiser. As Yorgo the waiter brought raki, beer, dried fish, and fried red mullet to the table, he heard fragments of their conversation.

"...they've overthrown the demon."

"Get out of here!"

"Who?"

"Don't jump to your feet, you'll attract attention. Sit down!"

"Who deposed him?"

"Our Thessaloniki army."

"How could that have happened?"

"For God's sake, tell us what happened."

"They got a fatwa from the shaykh al-Islam."

"What?"

"Here's the mind-boggling part. He's accused of harming Islam, causing Muslims to kill each other and banning religious books..."

"Was it Abdülhamid who was doing this?"

"That's what I heard from a friend who just arrived from Istanbul."

"I hope it's true, brother, but...if I saw it in a dream I wouldn't believe it."

"So Hamid is gone, huh?"

When the officers couldn't help but jump to their feet in excitement, Yorgo withdrew because his fat boss was summoning him. When he returned, the officers were sitting, but they were still in a state of excitement.

"I don't know," said the doctor, "I didn't hear that."

"They probably strangled the demon."

"Hopefully!"

"I think they sent him to hell like they did his uncle. He died vomiting blood."

"That man will be cursed in every household in the nation."

"Still, I hope they send him into exile instead of killing him."

Yorgo realized they were talking about the sultan and became excited. Because "the owl of Yıldız" wasn't just a problem for the officers, he was a problem for everyone. In the end he couldn't contain himself. "Excuse me," he said, "are you talking about the sultan?" The officers, who under the influence of drink saw Yorgo as a brother, said, "Yes, the demon is finished."

Yorgo rushed away to tell his boss. A little later, the fat, mustachioed owner came out onto the stage, silenced the musicians, and shouted, "Tonight all drinks are on the house. Enjoy yourselves ladies and gentlemen."

That night, his heart still racing, the doctor made his way through the narrow cobblestone streets, receiving a salute from the night watchman, and entered the front door of a two-story wooden house. The house seemed empty, quiet, and lonely, as it did every night when he returned. He lit the lamp, took off his jacket, went to the table in front of the window with the crocheted calico curtains, sat down, took a sheet of paper and his fountain pen, and slowly and carefully began writing the following letter:

Don't think that a lover can be comfortable when he is separated from his loved one.

Light of my eye, I am the same, my dear, my angel.

Don't be too hard on me for beginning my nightly letter of longing with this couplet by Shaykh al-Islam Yahya. Because my soul yearns for you. Will I ever see you again in this lifetime? Until now I've been in despair because it seemed this wish would never come true. But tonight it is as if the sun has come out from behind the clouds, as if the darkness has been banished, and for the first time it seems possible that I might see you, which I want more than anything in the world. Because the demon who ruined our lives, who exiled your venerable father to Cyprus and put impassable mountains and rough seas between us, has been deposed. We don't know his fate, we don't know whether he's alive or dead. I thank God a thousand times for the happiness he has brought our nation tonight, and I hope this good news will bring an end to your longing and misery.

He carefully folded the flower-patterned paper, placed it in a similarly patterned envelope, sealed it, and put it in a drawer with hundreds of other letters that had not been mailed. All of the letters bore the same address: Nabizade Melahat Hanım—Cyprus. That was all, because all he knew about Melahat Hanım, whom he dreamed of day and night, was that she was on the island of Cyprus. In any event, he wasn't writing the letters in order to send them.

Princesses with stiff necks—Gas lamps—
Floorboards—Yogurt and pilaf—Tobacco box

THE MEMBERS OF THE imperial family, who'd spent their last weeks in Istanbul under siege by gun-toting revolutionaries, with little to eat and with the lights in the palace turned off, and who'd then been put on a train to Thessaloniki, were exhausted, and curled up in various corners. When they woke four or five hours later, they tried to remember where they were, but at the same time they wanted to forget everything. They'd spent their lives sleeping on down mattresses, and their limbs and necks were sore from sleeping on the bare floorboards. They turned their heads left and right, rubbed their arms and shoulders, and uttered groans that echoed in the empty rooms. In addition, the mighty mosquitoes of Thessaloniki must have found their noble blood delicious, because they were covered in bites.

The huge mansion was dim because the shutters were closed, but the light that streamed in here and there was enough for them to see. They went to whatever bathrooms they could find, looked at their tired yellow faces and dirty hair in the mirror, and were grateful for the dried, shrunken pieces of soap that had been left behind. Once they were able to convince themselves they were presentable, they knocked on the sultan's door. He told them to come in, and when they did they saw he seemed to be looking for something on the floor, they bowed and greeted him respectfully, wondering as they did so what he was looking for and why he hadn't ordered anyone to help him. The sultan looked at them, tapped the floor with his right hand, and said, "Whoever made this floor did a masterful job. Wonderful material and workmanship. Look at how masterfully the boards are joined. The floor creaks a little, but that's to be expected. It's damp here by the seaside." He stood slowly, brushed the dust off his hands, and said, "I couldn't have done a better job myself. Good morning. How did you sleep. I'm pleased to see that you're all looking healthy." Then he looked at the floor again. "To tell the truth, the only floor I've seen this good was in Buckingham Palace."

Only then did his wives and children realize that he was attempting to conceal his emotional turmoil. The tired, aged, shaken sultan was trying to show fortitude. They played along and gave their attention to the floorboards.

No one mentioned how hungry they were because they didn't want to upset one another. In any event, toward noon the front door opened and soldiers brought in yogurt and pilaf. Once again, there was no cutlery.

Were they trying to humiliate the imperial family, or did they fear that they would use the metal to harm themselves? Perhaps it was simply an oversight. They never spoke of it, and when, three days later, the food came with forks and spoons (but no knives) they no longer had to eat with their hands or remember their noble cat.

That afternoon soldiers brought bedsteads, chairs, sheets, quilts, pillows, and towels. The furniture was shabby and dirty, but to the new inhabitants of the Alatini mansion it seemed beautiful. The commander told them he'd procured it all from hotels. Who knew who had slept on these sheets without knowing the next users would be a deposed sultan and his entourage. The servants set up the sultan's room first, on his instructions placing the bed as far as possible from the windows, then they moved on to the other rooms, and slowly the mansion began to look like the abode of a poor family, far from its original splendor and from the conditions they were accustomed to. Still, the sultan's wives and daughters had something to occupy themselves with, some tried to wash the sheets with the scraps of soap in the bathroom, some struggled to put mattresses onto broken box springs, some contented themselves with ordering servants around, but they all appreciated the distraction from their harsh conditions.

They were delighted when the sullen soldiers brought lamps in the evening, those four or five weak lamps seemed like a festival of light to them.

On the second night the sultan went to his room, his five wives and three daughters went to the hall on the second floor, the sons to another room, and the eunuchs and servants to two separate rooms. Meanwhile his daughter Şadiye Sultan, who'd pleased him so much when she gave him the yellow bag full of jewels, was able to give her beloved father another gift. She knocked respectfully, entered, and found him standing in front of the window as if the shutters were open, leaning on his cane. He greeted her lovingly, then she watched his face light up when she gave him the cigarettes, tobacco, and rolling papers she'd managed to grab as they were leaving the palace.

Abdülhamid couldn't manage without tobacco. He was adept at rolling the fine, strong, aromatic amber-yellow tobacco and would line up his cigarettes side by side. His tobacco box, of mahogany inlaid with jewels, was a work of art in itself. Like many of the cabinets, tables, and bookcases in the palace, it was his own work.

Perhaps his happiest hours were those he spent in his carpentry workshop. He was particularly pleased by the mastery he displayed in making furniture. He would proudly show his work to the people of the palace, he would expect their admiration, and sometimes when he was very pleased with himself he would compare himself to the eighteenth-century cabinet-maker Thomas Chippendale. He'd been deeply influenced by his visits to France, England, and Germany with his uncle Sultan Abdülaziz. He often spoke about the English to his family in the evening. He seemed to be a bit frightened by them.

When the sultan saw his tobacco box he snorted with delight as if he'd been reunited with an old friend; he immediately rolled a cigarette, lit it, and inhaled deeply, enjoying the moment and squinting his eyes with pleasure. He held the smoke in his lungs like a jealous lover, then exhaled slowly through his famous nose, the "imperial nose" that was mocked in foreign periodicals. Then he said, "I thank you from the bottom of my heart, my child. This is one of the things I missed most, no other tobacco is as strong as this, I've become accustomed to it, I can't smoke anything else. I miss my parrot too, and my carpentry tools. They're like extensions of my hands. I feel incomplete without them."

Then the sultan laughed and coughed at the same time. When he'd caught his breath he turned to his daughter, who didn't know why he'd laughed. "Life is full of coincidences," he said. "The merchant Alatini Efendi, who had this mansion built, brought me the best tobacco to give as a gift to the Emperor of Japan. May he prosper, for years he kept me supplied with tobacco, and now we're living in his house."

Şadiye didn't quite understand, but she was so happy to have pleased her father that she bowed deeply. In a sense she'd made up for the favor her sister had gained by singing *La Traviata* the night before. What had the soldiers patrolling the garden by lamplight thought about the foreign music that had drifted from the mansion in the middle of the night? During the chaos at the palace, Şadiye had managed to retrieve both the yellow "water" bag and this precious box. It was no secret that this tobacco aggravated his bronchitis, but he probably couldn't live without it.

The young princes solve a difficult problem
for the caliph

THAT DAY THE SULTAN'S daughters realized they'd made a big mistake. Even though Müşfika, Sazkâr, Peyveste, Fatma Pesend, and Saliha Naciye were their mothers, these tall Circassian beauties with eyes like gazelles were also the sultan's wives and by staying in the same room with them they deprived them of the opportunity to go to and from their husband without being seen. They regretted this situation.

The sultan had many wives and concubines at the palace; he would choose who he wanted and go to one of the many mansions on the palace grounds, and although this was customary, it was always done as if in secret. He would invite the woman through one of the eunuchs, she would sneak down the corridors to the sultan's room, or flit like a spirit among the linden trees to one of the mansions, seen by no one but the eunuchs and the guards, who in any event weren't considered human. She then shared the sultan's bed in secret, and when dismissed, would scurry back to the harem, her heart fluttering like a bird's at the prospect of becoming pregnant with a prince or even a sultan.

The sultan's daughters admired these women, some of whom were the same age as them, for their beauty and grace. Indeed some of the wives were younger than them. Did they have the right to deprive their father during this most difficult time? Since the five wives, some of whom were their mothers, had joined the exile in Thessaloniki, it was the daughters' duty to see that they were as comfortable as possible. Their venerable father had the right to call one of his wives whenever he wanted. This was a sultan's most natural right.

The daughters were all thinking about this, but it took a great deal of effort to speak of the private affairs of the mighty Caliph of Islam in a delicate and seemly manner. It was as if they wanted to resolve this sensitive issue, of which they pretended not to be aware, in a sublime and noble manner without having to put it into words.

In the end Şadiye Sultan found a way to mention the issue and to give it a name. "The issue of love is important," she said. "This is the only way the Ottoman dynasty will not be left without an heir. Otherwise, God forbid, the dynasty would wither away. So we have to resolve the issue of love."

Ayşe Sultan said, "Yes, love is truly important."

Refia Sultan hadn't been paying attention and didn't understand. "What's all this about love? Why are you going on about it?"

The two sisters looked at each other and wondered how they were going to explain in a seemly manner. Şadiye Sultan decided to resort to poetry. She drew close to Refia Sultan, looked her in the eye, and recited the following couplet:

From love Muhammed came to be
What is the result of love without Muhammed

Then she smiled faintly. Refia Sultan opened her eyes and said, "Of course. Yes, you're right." She seemed somewhat embarrassed to have been so slow to understand.

That day they moved their father's wives to another room on the top floor. The caliph could now send for the woman he wanted. Of course everyone in the mansion would hear doors opening and closing and the creaking of the steps, they would see the lamplight under the doors and would know who had a tryst with the sultan, but in keeping with the traditions and manners of the palace, no one would know anything.

The mansion had only sixteen rooms and halls, and it would take the denizens of the palace some time to get used to it.

The unlucky brother's bulging eyes—
Morning bath—The imperial nose—
The scourge of boils

HE'D WOKEN EVERY MORNING as sultan for so many years and was confused at first about where he was, then when he realized he was no longer emperor and caliph, he felt as if he'd been stabbed in the heart. They must have put his brother on the throne, what were they thinking? He thought his brother was a complete fool. He was also unlucky and brought bad luck to everyone around him. When they were young he'd shown his brother a parrot he'd grown attached to: "Look, Reşad, how beautiful it is." The blessed bird died suddenly that evening. Prince Hamid wept for his beloved parrot, but it didn't occur to him to suspect Reşad.

Sometime later he showed Reşad his favorite horse, and when that magnificent animal died suddenly a few hours later it was clear that it was the result of the evil eye, of the envy and malice in Reşad's bulging, spooky eyes. He never again showed any of his animals to his brother.

His brother was also an ingrate. During his long reign he'd allowed Reşad and Murad to remain in Istanbul and to live a life of luxury in their palaces with their wives, concubines, and servants, but on his first day in power Reşad had no qualms about sending his elder brother to Thessaloniki. Nevertheless, he was the sultan now, and he and his family were at his mercy. Reşad had only to say the word and executioners would descend on them like birds of prey. That's why he couldn't share his thoughts with anyone, not even his family. His only recourse was to pray constantly. But the rebels would tear the empire apart, and his brother would watch like a puppet as it collapsed. He was certain of this. Because unlike him, Reşad didn't have the political skills to play the rulers of France, England, Russia, and Germany against one another. Murad was different, he was clever, but after he'd had their uncle Abdülaziz killed by having his wrists cut, he vomited constantly for a day and a half and then lost his mind. No doctor had succeeded in curing the seizures and vomiting. Then the poor man went mad; he would talk to the walls and laugh to himself. They even had trouble getting him to come to the sword-girding ceremony because he was terrified of everyone. Three months later, when it was clear the madness could not be cured, he was deposed, and Abdülhamid became sultan at a moment when he least expected it.

When the sultan let it be known that he wanted to take a bath, there was panic in the mansion because there was no hot water, and the towels hadn't arrived. His family tried to convince him not to take a bath, to wait a day or two, but he stopped them by saying, "Do you remember a single morning when I didn't bathe? I take lukewarm baths in winter and cold baths in summer, sometimes twice a day. This is my most important habit. I have no intention of changing this. And there's no need for hot water, I prefer cold water in summer."

When they realized they couldn't convince him, the eunuchs took the sultan to the bathroom upstairs. There was a small dressing room and a steam bath with a marble basin. In the dressing room there was a mahogany closet, a small sofa, and, directly across from it, a large mirror. "Ah," sighed the sultan, "how I miss my wonderful bathhouse." That bathhouse in Istanbul had been designed by Raimondo Tommaso D'Aronco, who had served for sixteen years as the imperial chief architect. This brilliant architect had erected buildings all over Istanbul, including the sultan's palace, which employed twelve thousand people. Of course the sultan had showered the Italian architect with money and praise.

He locked the door carefully, undressed, and when he was naked he couldn't help looking at himself in the mirror. Mirrors of this size weren't seen in the palace, and there were certainly no mirrors in the bathhouse. When he took off his fez, frock coat, and

underwear, he felt more than physically naked; he felt
as if his soul had been exposed. In the mirror he saw
a hunchbacked ghost with deep-set, languid eyes. A
thin, pale body with little hair; a head that seemed too
big for his body, a sunken chest; purple burn marks on
his throat, chest, and abdomen from the red-hot metal
he used to try to alleviate his bronchitis and stomach
pains; it was as if there was a pressure on the back of
his neck that pushed his head forward and forced him
to hunch his back; broad but weak shoulders; his beard
dyed black, with occasional patches of white; and then
his most salient feature, his nose. That world-famous
nose. The imperial nose that was mocked in French
and English newspapers, that had been in the middle
of his face all his life, that couldn't be concealed or
ignored, the nose that had been a symbol of the empire for thirty-three years. It had been so many years
but he still couldn't get used to it. His father, Sultan
Abdülmecid, had been an elegant, slender, handsome
man. Indeed, when he wore his cape and ceremonial
clothes, he was as dazzling as a fairy-tale prince. His
uncle Sultan Aziz wasn't slender like his father; he
was a fair-skinned, gray-eyed wrestler who seemed
to make the ground shake when he walked. When he
went to Paris with his uncle, he noticed how the ladies
of the court, and particularly Empress Eugénie, looked
at him. Everyone was looking at his uncle and Murad.
Murad was slender and elegant like their father; he
was a crown prince with a likable face. His French was
fluent and he was skillful on the piano, often playing

waltzes and rondos of his own composition, and he became a favorite of the ladies of Paris and London. It was said that even Queen Victoria took a fancy to him. As the Ottoman prince most amenable to the West, Murad gave European courtiers great hopes for the future. In any event, he had the English national anthem played at his ascension ceremony.

Meanwhile, no one noticed or took an interest in the other prince, who wore a gray Istanbuline frock coat that came down to his knees. The Europeans were dazzled by his uncle and his brother, but treated him as if he were invisible. In a way, he found this to his advantage. The young Hamid had the opportunity to examine and reflect on everything and everyone he encountered.

As he looked at himself in the mirror, he asked himself why. For six hundred years his ancestors had married the most beautiful Russian, Ruthenian, French, Circassian, Polish, and Italian women, so how had he ended up with this nose?

He believed it was his ugliness that had lost him the love of his life, Firdevs, for whom he had been pining in secret for years; indeed he still couldn't go to sleep at night without uttering her name. She hadn't said this, she'd given a completely different explanation, but he felt that this angelic Caucasian girl had rejected him solely because of his nose. Why else would this tall, green-eyed flower, who'd been raised with expectations of being sent to the imperial harem, and indeed had been trained in religion, music, dance, and needlework, turn down the opportunity to enter the emperor's bed, give him a son, and perhaps in the future become the sultan mother, the highest rank a woman could reach in the empire?

From time to time he looked at portraits of his ancestors and tried to find a resemblance. Most of these centuries-old paintings were not accurate depictions, but some, like that of Mehmet the Conqueror, had been painted by Italian artists. His illustrious ancestor had a nose like an eagle's beak, it curled down almost above his mouth, but at least it was slender. It didn't distort his face.

The sultan was so obsessed with this that the word "nose" had been banned for decades. There were countless phrases that could no longer be used, and people had to be creative in finding substitutes.

The nose was one of the most important topics for the people of the empire. However, the issue of population was a bit complicated; the population had been higher at the beginning of his reign but had gradually been reduced to twenty million after the empire lost one and a half million square kilometers of land, including Tunisia, Egypt, Cyprus, Serbia, Montenegro, and Romania.

The skin under his right shoulder was red and swollen, and itched terribly. It was probably one of the boils that emerged from time to time in various places. He felt it. At the moment it was quite hard, but later it would grow softer, it would mature, it would fill with pus, then it would burst. He knew he had to wait patiently for this moment or he would share the fate of his heroic ancestor Yavuz Sultan Selim, who died because he squeezed a boil before it was mature. When the boil reached that point he would immediately call Hasan, an amateur surgeon who'd trained in the military. Hasan would put his mouth on the sultan's boil and suck. Hasan was so good at his job that the sultan promoted him to a high rank; he never left even a drop of pus. But unfortunately Hasan was not here. He didn't know what he was going to do when the boil matured.

After washing in cold water, he banged on the door, took a piece of flower-printed cloth from the eunuch, dried himself as best he could, then put on his Istanbuline and his fez. He would later learn that this primitive towel was cloth that had been torn from one of his wives' dresses.

After his bath he spent some time examining doorjambs, hinges, windows, and floorboards, behaving more like an engineer than an exiled sultan. Then he said, "I'd like to meet the carpenter who did this work. He's probably an Istanbul Greek or an Italian. The work is superb." Then he added, "In fact it would be easy to find out. All we'd have to do is pull up a couple of floorboards." This alarmed the others in the room. He said that Istanbul Greeks put coal dust under the floorboards to prevent woodworm and termites. Istanbul Greeks were the only people in the world who did this. If they pulled up one or two floorboards, they would be able to determine the carpenter's ethnicity.

If there was coal dust beneath them, they would know this work had been done by an Istanbul Greek. His daughters begged him not to do this, they feared arousing the suspicions of the ill-tempered soldiers patrolling outside the shutters. They knew he was trying to conceal how badly shaken he was by the blow he'd received, but still, they couldn't start tearing up the floorboards. They begged and pleaded until he changed his mind. He went to his room, calculated the direction of Mecca, then prayed on his prayer rug. Then he called the chamberlain and said, "Could you politely ask the guards at the door if I might have a word with the commander." He was no longer thinking about the floorboards.

Meanwhile at Yıldız Palace—
The eunuch's secret—Jewels like pebbles—
Long live the sultan!

AS THE SULTAN WAS thinking these things, mind-boggling events were unfolding at Yıldız Palace. The new government had arrested six thousand of the former sultan's men and had seized all of his property. The eunuch Cevher, who'd been castrated when he was brought from Africa as a slave and sold to the palace, where he rose to the rank of chief eunuch, was hanged from a lamppost on the Galata Bridge, and was left swaying in the breeze for days as an example. When they raided his mansion on the Bosphorus, they found a young slave girl who was beautiful enough to make the angels envious. They saw her weep bitter tears of grief. "My man is gone!" cried the Egyptian girl, and the mustachioed Ottoman men felt offended. Because despite their masculinity and their carefully groomed mustaches, no girl had ever been this much in love with them.

Even stranger events were taking place at Yıldız Palace, which had been ransacked and looted, and where soldiers had smashed and broken random objects in righteous indignation. After Cevher Ağa had been executed, a government delegation went to the palace to interrogate Nadir Ağa, who under torture revealed all of the places where Abdülhamid had stored his wealth. Incidentally, they were quite impressed by the former sultan's carpentry skills. They were amazed by this beautiful furniture crafted from mahogany and Lebanese cedar; not only was it beautiful but some pieces contained secret, invisible mechanisms and hidden compartments with locks that could not be opened. If Nadir Ağa hadn't cracked under torture, they would never have found these secret compartments. Each one they opened contained stunning amounts of gold and cash in various currencies. There were as many jewels and precious stones as pebbles on a beach. The delegation was mesmerized by the mystical shimmer of the sapphires, rubies, diamonds, and emeralds that had been brought up from beneath the ground.

As the delegation, accompanied by a squad of soldiers, inspected every corner of the deserted palace, they became aware of strange sounds coming from one of the rooms. Who could have remained in a palace that had been emptied and sealed? They looked at one another in surprise. They banged on the door and asked who was there, and dozens of voices shouted, "Long live the sultan!" Was this a detachment of guards determined to protect their sultan to the last breath? Perhaps these reactionaries were prepared for a final suicidal attack to kill as many rebels as they could before they died.

One of the delegation shouted, "Who's in there?" and again there were shouts of "Long live the sultan!" "Surrender!" they shouted, and once again the reply was "Long live the sultan!"

"There's no way out for you, try to think clearly, don't throw your lives away, your sultan is gone, those days are over, no one is going to protect you," they said, but it didn't work. The only response was the repetition of the same slogan. However, they noticed something strange. The shouting voices were odd; they weren't female voices, but they didn't seem like men's voices. Could they be eunuchs?

In the end the delegation lost patience, and ordered the soldiers to break down the door while they hid around the corner. They were to arrest everyone in the room and shoot anyone who resisted. The soldiers didn't hesitate to ready their rifles and kick down the door. Then the delegation and the soldiers received a great surprise.

The room was full of parrots, maddened by hunger, flying around the room screeching "Long live the sultan!" as they'd been taught. They were all white, and white feathers flew as they fluttered here and there. Some of them flew out the open door, while the rest continued fluttering about the room. The soldiers stood there with their rifles, looking at their young commander. The commander looked at the delegation, waiting for orders. If they were ordered to shoot these parrots who insisted on repeating this forbidden slogan, they were prepared to do so.

Once the delegation had recovered from the surprise, they decided to let the parrots fend for themselves. They opened the windows and the hungry parrots flew out across Istanbul looking for something to eat. Whether it was the will of God or a homing instinct, the parrots found Yeni Mosque, where the merciful citizens of Istanbul sprinkled grain for them, then they fluttered around the minarets of the mosques of Sülaymaniye, Sultanahmet, and Hagia Sophia, confusing the muezzins as they cleared their throats to recite the call to prayer. Because they heard shouts of "Long live the sultan!" It seemed to them like a bad omen. Which sultan were people hailing? Were they praising the new sultan or did they want the old one back? They didn't know, but they had enough experience to know that nothing good would come of this. The wisest thing to do was to finish the evening call to prayer quickly, climb down from the minaret, and hide in some corner. As the call to prayer mixed with the slogans, some of the muezzins panicked and stopped before they were finished. Some of the congregation left the mosques and rushed home, just in case.

On the day the palace was seized, hundreds of animals, terrified by the sounds of guns and cannons, broke free and fanned out through the city.

The sultan's famous horses galloped away, and even Mennan, who was famous for dragging his wounded owner off the battlefield with his teeth, had been seen grazing in the wilderness. Zebras, people called them "donkeys in pajamas," roamed calmly through the streets, but the strangest sight was a giraffe crossing the Galata Bridge.

Astounding requests—Baby snake— A compassionate commander—Forbidden names—Star-shaped noodles

* Pine water
* One brick
* My parrot
* My cat
* A piece of iron ten centimeters long and two centimeters wide
* Whatever clothes belonging to me and my family that remain in Yıldız Palace
* Black beard dye
* Furniture for the house
* Carpentry tools from my workshop at the palace
* A dozen bottles of Atkinson cologne

This list of requests, which he presented in person to the commander, aroused a sense of pity because it was clear that, however much wealth and power he'd once had, the man was mentally ill. Major Ali Fethi looked at the list in surprise, then managed to ask, "Are you certain?" When the man nodded his head and said, "Yes, yes," the commander couldn't think of any response. He tried to avoid direct contact with the former sultan, because each time he met him he was left with a deep sense of uneasiness. Besides, he wasn't sure how to behave toward the man, how to address him. He was a former sultan, but now he was a prisoner, an exile, a shadow of a man under house arrest with his distraught family, and all of them had suddenly become his responsibility.

Ali Fethi Bey was a compassionate man; he now had the person he'd seen as the empire's greatest problem, who'd darkened his life for years, against whom he'd whispered on many nights and whose death he had wished for, but for some reason he couldn't feel any hatred toward this old man. When he'd approached the sultan's room, he'd seen through the half-open door that he was praying on his prayer rug; he waited until the sultan was finished and then entered. He was wearing a cardigan over the underwear he'd probably slept in, his long beard now had patches of gray, and the faraway look in his eyes showed he hadn't recovered from the blow he'd received and probably never would.

After looking the commander over for some time, the sultan said, "You're a good man, officer, I know people. You give me confidence in these disastrous times. This is why I ask you for God's sake to tell the truth. Are our lives in danger?"

When Ali Fethi Bey said, "Of course not, sir, you and your family are under the protection of the army," the sultan wasn't satisfied, and a shadow of doubt fell across his face.

"How can I be confident?" he asked. "Two days ago I was the sultan of all these lands, I was the father of all these peoples, I was the caliph of all Muslims. Look at me now."

Ali Fethi Bey wanted to say, *Then you should have behaved like a real father, you shouldn't have let your pashas rob the people blind. You shouldn't have had the grand vizier strangled*, but he couldn't bring himself to do so and suppressed his rising anger.

Now the deposed sultan insisted on a guarantee. "I would like the army to inform me in writing that I am under its protection."

"I will pass your request to the highest authority."

As he was leaving the house, it occurred to him that he was not showing the sultan the same respect he would have in the old days. Even though he criticized him internally, he addressed him as "Your Majesty" and "my sultan," stood at attention, and did not look at him when he spoke. However, he should have spoken to the sultan as if he were in awe, as if he were addressing the shadow of God on earth. There was a whole list of flattering, obsequious titles he should have used, and he should have referred to himself as "your servant" and "the dust beneath your feet." But the commander couldn't bring himself to speak this way. He could not behave like a flunky. He was determined to show the respect that was due, but in a cold and distant manner. But the sultan stood to greet him like a caring father, and insisted he sit in the armchair across from him. The commander sat, but according to palace etiquette he should have waited until the sultan asked him three times. He couldn't be rude as other soldiers might, his nature prevented this. He'd heard some of the officers in the garden refer to the sultan's three-year-old son as a baby snake and say, "The baby snake will be a snake one day," and this had upset him.

The man had so many titles: Sultan, His Excellency, the Great Khan, emperor, the Caliph of the Earth, the Commander of the Believers, the Father of the Kurds, but now he was called Stingy Hamid, the Red Sultan, the owl of Yıldız, the Tyrant, the Demon, and now the "dethroned monarch." It had long been forbidden to use the word "dethroned," or indeed any word that vaguely resembled it.

It had also been forbidden to mention the names of Abdülhamid's brothers, Murad and Reşad. Those names had once been common but they'd been forgotten in the darkness of the past thirty-three years; no one gave those names to their children, and anyone who'd been given those names had changed them. In 1904, when the Muradiye Mosque in Bursa was reopened after repairs, the newspapers referred it as "the mosque honoring the father of Mehmed the Conqueror" in order to avoid using the name Muradiye. Foreign leaders who had been assassinated were reported to have died of natural causes, the French president was reported to have died of a heart attack, the Austrian emperor of shortness of breath, and the American president of a carbuncle. When the King and Queen of Serbia were assassinated, they were reported to have died of indigestion. Anyone who had the name Murad changed it to Mirad, and anyone who had the name Reşad changed it to Neşed.

The word "dynamite" was forbidden, as were the words "rebellion," "socialism," and "nihilism." It reached the point that a poor resident of Istanbul was exiled for life for ordering "star-shaped" noodles. The word "star" (yıldız) was forbidden because it evoked Yıldız Palace.

Still, the commander felt sorry for the downtrodden family. He couldn't bear seeing the children in that state, the look of fear bordering on terror on the faces of the young girls broke his heart, and he was uncomfortable with the way the sultan stood to greet him, asked after his health, pulled out his silver cigarette case to offer him a cigarette, then took the trouble to light it for him. He didn't know how to behave or what to say. He'd been placed in a strange situation. And what if—God forbid—the order came from Istanbul to execute the emperor? He would carry out the order, of course, but when the possibility occurred to him, Ali Fethi Bey trembled and prayed that a disaster like this didn't befall him.

A dead princess's soul—Parrot— Pasteur Efendi

WHEN THE COMMANDER SHOWED this strange list to his fellow officers, they didn't believe it at first. They tried to make sense out of the brick, the parrot, and the piece of metal.

Someone said, "He's being crafty, he's trying to trick us."

Another said, "I think he's going to make a bomb out of all of this."

"You call yourself a soldier, how could he make a bomb out of this stuff?"

"Who knows what's going on in that mind of his?"

"Isn't dye a flammable material?"

"And the cologne?"

"Do you think he's lost his mind?"

"If they came one night, took you by the arm, and threw you out of your palace—"

"I think the whole family has gone mad. In the middle of the night we hear the unbelievers' music coming from the caliph's house."

The commander, the most coolheaded of the officers, said, "I think I'm going to have to ask him for a reasonable explanation."

When he went back to the mansion, the sultan was sitting in the hall in one of the large green armchairs, reading a book by the light that came through the one window that was no longer shuttered. With glasses on his famous nose and a sweater draped across his back, he looked like a retired civil servant. He glanced at the commander over his glasses, then he closed his book and stood, his body looking even more bent over than usual. Like a polite host greeting a guest, he said, "Welcome, commander." Then he showed his book and added, "I read the Sahih al-Bukhari every day. It's very valuable. I used to have tens of thousands of them printed and distributed to mosques. I'm glad I had a copy with me. Welcome, what can I do for you?"

His voice was strong, soft, and persuasive. He smiled when the commander asked about the list. "So the list seemed strange to you," he said. "You're right. That's because you don't know my customs. Let me explain. Please, sit down." He gestured to the chair across from him. As soon as the commander sat down, the sultan took out his silver cigarette case and offered him a cigarette. He took the cigarette without thinking, as if in a dream, but when the sultan took out his lighter, he stood. He tried to take the lighter and ended up holding the sultan's hand. His hand was warm. He had a cloth wrapped around his neck, and he guessed the man was ill. The sultan took the list and both of them sat.

"This tobacco is very special," he said. "It's difficult to find." Then he laughed. "How strange life can be, commander," he said. "Do you know where this rare tobacco comes from? From Alatini Efendi, the owner of this mansion. He was the owner of the largest tobacco company in the Thessaloniki area, and every year he'd deliver this golden tobacco he'd had cut especially for me and write a letter declaring his loyalty to me... Now about the list. I rub pine water on my face every morning. I've been doing this for years and I'm accustomed to it. It tightens the skin and erases the signs of aging."

The commander couldn't help opening his eyes wide in amazement. Was the sultan that vain? It was said that Abdülhamid, like other Ottoman sultans, never appeared in public without makeup, but the commander had never given this much credence. It seemed it was true after all.

"I see that you're surprised," said the sultan. "But you should try it, you'll see the benefits. All your wrinkles are erased in a week. I recommend your wife try it as well. As for the brick, I always keep a brick at the head of my bed. When I wake in the morning I rub my hands on the brick as a dry ablution before going to the bathroom to perform my ablutions with water. So I don't get out of bed without performing an ablution. Sometimes they wake me in the middle of the night for important affairs of state. I immediately rub my hands on the brick and then attend to the matter at hand. No one is going to be consulting me about affairs of state any more, but still, I'd like to have it."

The commander knew that the sultan was very religious, but he'd never seen or heard of anyone performing dry ablutions with a brick. This man had some strange habits.

"The parrot," continued the sultan, "is my companion, he's been with me for years. I've grown accustomed to him and can't live without him. You wouldn't believe how smart that bird is. I experienced an unfortunate incident in my youth, my six-year-old daughter was playing with a candle and her taffeta skirt caught fire, she wasn't able to call out, but the parrot flew around shouting fire, fire, and this brought people running."

The commander said, "Now I understand why you value the parrot so much. He saved your daughter's life."

The sultan's face fell, his eyes moistened, and in a trembling voice he said, "No, unfortunately they were too late. Her mother tried to save her, she threw herself on her, burning her face, hands, and arms, but she didn't succeed. Unfortunately we lost her. I wasn't in the palace, I was out, I rushed there as soon as I got the news but ... anyway, it was fate. But I still feel grateful to the parrot. If they'd paid attention to him sooner my child would have been saved."

They both fell silent for a time, and an air of mourning descended on them. As if the dead princess's soul was floating above them, moving the curtains with a slight breeze. The sultan inhaled deeply on his cigarette. "Forgive me, commander," he said, "I have distressed you. Let me tell you about my parrot's other skills. The servants got fed up with looking after him so they decided to feed him pastry with parsley so he would die and they would be rid of him. The parrot flew to me and told me what they were going to do. I asked who, and he gave me their names. I believed him and investigated the matter, the guilty confessed; it seems they really were planning to kill this innocent animal. He would wander around the palace all day, and in the evening he would tell me what he'd heard."

He spoke as if he was relating something ordinary, and as the commander looked at him in astonishment, he looked down at the list and continued.

"It's the same with my cat. She means a lot to me. A white Angora cat. She's very noble, she won't eat anything unless it's given to her with a fork, she would rather starve. If she were here...under these conditions..." (He gave the commander a look of reproach.) "Anyway, I miss her a lot.

"I imagine you're wondering about the piece of metal. In fact it's quite simple. Commander, I have an advanced knowledge of science. I don't trust doctors too much because they make mistakes. They gave one of my wives an injection of morphine, and the poor thing died. One shouldn't believe in scientific medicine. I take precautions against disease. I have constant indigestion, so I eat little and drink senna tea.

Whenever I have bronchitis, a sore throat, or pain any-where in my body, I make a piece of metal red hot and cauterize the affected area. Here, look."

As he said this, the sultan pulled down the cloth around his neck to show the commander the burn marks. The commander couldn't believe his eyes, and the sultan seemed to be enjoying his surprise.

The sultan continued: "They were in such a rush to get us out of the palace that we weren't able to bring our personal belongings and clothes. My daughters wash what they're wearing in the bathroom, then sit and wait for their clothes to dry. That's what I heard. Oh yes, there's the beard dye, but there's no mystery about that. I've been dying my beard for a long time, a white beard makes a monarch appear weak. Since we're talk-ing about hair and beards, let me tell you an interesting story. Once, the English and the Russians were squeez-ing me into a corner. I heard that Bismarck, the iron chancellor, said, 'These two nations are treating the Ot-toman Empire like the poor man in La Fontaine's story who was caught between two mistresses.' One of the mistresses in La Fontaine's story pulls out the man's black hairs and the other pulls out his white hairs, and in the end the man is bald. Strange, isn't it? Bismarck was comparing us to this man. Since then I've taken care not to have any white hair. I'm half joking when I say this, commander. As for the furniture, I don't think I need to explain; a family can't live like this."

The sultan then explained how much he needed his carpentry tools.

"I used to spend a good part of each day making furniture," he said. "Being a monarch is a matter of luck. It's not something you can boast about, but craftsmanship is different, it's a matter of personal skill, and I'm proud of my carpentry. I'm a master carpenter and woodworking is the only thing that relaxes me, that and the detective novels I have read to me at night." A strange smile spread across his face. "In fact I'm a world-class furniture maker," he added. The commander sensed pride in the sultan's tone, or rather an attempt to ease his broken pride.

The sultan continued: "Atkinson cologne is an important part of my life. I'm a particular man. One bottle of cologne a day isn't enough for me. Whenever I touch anything, a book or a document, I immediately disinfect my hands with cologne. You can't ignore microbes, commander. At a time when no one in Paris had any faith in Pasteur Efendi, I sent him a lot of money, I gave him ten thousand francs and the Order of the Mecidiye and asked for his support. Monsieur Pasteur sent his right-hand man, Monsieur Chantimes. I had the man build a rabies hospital in Istanbul."

This man is such a braggart, thought the commander. *He tries so hard to prove what an important person he is. We all know who he is. Anyway, most of his requests are reasonable. Especially about the personal belongings in the palace.* But he had to give the man credit, the story about the parrot informant was brilliant. He'd gotten everyone in the palace to believe it was true.

The dangers of Thessaloniki—The Girl Incident and the lynched consuls— Lament for the hanged

NO ONE COULD SAY that Thessaloniki was a tranquil city: The nightlife was seductive, the population was cosmopolitan, there were daily newspapers in five languages, and people engaged in fiery debates. As the central authority in Istanbul grew weaker, there was increasing unrest in Greece, Montenegro, Bulgaria, Bosnia and Herzegovina, and Serbia, and all signs pointed to the coming of a period of turmoil. One such incident, which took place just before Abdülhamid became sultan, was the "Girl Incident," a tragedy that unfolded when a Bulgarian girl named Helen fell in love with a Turk. The doctor, who since his first day in Thessaloniki had taken the trouble to record everything he saw and learned about the city, had the following to say about this incident:

According to the story, a young Bulgarian girl from Avrethisar fell in love with a Turkish lieutenant, converted to Islam, and began wearing an abaya. The girl's family didn't accept this, and insisted that her conversion had been forced. The lovers traveled to Thessaloniki (apparently accompanied by the man's mother, an imam, and a Black servant) to make their marriage official. A group of a hundred and fifty Orthodox had gathered at the Thessaloniki train station, and when they saw the girl they caused a commotion, ripped off her abaya, and, despite her shouts of "Let me go, I'm Muslim!," abducted her and brought her to the American consul's house. Crowds of angry Muslims, believing the girl had chosen the right path by converting and determined to bring their new bride back to the community, took to the streets, swinging their long prayer beads and shouting *Allahu Akbar* as they made their way to the Saatlı Mosque. The French and German consuls decided to attempt to calm the crowd and made the fatal mistake of entering the mosque courtyard. The French consul Mulen and the German consul Abot were lynched by the crowd.

After the murder of these representative of two great powers, things slipped out of control. The incident was on the front pages of European newspapers. *Le Journal de Deba*, which I found in the library archives, had the following to say: "The lesson to be learned from the bloody incident in Thessaloniki is this: The misrule of the Ottoman state has reached a catastrophic level."

Three prime ministers met in Berlin and issued the following statement: "The Thessaloniki incident has made it clear that foreign nationals and Christians are not safe in the Ottoman Empire. The great powers may send naval forces to dangerous areas to prevent the recurrence of such incidents."

Warships from the five great powers entered the harbor of Thessaloniki and aimed their cannons at the city. In the end, six Turks who were alleged to have killed the consuls were hanged in Eleftheria Square, and their bodies were left to swing gently in the sea breeze for days. Many others were tried and convicted. This incident also led to an uprising of students of the Enderun School, which had deposed Sultan Abdülaziz.

Thus a Bulgarian girl and her Muslim lover unwittingly changed the fate of Abdülhamid, who had envisioned a life in commerce. The city of Thessaloniki, which he'd never seen, played an important role in his life. As a result of this incident his uncle was overthrown and his brother Murad ascended to the throne, but when he in turn was overthrown three months later, the Ottoman Empire was left to Hamid, who had never expected to come to power.

How strange history is, thought the doctor. *This time an army that had set off from Thessaloniki deposed him, and he's been sent into exile in this city. The city named after the unfortunate, motherless queen. Perhaps this was Thessaly's vengeance.*

There was another aspect of this story that caught the doctor's attention. Two thousand four hundred years after Helen of Troy, the beauty of another Helen caused, if not a war, the overthrow of an emperor.

After he'd finished writing and put away his notebook, Atıf Hüseyin Bey lay on his bed and lit a cigarette, feeling the excitement and anxiety of witnessing history. As he watched the cigarette smoke rise to the ceiling, he thought of Melahat Hanım. Had his mind been playing tricks on him that spring evening when he fell madly in love with a graceful girl in a pink veil? Had he fallen in love with an illusion? But in the Islamic world, wasn't love always like this? There was no chance he would ever see or meet Melahat. He could only see her from afar. And sometimes this was enough.

A child's fear—Romaine lettuce

BOTH THE SULTAN AND his young son had become ill, and their dry coughs echoed through the empty mansion. The little boy's tonsils had become infected, and he had a fever. The sultan had a fever as well, but he was more concerned about his son than about himself. He prayed as he paced up and down the large hall, begging God to forgive him. He was also deeply concerned about his six-year-old daughter's fever.

The worn-out mattresses that Ali Fethi Bey had procured from the hotels were placed on battered box springs that had been left upstairs, and the monarch no longer had to sleep on the armchairs. However, he put his son in that bed, and spent his time either pacing in the hall or reciting prayers by his son's bedside and blowing on his red face to ease the fever. Meanwhile he was watching the front door. When he saw that no one was coming, he called the eunuch and said, "Tell the commander that I require a spoon." This reasonable request was quickly granted. What could be more natural than for a sultan to want to eat with a spoon? But the monarch's intentions were different, he couldn't think about food when his son was in this condition. When food was brought at noon, all he took was some of the romaine lettuce he'd noticed. He wrapped the head of the spoon with a handkerchief, then held his lighter under the handle until it was bright red. When it was glowing he started to bring it toward his son's neck, but the boy started howling. The boy screamed and struggled, but the sultan kept trying his hardest to bring the handle of the spoon to his throat. There were tears in his eyes now. The family watched in horror from the doorway, but no one, not even the boy's mother, said anything. After what seemed a long time but what was in fact only seconds, the monarch pulled the spoon away; the boy was sobbing in fear, tears were pouring from his eyes, his little hand pointed to his father in reproach. The sultan took out the lettuce leaf and pressed it firmly onto the boy's neck, which was quite warm from having the hot metal held so close to it. The boy began to wail even more. The monarch tried to console the boy by saying, "My, son, light of my eye, you are an Ottoman, grit your teeth, hang on. This will heal you." Then he gestured to the boy's mother to come hold the lettuce against his neck. The tearful young woman did as he wanted. She tore off a piece of her dress, placed the lettuce in it and wrapped it around the boy's neck.

The sultan said, "Actually, you should use aloe, it takes the pain away immediately, it moisturizes and heals, but unfortunately we don't have any. This is better than nothing." Then he made the handle of the spoon red hot again. "Look, my lion, your father is going to do the same thing to himself, and I won't just hold it close the way I did to you, it's going to touch my skin." He placed the glowing metal against his throat, his hand didn't even tremble. After holding it there for some time, he pressed a lettuce leaf against his throat and smiled. "My lion," he said, "does it make you feel better to see me suffer the same pain? Now, God willing, we'll both get better."

His family was accustomed to the sultan cauterizing various parts of his body, but this was the first time they'd seen him do this to a child, even if only partially, and they were terrified for the little prince.

The doctor's heart palpitations—A test— The first visit to the mansion

AFTER A RESTLESS NIGHT, drifting in and out of sleep, wondering obsessively if the tyrant had really been deposed and experiencing heart palpitations, the doctor set out early, passing through Eleftheria Square, where six Turks had been hanged thirty-three years earlier, to get to the hospital, where he hoped to learn more details about the fate of the sultan. This was a momentous event that affected the lives of everyone in the empire, whether they were Turks, Jews, Bulgarians, Armenians, Greeks, or Serbians; no one could stay calm and go about their business as usual.

Early in the morning, the streets of Thessaloniki began to fill with groups of excited people who whispered and read aloud from newspapers. This could only mean that the tyrant who had oppressed and suffocated everyone for so many years had been overthrown. And he had been overthrown by the young officers of the Third Army, who they'd seen so often on the streets of Thessaloniki. It was difficult to believe.

The greatest celebration Thessaloniki had seen was on the day Abdülhamid proclaimed constitutional monarchy after coming to power. As in every city in the empire, there were official parades, and people of all nationalities, religions, and sexes poured into the streets throwing flowers and shouting, "Long live freedom!"

Now, in spite of everything, the Thessaloniki newspapers announced the sultan's overthrow in a timid and cautious manner. It was not going to be easy for people to become accustomed to this new period.

As he passed through the square the doctor mumbled, "The bastard! He destroyed our lives," then continued on toward the hospital as he did every morning. The Third Army Hospital was full of soldiers and officers who had been severely wounded in clashes with Balkan guerillas. He was so busy that the nurses wiped the sweat from his brow as he performed surgery. He would have to treat dozens of patients that day, this was the price of being a senior military doctor. He pushed his way through the anxious crowd of relatives waiting outside the hospital door. He'd just put on his white jacket and hung his stethoscope around his neck when he was given word that the chief doctor wanted to see him. He wondered why he was being called in so early in the morning. The chief doctor didn't like him much because he was too close to the dissident officers. In any event, the doctor never concealed this. He fully supported those who wanted to overthrow Abdülhamid and bring freedom to the nation. He was in the habit of reciting Namık Kemal's nationalist poetry in a deep, full voice.

The chief doctor greeted him with an odd, almost devious smile. "Good morning, doctor," he said. "You have a new assignment." Then he handed him a telegram from the Ministry of War in Istanbul, announcing that Captain Atıf Hüseyin Bey would now serve as doctor for the deposed sultan and his family, who were under house arrest in Thessaloniki.

The composure he had gained from his training and experience as a doctor prevented him from fainting on the spot, but his head spun and his hands trembled. His heart was beating in his throat like a hunted bird. As he returned to his own office he kept wondering how this had happened.

He was dazed, but he had no choice but to take off his white jacket and put on his uniform jacket. He read the telegram again several times. There was no mistake, the telegram said that Captain Atıf Hüseyin Bey was responsible for the health of the deposed monarch and his family, who were being held at the Alatini mansion. His greatest enemy's health had been entrusted to him. He put his stethoscope in his bag and left the hospital.

The doctor liked walking the streets of Thessaloniki, he usually walked everywhere, but now, as he was on official duty, he got into the military car that was waiting for him at the front door. The roof of the car was open and it was a bright spring day, but he was so dazed that he barely saw where he was going.

He did notice that they passed Hamidiye Avenue and Hamidiye Fountain. The dictator's name was everywhere, wherever you turned you were faced with his heavy, sinister shadow; presumably this would change now that he'd been overthrown. These avenues, fountains, and neighborhoods—yes there was a Hamidiye neighborhood in Thessaloniki—would later be renamed Reşadiye after the new sultan.

As they approached the mansion, he saw that soldiers had blocked the streets and weren't allowing anyone to pass. The doctor was only allowed to pass after the driver showed the guards his official pass. The area had been closed to all civilians. This three-story, red-brick mansion with its large garden full of century-old trees was one of the most beautiful buildings in Thessaloniki, and one of the Italian architect Poselli's masterpieces. There were also sentries at the garden gate. He noticed soldiers with rifles every twenty paces, and officers wandering here and there smoking cigarettes. In the flower bed in the middle of the garden was a sign that read *Liberté, Egalité, Fraternité*. It had probably been put there by officers excited by the overthrow of a dictator. The doctor spoke with the commander, gave him his assignment papers, then sighed as he looked toward the front door. "This is a test," he said to himself as he climbed the front steps. "God is testing me."

The sultan and the doctor meet—The New Ottomans—Armenians—Assassination attempt—National poet Namık Kemal

WHEN THE DEPOSED SULTAN saw the officer, who the eunuch had announced, he raised his eyebrows in surprise, then his suspicious nature led him to feel uneasy. He looked at the captain, a sandy-haired man of medium height who had a fashionable handlebar mustache that made him look like a French doctor, and wondered what he was doing there. Had he been appointed to replace Ali Fethi Bey? Or was he here to harm him and his family? When the captain explained that he had been appointed as doctor to the imperial family, the sultan's suspicions were not allayed. He shook the man's hand and gestured for him to sit, but dozens of possible scenarios raced through his mind. Was this doctor, who had appeared so suddenly, a government spy who'd been sent to murder them discreetly?

Despite his misgivings, Abdülhamid greeted the doctor not just politely but with the dignity of a ruler.

He answered detailed questions about his own health and that of his family. The doctor took out a small notebook with a Bayer logo and wrote down the details of the sultan's constipation, bronchitis, indigestion, insomnia, neuralgia, and hemorrhoids, and the medical status of his wives and children. Later, when the sultan insisted, the captain took a cigarette from a case inlaid with diamonds and precious stones, then sat and listened to the old man in defensive silence.

"From outside, everything seems easy, doesn't it, doctor? Especially being a head of state...You can take care of everything with a single command, hang or behead whomever you want. The public might think this, but that isn't the case. In fact the monarch is a prisoner and slave to the throne, he can't do everything he wants. There are a lot of people running the state, and they play all sorts of games behind his back. Among them are traitors in the pay of other nations, viziers who want to put another member of the dynasty on the throne or even take it for themselves, all of them making devious plans to overthrow the ruler. Oh how I wish I could have lifted this nation up with a single command. I visited France and England when I was twenty-four, and I was amazed by the scientific progress they'd made. I was with my uncle and my brother, we saw with our own eyes that they were so far ahead of us we could never catch up. Those factories, those trains rushing past, lamps that turn night into day, clean, well-illuminated cities where men and women live and work together."

The doctor couldn't contain himself and said, "This is exactly what we were trying to say. All we wanted was for the Ottoman Empire to be like Europe, to experience development based on science. But instead of following this path you had your spies watch us and imprisoned and persecuted anyone who spoke up."

"That's why I said it looks easy from outside. There was nothing I could do! Such a huge empire, so many millions of citizens. Everyone has their own ideas. The ulema says one thing, and admirers of Europe say another."

"If you hadn't silenced the intellectuals, they could have enlightened the people."

"No, no," said the former sultan, "it wouldn't have worked. Look, let me tell you something. A university professor put a pigeon in a box to see how long it could live without air. Then, using religion as an excuse, some of the conservative officers attacked him. We were barely able to save him. Faith and science are incompatible."

In helplessness he held out his hands, shrugged his shoulders and raised his eyebrows. "What could I have done? Things had been going badly since the time of my grandfather Murad. The Russian tsar, the French and British Empires were trying to carve us up like a hunted animal and take the tastiest pieces. And what did I do? I acted as if I didn't know what was going on and set them against each other. And I drew the German emperor to my side. The people you call the New

Ottomans aren't aware of this; they talk about freedom but not about anything else. But I know that this word will make our lands miserable and tear apart the state. I kept this state afloat for thirty-three years but no one appreciates me. They ignore all of my achievements. That's my destiny, what can I do? The will of God…"

There was a long silence. There was no sound but the cheerful chirping of the birds in the garden. The doctor thought he should report what the man had been saying, these were significant statements. But he noticed that the man had said nothing about the new regime or the new sultan they'd put on the throne.

The doctor asked, "And now?"

The old man immediately grasped the situation, and he dropped the tone of grievance he'd been using. "You can be sure that my brother and your new government will do everything in the best possible way. I'm nothing more than an old man who prays for their health and wishes the best for the nation. I swear I have no intention of trying to return to power. In fact I wanted to retire from office but the people around me wouldn't let me. My only desire is to live a calm, quiet life in this corner of the empire. May God protect my brother the sultan and may all go well for him."

You liar, thought the doctor. *This man is terrified. The fear is driving him mad. All the greatest monsters are like that.*

The sultan was perceptive enough to know what the doctor was thinking.

"You've misunderstood me," he said. "Or rather, both you and the Europeans misunderstood me. They depicted me as a bloodthirsty tyrant. They had to do that in order to carve up the empire. I'm the world's most compassionate man, believe me when I say this, I'm being sincere. Contrary to my family's custom I didn't kill my brothers or any other relatives who were contenders for the throne. In thirty-three years I approved only four or five executions; those weren't for political reasons either, they were monsters who had slaughtered their parents or their children. At the palace I had only one person executed, a eunuch who committed an act of astonishing impudence. Our history has not seen a period of such benevolence. But what did they do, they depicted me as an executioner covered in blood."

The doctor was so annoyed at how this man was trying to portray himself as an angel that without intending to he interrupted the sultan. "Oh, come on," he said. "You sent all the intellectuals into exile. You had Grand Vizier Midhat Pasha killed in Yemen. The European newspapers depicted you covered in Armenian blood. You massacred thousands of our Armenian citizens. Are these lies?"

"I don't accept this!" The sultan stood suddenly. "I don't accept this, I can't be blamed for these things. History will show this."

"Don't get excited," said the doctor. "It's not good for your blood pressure."

"How can I not get excited?" asked the sultan. "What could be more provocative than calling a compassionate man a monster. The Armenians...Not ordinary Armenian citizens, of course, but don't you know that Armenian terrorists tried to assassinate me?"

The doctor nodded. The sultan, still on his feet, continued.

"Three years ago they tried to blow me up with a bomb. As I was returning from Friday prayers, they blew up a carriage full of explosives, twenty-six innocent people were blown to pieces. I survived because I took a moment to speak to the shaykh al-Islam and I was late. Otherwise I would have been blown to pieces. The perpetrators were caught, their leader was a Belgian named Joris. You know about all this, don't you?"

"Yes."

"Now tell me what monarch wouldn't have these monsters executed? Think of all civilized nations. In which of them would this crime go unpunished? None of them, of course. They would have tortured those assassins to death, but what did I do, doctor, what did I do? I let them all go, I sent them abroad. I even gave them money."

The sultan offered the doctor another cigarette, but he didn't take it. Then he lit his own cigarette, inhaled deeply twice, blew the smoke out of his famous nose and said, "When Armenian terrorists armed with guns and bombs took over the Ottoman Bank, killing innocent people and threatening to blow up the bank and start a revolution, what did I do? Do you remember, doctor, did you read about it in the newspapers? I allowed these violent terrorists to calmly board a yacht and leave the country. Look it up, it happened exactly as I said it did. Does all this forgiveness make me a murderer and a monster, or a compassionate ruler?"

The doctor began to feel overwhelmed by what the man was saying. He realized he could not argue with a man who had spent his life debating politics with the entire world; he was almost at the point that he had to admit the sultan was right because these were historical facts that could not be refuted. Indeed this sultan was compassionate in comparison to his ancestors, one of whom had nineteen of his brothers strangled when he came to power, and it was true that he had pardoned the terrorists. Indeed sometimes he paid salaries to the intellectuals he had exiled.

The doctor left the mansion in a state of confusion. This was the man's greatest skill as an emperor; he confused people. This man, who was known to the world and to the opposition in the empire as a butcher of Armenians and was depicted in foreign newspapers as a symbol of death, had turned everything around by saying he had spared even those who had attempted to take his life. The best way for the doctor to alleviate his confusion would be to discuss all of this with his friends in the evening. Perhaps they could help him make sense of it. In any event, they were waiting excitedly to hear everything he had to tell them. It wasn't just them, all of Thessaloniki was bursting with curiosity. He thought about Melahat the whole way home. She must have heard that the tyrant had been overthrown, there must have been as much joy and surprise at this development in Cyprus as there was in Thessaloniki. Not just in Cyprus but all of the Turks, Greeks, Jews, Armenians, Kurds, Serbs, Montenegrins, Bulgarians, Roma, Arabs, Georgians, Crimeans, Wallachians, Pomaks, Albanians, Bosnians, and Levantines of the empire were experiencing the same thing. Yet it was going to take time to get used to a world without Abdülhamid. Most people couldn't remember a time when they didn't feel his cruel breath on the backs of their necks, even though they never saw him and he kept himself hidden behind the high walls of his palace. They were going to continue whispering for some time. Because, after all, what if the man was able to seize power again? This wasn't a possibility to be discounted. What the doctor wondered about most was whether the new government would pardon those whom Abdülhamid had exiled. Presumably they would, in fact they surely would. This meant that Melahat, for whom the doctor pined day and night, would return to Istanbul soon. The doctor had been madly in love since the first time he saw her on that evening that smelled of lilac and the sea. When he learned that Melahat, who lived in the same neighborhood, was not indifferent to him he began walking on air. Unfortunately her father, Saadettin Bey, who was a high official in the police department, ran afoul of the palace and was abruptly sent to Cyprus, where

Namık Kemal Bey was already living in exile. If only the great poet Namık Kemal, whose beautiful nationalist poems challenged the despot and introduced the word "freedom" to the youth of the nation, had lived to see this day. For years, Namık Kemal's poems of freedom had represented resistance in the hearts of the youth, and in the end it was the poet and not the cruel sultan who had emerged victorious. Indeed it was said that a certain courageous officer had taken the surname Kemal out of admiration for the poet.

The doctor laughed happily and lit a cigarette, then remembered that Namık Kemal and Abdülhamid had once been friends. In the beginning, at least, they'd spoken well of each other. The sultan had invited the poet to join the committee that drafted the first constitution, and had also assigned him to a number of other duties. It was interesting that while reformist poets like Namık Kemal and Tevfik Fikret initially supported the sultan, he was at first severely criticized by the conservative poet Mehmet Akif, who called him the Crimson Unbeliever.

The doctor drew deeply from his cigarette and thought, *We're all full of contradictions. Myself included.* But the strangest was the old man he'd just met.

Curious young officers—What kind of man
is the Crimson Unbeliever—Armenians
circumcised after death

THAT EVENING AS THE officers sipped their drinks and
ate fresh, crispy red mullet at the Olympos, which
seemed brighter and more attractive than usual, the
doctor tried to answer his friends' many questions.
How did you go there, what did you say, what did he
say, did you examine him, how did he greet you, is he
miserable or is he still proud, did you touch him? The
questions came at him so fast and steadily that he had
to speak quickly in order to tell them everything.

"A weary, miserable old man in an old sweater
came into the hall. Anyone who had seen him on the
throne during one of the celebrations at the palace,
where hundreds of government officials didn't dare
to approach or speak to him, or indeed even look
directly at him, and where the highest-ranking viziers would bow down to kiss a cord that extended
from the throne and then back away slowly, wouldn't

believe it was the same man. A man of medium height, hunchbacked, as you know, and that famous face we've all seen in our nightmares...But somehow his nose didn't seem as big as I'd thought it would be. Yes, bigger than an ordinary nose, but...maybe because it's so exaggerated in the European caricatures it didn't seem that big to me.

"He greeted me politely, shook my hand, and sat me across from him. He immediately took out his cigarette case and offered me a cigarette, but I didn't take one. Then I told him who I was, and that I had been assigned as his doctor. I told him I'd received an order from the Ministry of War. 'If you have no objection, might I see the order,' he asked timidly. I showed it to him and then said, 'I have to examine you, where's your room?' He brought me to an empty room in the empty mansion. It looked like a room in a boarding-house; there was a simple bed, and the old sheets and quilts gave it a shabby air. I asked him about his medical complaints.

"He told me about his indigestion, bronchitis, frequent colds, throat inflammations, constipation, and various joint and muscle pains. There was a cloth wrapped around his neck. When I asked him what it was for, he smiled and said, 'Doctor Marko Pasha and Doctor Mavroyani Pasha were the doctors who served me longest, but, begging your pardon, I don't trust doctors much. I've seen how many mistakes they make. That's why I prefer, if possible, to treat myself. When I have throat inflammations I put red-hot metal to my neck.' Then he took off the cloth and showed me the red burn marks.

"I asked him to disrobe, he took off his sweater and his underwear and sat on the bed. I listened to his lungs, they were quite congested, and when I touched his cold, clammy skin I had to remind myself that this man had been sultan and caliph. Because I still didn't believe it. When I told him to cough he coughed, when I told him to take a deep breath he did so, I told him to hold his breath and he did, when I told him to stand up he stood. When I asked about his bowel movements and frequency of urination, he told me . . . I almost got the giggles, it was unbelievable, was I really touching the caliph? I would never have believed that one day I would have this experience.

"There were black-and-blue burn marks all over his torso, and when I asked about them he said they were from the hot iron. I thought this was a crazy thing to do but I didn't say anything. I took his blood pressure, which was a bit high. I asked what medications he took, and he said he seldom took any. He occasionally took sulfates and used spirit or cupping, and of course there was the cauterization. Nothing more. I told him I would bring some medications the following day. I told him I was also responsible for his family and entourage. He told me he had five wives, three daughters, and two sons as well as the servants. I was surprised because I hadn't heard even the faintest sound. I told him I would have to examine them all. He thanked me, and said he would inform me if he had any medical complaints. Then he got dressed and invited me to join him in the hall.

"He said that if we'd been in the palace he would have offered me some very good coffee, and apologized for not being able to offer me any. Once again I didn't take the cigarette he offered me. He seemed to be trying to ingratiate himself. He began telling me how well he'd administered the empire and about how compassionate he was. Can you imagine? The Red Sultan compassionate . . . It's laughable. He claimed not to have massacred Armenians. He told me about how he'd pardoned the people who'd tried to assassinate him. I got a bit confused at this point. I couldn't say he was lying, because I knew it was true."

Major Saffet, who was somewhat older than him, said, "Yes, you remember correctly, but these are the man's tactics. Nothing but intrigue. He does things and acts as if he didn't. How many thousands of Armenians were slaughtered in Istanbul after that assassination attempt? He pardoned the would-be assassins because he was pressured to do so by the embassies of the great powers, then he secretly provoked, or even secretly ordered, elements of the civilian population to attack the Armenians."

The poor waiter hovered around them, trying to listen to what they were saying so he could tell his boss, but he wasn't the only one. Everyone in the restaurant was looking at them and trying to hear what the doctor was saying. Thessaloniki was a small city, the news had spread quickly, and no one was talking about anything else.

Major Saffet said, "What happened in the east was even worse."

Captain Nihat said, "Yes, major, but didn't the Armenian terrorists, the Dashnak, stage an armed rebellion and commit massacres?"

"Yes," said the major. "There were armed uprisings in Istanbul, they took over the city of Van; there were massacres in Sason, Zeytun, Bayburt, and Erzurum. Thousands of innocent Muslims were killed but the sultan didn't punish the terrorists who did this, he punished the civilian population."

Nihat objected again. "It was the Kurds and not the Turks who put down those rebellions."

"Yes," said the major, "you're right, but who organized the Kurds, who recruited and armed thousands of Kurds to form the Hamidiye Regiments, who promoted Kurdish feudal lords to the rank of pasha? This is what I want to explain to you. The tactics of a devious man, he sets everyone against each other, then sits back and watches it all with an innocent expression. The Bulgarian church, the Greek church, and the Serbian church have been in conflict for years. Why? Because if they were united they would constitute a threat to the empire. My friends, you're up against the craftiest man in the world. Don't believe a word he says."

The doctor said, "Don't you realize that what you're saying is in favor of the sultan? He set people against each other to put down rebellions and save the empire…"

A thin young man with wire-frame glasses and a thin mustache approached the table.

"Excuse me, commanders," he said. "I was sitting right behind you and I couldn't help overhearing your conversation. Forgive me."

"Fine," grumbled Saffet.

"I'm an Armenian from Van," said the man. "My name is Agop Demircian. With your permission, there's something I'd like to say."

The officers nodded.

"They circumcised my father!"

"How could that be?" said Captain Nihat. "Why would they circumcise a Christian citizen? Everyone is free to practice their own religion. I've never heard of anything like that."

The nationalist officers thought that this was Armenian propaganda and adopted a distant attitude, but Agop said, "Listen to me for a moment commanders, I implore you, not only did they circumcise my father, they did so after he was dead."

The officers looked at one another as if they were trying to understand what the man had said.

"As you were just saying, there have been some major clashes between Armenians and Muslims, thousands of people have lost their lives. My father was among those who were killed in Sason. My mother found him among hundreds of bodies in the square. His pants had been pulled down and my mother could see that he'd been circumcised. She shouted out, 'This is my husband, Kirkor. Last night he was a Christian but today he's become a Muslim!'"

The officers must have been interested by what the man had said, because they invited him to sit at the fourth, empty seat at the table. "Tell us more, Agop Efendi," they said.

Agop whispered, "It's all because of the individual you were talking about earlier." He glanced around in fear as he said this.

"The sultan? How so, what does this have to do with him?"

Still whispering, Agop said, "The great powers of Europe sent observers to report on the conflict. They looked at whether or not the victims were circumcised to determine whether they were Muslim or Christian. The number of Armenian victims was always higher than the number of Muslim victims, but the government forces circumcised most of them so they would be recorded as Muslim. After the clashes in Sason, they called in a man named Ilyas who circumcised five hundred Armenian bodies. My poor father, Kirkor Demircian, went to the next world circumcised."

Even the officers were surprised by this level of intrigue; they didn't believe what they'd heard. This sultan was a diabolical politician, indeed he could outwit the devil himself. Somehow the doctor couldn't see the miserable man he'd examined that day, and who'd offered him a cigarette, in this light, but he'd been in the presence of an emperor who had the whole world wrapped around his finger. He was a monster, a clever, devious, calculating monster.

"That's too much," said Major Saffet. "It's difficult to believe."

Captain Nihat, who'd been having difficulty containing himself, turned angrily to Agop and said, "Look? Are you a terrorist? Dashnak, Hinchak... Do you have anything to do with these organizations?"

"No, sir," replied Agop in surprise.

"Where do you live? Thessaloniki?"

"No sir," said Agop in a trembling voice. "My family is in Istanbul. I come to Thessaloniki to buy tobacco, then I sell it in Istanbul. I'm an independent merchant."

For a time Nihat continued to stare sternly at Agop, and the atmosphere at the table became tense. Then he said, "Look! Did you take part in the raid on the Ottoman Bank?"

"Wha— No, commander."

"Tell the truth!"

"I am telling the truth, commander."

"Okay, did you take part in the Armenian raid on the Sublime Porte?"

"Perish the thought. Of course I didn't, commander. I don't have anything to do with those organizations."

"So you weren't involved in any of those incidents."

"No, commander. I'm an independent merchant who works to feed his family."

"But your father took part in the uprising," said the captain.

Somewhat taken aback, Agop stuttered, "Y...yes. But I haven't been back to my native lands in years."

Nihat suddenly leaned across the table and seized Agop by the collar. "You're lying," he said. "You're an Armenian terrorist. Everything you said is a lie, it's slander! So they circumcised them, and five hundred people at that, so what about the blood, how are they going to conceal the blood?"

His voice was so loud that everyone in the restaurant was looking at them in deep silence; the waiters were frozen in place, there were no sounds of knives and forks and clinking glasses.

The doctor noticed that Nihat was trembling in rage and that his hand was moving toward his pistol; he stood and removed Nihat's hand from Agop's collar. He apologized politely to the young man, who didn't quite understand what was going on, and invited him to leave the restaurant. Agop was quick to comply with this request, and disappeared as fast as he could.

When the doctor sat down, Nihat lit a cigarette and smoked in an irritated manner. Major Saffet tried to calm him. Nihat turned to the doctor and asked, "Why did you defend him? It's clear that he's lying, that he's defaming our state and our people."

"How do you know?" asked the doctor. "Haven't terrible things been going on for several years, haven't thousands of people been killed on both sides? It's a mess, everyone is at each other's throats."

"Yes, a lot of people have died," said Nihat. "But I just don't believe what he said, it's slander. When I asked him about the blood he didn't say anything, he couldn't answer. If they'd circumcised them, wouldn't they be covered in blood?"

The doctor raised his beer. "Come on, let's end the evening on a positive note. We're all very excited. We'll carry on tomorrow."

The three tipsy officers left the restaurant and went their separate ways. Even if the evening had gone a bit sour, it had ended on a good note. The doctor wanted to get home as soon as possible, because he had his nightly letter to write. He was going to tell Melahat about everything that had happened. "It depends on the time of death, Nihat," he murmured. "If enough time has passed, dead bodies don't bleed. And in any event, those bodies would already have been covered in blood." But he had no intention of telling Nihat about this medical fact and getting into an argument about the conflict between the Armenians and the Muslims. After all, they were citizens of the same country.

The secret notes of a doctor who suddenly became famous

BEFORE HE'D EVEN BEEN able to digest what was happening, the doctor had suddenly become the most famous man in Thessaloniki. When he walked the streets and squares he'd known for years, people stopped talking and stared at him as he passed, though no one had the courage to approach him. It was as if there was an invisible bell jar over the doctor. The only thing everyone from seven to seventy talked about was the sultan having been exiled to their city. Everyone's heart was racing, and everyone wore an indelible expression of surprise. It was as if they were dreaming a shared dream. The doctor was the only person who could enter and leave the sealed area, the only person who saw the former sultan every day and then walked among the people. This made him seem like a mortal who went to Mount Olympus to visit the gods. Though in fact he only went to the Olympos nightclub. He continued to work at the hospital, he met his friends frequently, and every night when he went home he wrote to Melahat. The only deviations from his old routine were his visits to the Alatini mansion and the notes he wrote on what he saw and heard there in the little notebooks distributed by pharmaceutical companies. He wrote about his conversations with the sultan, and although he didn't think these notes would ever be published, he felt it was important to keep a record for posterity. The man felt the need to talk to someone and was telling him amazing things; he had a feeling there was more to come. Still, he felt it best not to mention these notes to anyone, and indeed to hide them where no one could find them. It was strictly forbidden for the former sultan to have any relationship with the outside world, to receive or send any news. If the new government heard about it, he might even face a court-martial. The sultan's brother Reşad, whose name had been banned for thirty-three years, had come to the throne as Mehmet V Reşad, male children would now be given his name, but everyone knew that Reşad was a puppet controlled by the army. The leaders of the Committee for Union and Progress had taken over the administration. He wouldn't be surprised if they shed so much blood that people would miss the old sultan. The "sick man of Europe" needed surgery, and unfortunately surgery was a bloody business.

As the doctor wrote his spidery notes in the Bayer notebook he occasionally felt spooked, as if he were being watched, and he would glance around the room and out the window. At the moment, even mentioning the sultan's name was a great risk. On the first page of the notebook he wrote: "The words of the deposed monarch Abdülhamid." On the first page of another notebook he wrote: "Concerning Abdülhamid's medical condition."

He had to be careful about his phrasing. Then later he thought to himself, "His tyrannical reign is over, why am I so worried?" After all, had freedom not arrived, had the oppressor not been overthrown? Yes, power had changed hands, but a voice within told him to be even more cautious in this new era. The former sultan used to send his opponents into exile, but these people gunned their opponents down in the streets. He'd seen everything with his own eyes in Thessaloniki.

Bored ladies—An opera at the palace—
A beauty who was often pregnant—
Sarah Bernhardt

THE MANSION WAS EMPTY, the imperial family had no
one else to talk to, they were under a military block-
ade, they were only allowed to open one or two shutters from time to time so there was usually little light;
they missed all the fun they used to have in the palace, the private operas, the exotic animals, the joy of
opening the packages of elegant clothes sent by the
ambassador in Paris; they all had long since moved
past being bored to tears and were now on the verge
of a nervous breakdown. The daughters were careful
not to make any sound apart from music so as not to
disturb their father, but they desperately had to find
some solution or they would not be able to endure this
prison. The mothers, who were experiencing the same
boredom themselves, didn't know what to do to amuse
the young girls. They took turns at the piano, playing both Oriental and Occidental music, and rondos,

barcaroles, and waltzes. Unfortunately the music was not enough to entertain them, and indeed it could be irritating because the piano, which was flanked by two large candelabras, was out of tune.

One afternoon when they were languishing on the top floor, Şadiye Sultan suggested playing a game. Let's see who knows how many rooms, halls, and bathrooms there are in our palaces. All of them, and particularly Ayşe, thought this was a good idea. In any event, they were only interested in themselves. For them, the word "Ottoman" described a family rather than an empire. The family was a closed world, they felt they were above everyone and everything and their lives were completely filled with concerns such as who wanted to marry whom, which princes were at odds with each other, who had how much money, who was in love with whom, which prince had a bright future, the newborn members of the dynasty, the magnificent circumcision festivals, who was wearing the nicest jewelry, clothing brought from Paris, furs, cloth, earrings, necklaces, broches, makeup, perfumes.

"Shall we start with Dolmabahçe Palace?" asked Ayşe Sultan.

"Why not," said Naciye Hanım. "You start."

Ayşe looked up at the high, decorated ceiling, and after thinking a while said, "First the number of rooms. Dolmabahçe has two hundred and eighty-five rooms. There are forty-four halls. There are also sixty-eight bathhouses and sixty-eight toilets."

Her mother, Müşfika Hanım, said, "Good for you. How do you manage to keep so much information in your head? That's amazing."

Şadiye Sultan said, "Fine, so how many tons of gold were used in the ceiling decorations?"

"Fourteen tons," said Ayşe Sultan, and once again she was congratulated.

"How many lightbulbs are in the chandelier in the great hall?" said Refia Sultan, thinking she was asking an impossible question, but Ayşe Sultan answered at once, "Seven hundred and fifty lightbulbs. The chandelier was a gift from Queen Victoria. It weighs four tons. It's the largest chandelier in the world."

"That's wonderful," said Fatma Pesend Hanım. "You've become an expert on palaces."

Ayşe Sultan smiled in gratitude, but didn't feel the need to say that the information came from a page from an old French magazine she'd grabbed as they were leaving the palace, and that she'd read over and over again out of boredom. It contained a sentence she hadn't repeated—"Dolmabahçe Palace alone was enough to bankrupt the already indebted Ottoman treasury." Customs officials had cut this page out of the magazine and sent it to the palace. All books and magazines sent from abroad were censored in this manner. All customs officials had the right to remove whatever pages they wanted. They cut out pages they sensed were subversive and sent them to the palace. Ayşe Sultan had been in the habit of reading these pages whenever she managed to get her hands on

them. A book titled *The Laws of Thermodynamics* had
been sent to the palace because a customs official
had mistaken the word "dynamics" for "dynamite,"
which was one of many forbidden words. Ayşe Sultan
had never quite understood why the book had been
censored.

In fact the issue of censorship went far beyond
what a young girl who loved her dear father could
see. The sultan was constantly restricting the press; he
wouldn't allow people he didn't like to publish newspapers; he had writers fired, exiled, or imprisoned, but
he lavished gold on newspapers like *Sabah* that constantly praised him. He also undermined opposition
publications by buying up the newspaper's shares. As
if this wasn't enough, he paid a lot of money to foreign
newspapers to cut articles that were critical of him. He
owned the *Korrespondans* newspaper in Vienna and
the *Oriyent* newspaper in Paris.

The magazine page in Ayşe Sultan's pocket was
the only souvenir of the "home" that they could now
see only in their dreams, that they'd left to the sound
of cannon fire as the Guard Corps surrendered to the
Movement Army from Thessaloniki, people rushing
this way and that, animals scampering to escape the
noise, and from which they'd been taken by force and
loaded into brougham carriages. When they heard
the approaching rebel army, the night watchmen, Albanian doormen, gardeners, butlers, cooks, eunuchs,
chamberlains, and minor officials all disappeared
into the night. When the guard unit of the Second

Army, which had been assigned to protect the palace, began to arm themselves, the sultan said, "Put those arms away, not a single shot will be fired, I will not shed Muslim blood," so they surrendered to the rebels.

The palace wasn't a single building, it was a city. It was a city inhabited by thousands of people, with its own mosque, police station, bank, hospital, guard unit, opera, theater, ceramic factory, carpentry workshop, and zoo. Every Friday her father boarded a solid-gold carriage flanked by cavalry or infantry to attend Friday prayers at the Hamidiye Mosque at the bottom of the hill. People would come from all over Istanbul, jostling one another and peering over shoulders to get a glimpse of him from a distance. It was on one of these festive occasions that they tried to blow up her dear father with a bomb. Twenty-six people and a number of thoroughbred horses were blown to pieces, but God had protected her father. Her dear father's heart was so strong, he was so fearless that amid the carnage he seized a whip and drove the carriage back to the palace himself, showing the people that their beloved sultan was still alive and could not be disposed of so easily. Some time after this incident he'd explained to his daughter why censorship, surveillance, exile, and other precautions were necessary. "We have so many enemies within and without, my girl. If you knew how many assassination plots we hear about every day, if I hadn't established such an effective secret service I would have died a hundred times already. They tried to enter the palace through the sewers, there were plans to smear poison on the arms of my throne during a holiday celebration, they've tried to incite the people to rebellion. Censorship is essential. The European press publishes slander cooked up by the nations that are trying to destroy us, some traitors at home repeat this slander because they've swallowed the hook of freedom that was so cynically thrown to them. The only thing the great powers want is to topple this great empire and share it out among themselves. Do you understand now, my girl? We're in danger because they know that as long as I'm alive I will not allow this. We have to keep our eyes open."

Ayşe Sultan was so moved by her father's words that she retired to her room and wept for hours, she cursed those who had tried to kill such a great and compassionate ruler, she prayed fervently till morning for God to protect him and smite his enemies. After all, he was accountable to no one but God.

Her compassionate father was depicted on the covers of European magazines as a bloodthirsty killer, but they didn't call King Leopold a barbarian even though he'd had thousands of people's hands cut off. These people were hypocrites. Her father was right.

The bored women of the mansion soon found a new way to entertain themselves. They played out scenes from the Italian operas they'd seen at the palace. They sang Verdi arias to the accompaniment of the piano, acting out grandiose scenes in their pitiful clothes, but it was enough to keep them amused.

At the palace, which now seemed almost imaginary, when the sultan went to bed in the evening, he would have novels read to him from behind a screen at the foot of his bed, but occasionally, when he didn't drift off to sleep, he would clap his hands and say, "Opera!" When word was sent to the Italian performers, who held ranks such as pasha, major, and colonel on the palace staff, they had half an hour to prepare to appear onstage. The director of the palace theater was Arturo Stravolo, an accomplished performer from Naples who had immigrated to Istanbul with his parents, his uncles and aunts, his wife, and his brothers, all of them also performers, and entered the sultan's service. The sultan did not want to see any play more than once, so one of Stravolo's duties was to travel to Europe, watch new plays, and decide which ones to stage for his master.

All of the performers were attached to a military unit and had to wear uniforms denoting their rank. Angelo was a lieutenant, Luigi the violinist was a captain, Gaetano the baritone was a colonel, and Nicola the skilled tenor was an adjutant major. When Aranda Pasha the conductor received word in the middle of the night that he was to perform *A Masked Ball*, the orchestra had to be ready to perform the piece in half an hour. On some days the sultan watched plays with family and guests, but at night he would sit alone in his box. If there was something in a play he didn't understand, or if there was anything about the performance that puzzled him, he would stop everyone with a gesture of his hand. Everything had to be explained in detail to His Highness before the performance could resume. Also, the sultan did not like unhappy endings, so the ending of every opera from *La Traviata* to *Il Trovatore* was changed. For instance, Violetta didn't die in the end but was seen dancing happily.

Sarah Bernhardt, the most famous French actress of the period, came to the palace theater to perform and was presented to the sultan. "Madame," he said to her, "it's said that in Paris you performed a death scene so realistically that the audience panicked because they thought you were really dead. Is this true?"

Bernhardt, flattered by the sultan's attention, said, "Yes, Your Majesty, what they say is true, and this evening I will show you."

The sultan, who had forbidden death scenes, hurriedly said, "No, no, madame, what I would like to request is that you not play this scene so realistically, or, if possible, to cut the scene altogether."

The actor the sultan most enjoyed watching was Arturo's beautiful wife, Cecilia. He wanted her to play the lead role in every play, but because for biological reasons this was not always possible, the troupe had to go to great lengths, using wigs, makeup, and dimmed lights to disguise another actress to resemble her. Because Cecilia was frequently pregnant, her growing belly would become unsuitable for the young female roles she played and she would stay away from the stage until she gave birth. However, it was worth the trouble; the Italian performers were paid well and lived in luxury, and Arturo the director became the first person in Istanbul to own an automobile. The caliph, the protector of Islam for whom the people of Anatolia prayed, was a fan of European culture. He used to say that Turkish music made him feel gloomy, but that European music cheered him. He would say, "They call it Turkish music, but it came from Persia and Greece. Turks have no music of their own except pipes and drums." He loved opera. The sultan was full of contradictions, though, and sometimes he would get bored halfway through the play. When Stravolo sensed that the sultan was getting bored, he knew enough to stop in the middle of a scene and bring jugglers, magicians, and acrobats onto the stage.

The snake's hands—Sherlock Efendi— Translation department

"THE NIGHTS IN THESSALONIKI are longer than they are in Istanbul," said the sultan. "I've always had trouble sleeping, but it's worse here. I sit in the armchair and smoke cigarettes until morning."

"Here you don't have the entertainments you had at the palace, that's why," said the doctor. There was a veiled mockery in his tone, and he seemed pleased with himself. "People say you had detective novels read to you in the bedroom and that when you were bored you watched opera. Is this true?"

"Yes," said the sultan, "that's true. Indeed I even established a translation department. Day and night they translated the latest books from Europe for me."

"Is it true that you admire Sherlock Holmes?"

"Yes, but I used to admire Rocambole. Have you heard of him, doctor? There was a famous French writer called Pierre Ponson, his lead character was a man named Rocambole who could do amazing things.

I used to like him better than Sherlock, but then I got angry at the man and stopped reading him."

"Who was it you were angry with? The writer or Rocambole?"

"Why would I be angry at my favorite character? I was angry at the writer, of course. I'd had his latest book translated, Ismet Ağa was reading it at the foot of my bed. There was a passage that read, 'It was as cold as a snake's hands.' I warned him to read it correctly, how could a snake have hands? He insisted that this was what it said. I immediately had the translators called in. They all came in the middle of the night, they were half asleep, they'd dressed hastily and they were disconcerted. I asked them to explain what they meant by snake's hands. I told them I was going to fire them all for such a blatant error in translation. They swore they'd translated the sentence accurately. 'That's what the author wrote, we were surprised too but we didn't change it.' I was confused. 'Fine,' I said, 'I'm going to look into the matter, if what you say is true you can stay on, otherwise I don't know.' They brought the book in the original French, they showed me the sentence, and yes, they were right, the man had actually written this: *Elle avait les mains aussi froides que celles d'un serpent.*

"Don't look so surprised, doctor, as children we were all taught French as well as Arabic and Persian. My French isn't as fluent as my elder brother Murad's was, but I know the language. If I had any French books here I could show you. Meanwhile, let me tell you that I'm not allowed to have any books or newspapers here. They won't even allow a sheet of paper. I wonder if there's anything you can do about this, doctor, I can't live without reading. At the very least they can give me some French detective novels.

"What was I saying? Later I found another non-sensical mistake that Ponson made: *D'une main il leva son poignard, et de l'autre il lui dit*... I remember because I couldn't believe a famous French novelist could make such a mistake and I read it over and over again. Do you know French, doctor? Good, then you understand. I asked myself why I should waste my time reading a man who could make such basic errors, and I never picked up another of his books. Then I discovered Arthur Conan Doyle and Sherlock Holmes. I had it all translated. These stories were more cleverly written. In fact Conan Doyle came to Istanbul and wanted to meet me, but it was during the month of Ramadan and I didn't have time. I awarded him the Order of the Mecidiye, and I awarded his wife a Medal of Compassion.

"I've suffered from insomnia since I was a child. When I listened to these novels I forgot the troubles of daily life, I put myself in the detective's place. I tried to solve the mysteries. And sometimes I did.

"Forgive me, I imagine I'm giving you a headache. Let's leave all that aside for the moment. There's a question I want to ask you, doctor. Please answer me, don't disappoint me. My request is sincere. I know that my brother Reşad Efendi is now sultan. May God give him long life. But who's running the government, who's the grand vizier? Suddenly, I no longer know anything at all. Who's the grand vizier, who are the other members of the cabinet, how are things going in the Balkans, please tell me. I'm just a nobody who does little but pray. What harm could I do anyone. Please."

Melancholy—A Caucasian bride's unfortunate prince—Cows in the mansion garden

HIS MISERY GREW DAY by day, night by night, until it was like a stubborn snake wrapped around his neck. He forced himself to focus on something else, he tried to bring more pleasant memories to mind, he thought of the activities he'd been so fond of in his youth—hunting, horseback riding, archery, swimming, running—to plant the seeds of some kind of hope for the future. He remembered that he'd once been able to run for miles, that he used to swim in the Bosphorus all the time, but now his body was in ruins, and he was amazed by the state he'd allowed it to fall into. Terell, the American ambassador, had given him wonderful saddles made in Texas. This gift of saddles and guns that had been specially made at the Colt factory had been reported in the American press.

"Ah, those were the days," he said. He had paid a high price for all those long years of intrigue, treachery, complications, and fear of assassination at the palace. The rebels from Thessaloniki had struck an unexpected blow, and there could be no recovery from this wound. He asked himself how this had happened to him, and, oddly enough, he put it down to not having exerted enough pressure. How could he not have seen the way that nefarious organization called the Committee for Union and Progress would grow and gain power? Had his secret service in Thessaloniki betrayed him? There was no longer any point in thinking about these things, what was done was done and the throne was now well beyond his reach. The despair and melancholy that had haunted him all his life had reached new levels during his first five days in exile, just as a bullet wound hurts more when the heat has faded. He would never forget how, when he was a child, his mother kept her distance from him out of fear of infecting him. He remembered how she'd looked at him lovingly, he remembered her sad, thin, delicate face, flushed with the fever of the tuberculosis that was raging within her.

He would never forget the look in her eyes. As he sat with her in a room in the cold and unpleasant Beylerbeyi Palace, he felt that she wanted to embrace him, that she was trying to close the distance between them with her eyes. They had to speak loudly, and their voices echoed. In her last days, the young woman told stories about her family, recited nursery rhymes from her childhood, and recalled legends about Mount Qaf, and these remained vivid in his memory for the rest of his life.

She wasted away before his eyes in that cold, sinister Beylerbeyi Palace, and after her death he felt out of place with the other princes, who were living happily with their healthy mothers. He spent most of his time in empty rooms, in closets, and under beds, wishing that his own death would come soon.

As he sat hunched in the armchair, smoking one cigarette after another until the room was thick with smoke, the former sultan thought that none of this would have happened if his mother hadn't died. *Not even this last rebellion. Being motherless is the hardest thing to bear in this world.*

He was seventy years old, but no matter what he did, he couldn't rid himself of the image of that little prince with his sad, drooping, drowsy eyes, watching from behind the door as the other children enjoyed themselves. Everyone talked about his half brother Murad; how cheerful he was, what a good horseback rider he was, his skill at the piano, the waltzes he composed, his masterful swordsmanship, how handsome he was. Murad was the star of the dynasty. He had never been able to compete with Murad, had never been able to get ahead of him. Murad was first in line for the throne, he was the heir apparent. At the time no one would have imagined he would lose his mind, that he would be deposed within three months and that Abdülhamid would be placed on the throne. When he was catapulted to the throne at the moment he least expected it, he experienced the intoxication of absolute power, he was lifted to the sky, for the first time he had surpassed everyone in the family and it gave him a singular joy. The orphaned son of an unfortunate Caucasian girl known as Tir-I Müjgan was now the head of the dynasty, he had surpassed all his rivals. If his mother in heaven had lived, she would be the sultan mother.

He'd seen the way Murad had been destroyed by drink. When they were both princes, Murad would suggest having a drink, Hamid would say, "Fine, but just one," but despite his promise Murad would have a second, a third, a fourth, and then lose count. When Hamid complained that he'd broken his promise, Murad would laugh and say, "I promised I'd have one glass of cognac, and I kept that promise. My second drink was chartreuse, brother, and the third was Armagnac." He himself would only have one drink, he didn't drink much. Once when he wanted to find out why Murad was so fond of drink, they went to the lodge in Maslak and drank like madmen, and at first he liked the feeling of light-headedness, the cheerfulness his melancholy soul was unaccustomed to, and the sense of rising up to the sky. The following day he was punished for this escape with vomiting and cramps, and from then on his wary nature guided him to be more moderate. A single glass of cognac or rum was enough to relax him.

The former sultan emerged from his reverie and looked around. If they weren't going to kill him, he had to find a way to get out of this mansion. He thought deeply about this, he looked at it from every angle, but the only conclusion he reached was that as a prisoner there was nothing he could do. The commander and the doctor were the only people he spoke to, there was no way he could get a message to the outside world. Help could only come from outside. The Muslim population of Anatolia was devoted to him; if they saw even the slightest opportunity they would put their caliph back on the throne. His closest friend among the foreign leaders was Kaiser Wilhelm. The kaiser had visited him in Istanbul twice, and they got along well. He'd given his own most valued property in Tarabya to the kaiser so he could build a summer embassy. The kaiser had built a wonderful fountain for him in Istanbul. Later on the kaiser had visited Jerusalem, and had gained admiration for dismounting from his horse and entering the city on foot. Abdülhamid had given his friend a valuable plot of land in Jerusalem on which to build a church, causing envy among the other European leaders. Perhaps the kaiser was already exerting pressure on the government to keep them from killing his old friend. He hoped this was the case; he'd put aside his dreams of regaining power, and all his hopes of remaining alive rested on the kaiser. He wouldn't have forgotten his old friend, the Germans were a trustworthy people.

Even though he was a prince, and perhaps because he'd lost his mother, he'd always worried about having enough money, and now this anxiety had returned. The amount of property and wealth he had, he owned land the size of a country, was incalculable. He had to be one of the wealthiest men on earth. However, he presumed it had all been seized by the new government. In these circumstances, he could only rely on the wealth he had in foreign countries. The gold and stocks he held in Deutsche Bank and Credit Lyonnaise must have amounted to quite a fortune.

His daughters' fiancés had remained in Istanbul. As a father, he should be arranging weddings for them and building the mansions where they would live. After that it would be his sons' turn. In addition, he had to support a family of nearly forty people at the Alatini mansion. Fortunately, with his usual prudence, he'd sent some of his wealth to foreign banks and had not kept it all in the empire. He knew that no matter how much he implored his brother, the man wouldn't give him anything. And perhaps the man was right. Because for thirty-three years he'd kept his younger brother Reşad under house arrest, he hadn't even allowed him to step foot outside. Now his time had come, and their positions had been reversed. After his older brother Murad had been deposed he was imprisoned for many years at Çirağan Palace, the poor man drew his last breath there. In the old days they would have been killed, they should have been grateful for being allowed to live. But of course the same thing could have been said for him. If it wasn't for his brother's compassion and the new customs, he would have long been dead and buried. Indeed they would have killed his sons as well.

Just as sunlight began to appear through the closed shutters, he heard the call to prayer. The sound spreading out in waves from the mosques of Thessaloniki brought peace to his soul. Now he would perform his ablutions and morning prayers. Praying calmed him even more. But something strange happened, just as he had finished his prayers and was folding his prayer rug, he was surprised to hear cows lowing outside. How had cows gotten past so many soldiers? Someone was calling to the animals and trying to calm them. The strange thing was that the voice sounded like that of Mehmet Efendi, chief of the dairy at the palace. He squinted through the shutters but couldn't see anything but shadows. Could these be the cows' shadows? Just then the cows lowed again, then he heard the dairyman's voice and the squeaking of a wheel. Now he was certain, however they'd got there, there were cows on the grounds of the Alatini mansion. The sultan was accustomed to having animals around him, and he felt a deep sense of peace. Indeed he could smell the horses and the cows.

The doctor's revolutionary anger— The miracle of heroin—The bombs on the ship— The doctor joins a secret society

WITH EVERY PASSING DAY, the doctor felt more anger toward the man he referred to as the "dishonorable dog"; that day, when he left the Alatini mansion burning with revolutionary anger, he muttered to himself that the man thought he was still the sultan. *I know French, I know this, I know that. What he'd studied, what he'd learned. Which emperors he'd been friends with...Boorish dog!* As the military car made its way through the empty streets he puffed angrily on a cigarette, then stopped and laughed at himself. He'd referred to a member of a dynasty that had ruled for six centuries, to a descendant of Mehmet the Conqueror, as boorish, but then when he thought about it, he realized that the man was in fact boorish. *He's not like his illustrious ancestors.*

The man was a braggart, his ego had been stoked for years, and now the doctor was the only person left

to whom he could brag. He'd come close to implying
that he knew more about medicine; in fact he actually
had implied this. He didn't approve of the medication he'd been prescribed for his cold; in addition to
resorting to frightful, idiotic practices such as cauterization, he did not hesitate to say that a folk remedy
he'd learned from the Circassians was the best medicine in the world. You crushed willow bark, mixed it
with yogurt, and spread it all over your body. Though
when the doctor remembered that willow bark con-
tains salicylic acid he felt a bit embarrassed. Just a few
years ago the Bayer company had introduced a new
wonder drug called aspirin. It had been invented by
a German chemist named Felix Hoffmann, and the
main ingredient was the acid in willow bark. But the
doctor thought Bayer's real wonder drug was heroin.
It eased people's pain, especially the wracking pain
of the rheumatism that was so common in this climate. Doctors were prescribing it left and right, the
pharmacies had trouble maintaining their stocks, he
used it himself on occasion. If the sultan or any of his
family were in serious pain he would prescribe it to
them, but for the man to come out and ask him if he
knew French was downright rude. Did he not know
that he was talking to a physician who had studied
at the Imperial School of Medicine, which the man's
grandfather had founded and where instruction was
in French? Had his grandfather Sultan Mahmud not
said at the opening ceremony that education would
be in French because that was the only way to learn

medicine? Had he not proclaimed that medicine in the East had fallen behind? Had the fanatics not dubbed him the "Unbelieving Sultan" for this? This wasn't the only reason, but it was one of the most significant.

He surprised the driver by saying, *"Oui Sa Majestie Imperiale, oui ta!* In your eyes I'm just a lowly doctor. Well, do you know what Le Sultan Rouge means?"

Then he laughed at himself. There was no need to take the man so seriously, no need to get so worked up, he was just a pitiful old prisoner. If he was a pitiful doctor, and he wasn't, the man was a miserable old prisoner. But the doctor had other matters to concern himself with. He shook his head, said *"Quelle malheur,"* and left the mansion. Ottoman soldiers who had been wounded in clashes with Bulgarians, Serbs, Greeks, and Montenegrins were waiting for him at the hospital. He would be able to heal some of their wounds, but he was also going to have to amputate some arms and legs.

Even though Abdülhamid's brother was now on the throne, the doctor knew that the sultanate was finished, that the Committee for Union and Progress had seized the nation's destiny.

It was springtime, and the trees of Thessaloniki were bursting with colorful blossoms as if to celebrate the sultan's overthrow. Their scent was intoxicating and nourished the doctor's hopes. Life is good, he thought, it truly is. Even though he'd been born, raised, and educated in Istanbul, he now felt like a native of Thessaloniki. If he wasn't transferred elsewhere, he would be content to spend the rest of his life in this beautiful city. If he could be united with his beloved, he would bring her here. In any event, the shadow of the sultanate had darkened Istanbul, and the domes, minarets, and palaces served as reminders of painful events from which it would take years to recover. Thessaloniki, on the other hand, was a city of cheer, youth, drink, music, and rebellion.

On account of this man, half of Istanbul had been spying on the other half, and people's faces had been darkened by the shadow of betrayal. Family members spied on each other, they ruined the lives of innocent people with unfounded lies in order to get the medals and bags of gold that were distributed left and right. Thousands of denunciations arrived at the palace every day, which were examined and taken seriously, and punishments were meted out without any regard to their veracity. The surest way to punish those with subversive ideas was to cast a wide net and sacrifice the innocent. This was the only way to ensure complete security.

A pasha's horse-drawn carriage collided with another carriage, and the passenger in the other carriage was identified as once having met Prince Reşad Efendi. Even though the accident was the fault of the carriage drivers, both passengers were exiled to Fezzan in the Libyan desert.

Once a report came that there were infectious microbes in the wind blowing from the Asian side of the Bosphorus, so the sultan closed all the doors and windows, had cotton stuffed in the keyholes, and didn't leave his room for days. One of the strangest denunciations concerned a ship that was sailing to Istanbul from the port of Marseilles. The denunciation, which had been sent from France, claimed that enemies of the sultanate had produced walnut-size bombs in a factory with the aim of assassinating His Imperial Majesty, that these bombs had been packed into crates and loaded on a ship called the *Niger*, of the Messagerie Maritimes Company, that they would attempt to unload the crates in Istanbul, and if this failed they would be delivered to the Black Sea port of Samsun. This denunciation caused quite a commotion at the palace, and His Imperial Majesty was beside himself. To prevent this treacherous attack, he set up a commission under the direction of a pasha, the *Niger*'s every move was tracked from the moment it left Marseilles, every port of call was reported, strict instructions were telegraphed to every Ottoman port in the Mediterranean that the ship was to be observed and that even the smallest item that came off it was to be checked. When the *Niger* arrived in the port of Istanbul, it was immediately surrounded by spies, officials, and riflemen. According to the rules of the capitulations, they could not board the ship and search it, but everything that came off the ship was examined in detail. In spite of this rigorous scrutiny, nothing resembling a crate of bombs was found. The commission was certain the bombs would be unloaded in Samsun, so they immediately boarded a ship and sailed there. The second part of the denunciation claimed that these bombs, which were small enough to carry in a vest pocket, would be brought to Istanbul on fishing boats, and then—God forbid—the assassination would be carried out. In the end the commission sent a coded telegram to the palace saying that the explosives had been seized. A container being sent to a merchant in Samsun had been labeled in the manifest as carbonic acid. The merchant was immediately arrested and sent to Istanbul, and the container was loaded onto another ship, which was sent to the waters north of the Bosphorus. After waiting there for a time, it was ordered to enter the Bosphorus and anchor off Leander's Tower. The bombs were then examined at a factory in Zeytinburnu. The report stated that the "bombs" were in fact carbonic acid capsules used in the manufacture of carbonated beverages, but they were nevertheless dumped into the sea and the sultan heaved a sigh of relief.

This was one of the true stories that spread through Istanbul by word of mouth. Istanbul was now a tainted city, Abdülhamid's rule had poisoned the city and its inhabitants. People who have been subjected to tyranny for a long time tend to rot, thought the doctor. He remembered the stirring lines he'd read in secret since he was a schoolboy and that always refreshed his hatred for the sultan, the palace, the ceremonies, the medals, the embroidered cords, the eunuchs, and the spies:

Cover up this disastrous scene...Cover it up, oh city
You're the greatest whore in the world, cover it all up
and sleep for eternity.

Thessaloniki, on the other hand—apart from its rebellious tendencies—was a young, cheerful city where free and beautiful girls had their skirts blown by the sea breeze. Officers with connections to the palace were being shot one after the other by bold rebels. Three years earlier a friend of a friend had put the doctor in a brougham carriage, blindfolded him, and brought him to an unfamiliar house in an unfamiliar neighborhood; when his blindfold was removed he found himself in a dimly lit room with a masked man, and he was asked to swear, with one hand on the Quran and the other on a dagger, that "he would struggle to restore the constitution of 1877 and that he was prepared to risk his life to this end," then the rebels took off their masks, saluted him, and said, "Brother, welcome to the community of New Ottomans." He would never forget that sacred moment, he would never forget the terrifying shudder that went through him when he knew he'd set off on a path from which there was no return and that he was prepared to sacrifice his life for these ideals. The situation had seemed so hopeless back then, but the sparks they'd ignited had turned into a conflagration, the dictator had been yanked from his palace, and the entire empire was freed from his iron grip. Now there was

nothing to prevent the empire from turning its face
to the West. The leading officers who had left Thessaloniki, such as Enver and Niyazi, would first unite the
peoples of the empire, establish equality between men
and women, then transform this enormous country
into a free, prosperous, civilized, and industrialized
nation like Germany, France, or England. And they
would do this quickly, too. Once again he recited the
lines he had memorized so many years ago.

> *I visited the infidel's lands, I saw towns and mansions*
> *I wandered the realm of Islam, I saw all of the ruins*

The strange thing was that even the imprisoned
former sultan thought this. Just yesterday he'd said,
"Unfortunately, the Muslims are the most backward of
my subjects. Their literacy rate is much lower than that
of Christians and Jews. Because our alphabet is so difficult to learn." He'd said that the alphabet needed to
be reformed. Another thing he bragged about was the
issue of the measurement of time. He had decided that
keeping the old system would be an obstacle to closer
relations with Europe. He wondered how people were
going to get used to the new system. It wasn't something you could just order people to do. "Then I found
a solution, I had elegant clock towers erected in the cen-
ters of thirty-two cities," he said. These clocks were set
according to the new system. So people would have no
choice but to use the new system, and they would grow
accustomed to it. This was so typical of Abdülhamid.

Fine, but if he's saying that we have to follow Europe in order to develop, why had he maintained Islamist policies for so many years? The doctor imagined they would have time to discuss this issue. His visits were not confined to matters of health; they would sit, smoke cigarettes, and discuss the issues facing the nation. The sultan was a very cunning man. He would steer the conversation toward politics and try to get him to say things, but he didn't succeed. As the doctor neared the hospital, he leaned back in his seat and said proudly, "After all, I'm a committee member."

A field of fish on the frozen Bosphorus

WINTERS IN ISTANBUL ARE occasionally quite severe. During one such winter, strange clicking sounds were heard in the sea off Kandilli. The noise was so loud that the wealthy inhabitants of the waterfront mansions and their many servants rushed to the quay or to the windows to look at what sounded like the end of the world. Despite the strong currents, the Bosphorus had frozen. The Muslim population of the Bosphorus muttered prayers, the Orthodox and Catholics made the sign of the cross, and the Jews prayed in their own manner. It looked as if the Bosphorus could now be crossed on foot, but this was not what had alarmed the people who had crowded along the shore. Fish had been caught in the ice with their heads above the surface, they opened and shut their mouths as they struggled, making a loud clicking sound; the sea had become a field of bonito. No one had ever seen or heard of anything like this. Everyone felt this was a portent of the end of the world, and many went pale with fear.

A few brave young men without superstitious beliefs walked out onto the ice, grabbed the fish by their heads, and pulled them out. The fish didn't come out easily and were lacerated when they did, but a number of people on the shore sprang into action when they saw this. They all rushed out onto what had become a field of fish to pull out the enormous bonito and carry them to the shore. Bonito of this size was usually pickled in brine to make lakerda; if they pickled these fish and stored them in jars, they would have enough to last for months. Those who were collecting the fish began having visions of lakerda, an Istanbul delicacy usually served with onions. It wasn't just the people of Kandilli, people from neighboring towns on the Bosphorus came to collect the fish that they saw as a gift from God. Waterfront gardens, private piers, and the quay were covered in fish. Some generous mansion owners allowed the poor who had arrived late to the feast to take as much fish as they wanted from their gardens.

Of course it was unthinkable for news of an incident of this magnitude not to reach the government and the palace. The sultan, who was frightened of ship horns and was suspicious of singing birds and the wind, was quick to take the situation in hand. Guards descended on Kandilli and the area around it; they forbade anyone to walk on the ice, and they brought some of the fish to the palace to be examined. The sultan gathered his doctors, astrologers, animal caretakers, and teachers of natural science and ordered them to get to the bottom of this incident as soon as possible. Until they achieved results, he would remain in his apartments under the protection of his Albanian guards. They were ordered to check if the fish contained bombs or carried infectious diseases, or if there were messages concealed in their gills.

While the scholars examined the samples, all of the fish that had been gathered were seized, placed into horse carts, and brought to a secluded location, where they were kept under guard. When no new orders came the fish began to smell and the guards, who had no choice but to remain there, vomited for days and swore they would never again eat fish.

In the end, word was sent to the sultan, who was waiting in fear in his apartments, that the committee requested an audience. The sultan received them in his office, and he was so eager to hear what they had to report that he dispensed with the usual formalities, such as the kissing of the hem of his cloak. According to the committee's findings, the sudden drop in temperature had caused water to freeze in the gills of the fish, forcing them to put their heads above the surface in order to attempt to breathe. The fish contained no bombs, messages, or any other suspicious objects, and the monarch and his government were able to breathe easily.

Peaceful cows—European gentlemen smelling of cologne—A lost fortune

WHEN ALI FETHI BEY returned to the Alatini mansion from Istanbul with some of the imperial family's belongings, two large cows, the chief dairyman Mehmet Ağa, and a white parrot that fluttered excitedly in its cage, the former sultan's face lit up with delight and he remembered one of his grandmother's sayings: "God first causes His beloved servant to lose his donkey, then causes him to find it." It seemed odd to him that, after having lost an empire, he was as delighted as a child to see two cows and a parrot. The poor man couldn't see the cows because he wasn't allowed out into the garden, but as soon as he lifted the cover off the parrot's cage, it immediately cried out, "Long live the sultan! Long live the sultan!" This gave him a feeling of excitement, the household must have felt the same thing because he heard people rushing down from the upper floors. When the soldiers outside heard the parrot, they became uneasy. But the commander was inside, they were sure he would wring the bird's neck.

The commander did nothing of the kind, he watched in surprise as the former sultan signaled for him to be quiet by putting his nicotine stained finger to his lips, then closed the parrot's beak.

Like all of the young officers in Thessaloniki, Ali Fethi Bey was a staunch committee member, but the old man was still the Prophet's representative and he felt he had to treat him respectfully. It wasn't in his nature to kick someone when they were down, and he was truly upset by the state the emperor was in. The man behaved so decently to him that it almost erased the image of the Red Sultan. When he saw this calm, mature old man up close, it was difficult to believe that he'd had Mithat Pasha and Mahmud Celaleddin Pasha strangled in the dungeons of Taif, that he'd shed so much innocent blood, that his network of spies that stretched from Belgrade to Yemen and from the Caucasus to Africa had darkened the lives of hundreds of thousands of people with their trumped-up denunciations. When he was praying, he looked like a retired civil servant.

Nevertheless, the commander could see that this was an act, he could see it in the way the sultan's eyes shone sometimes when he talked about world politics, the way he constantly reminded himself of his past glory, and the way he tried to justify himself.

It was fortunate that the poor man was completely cut off from the world; he didn't know that from the moment he'd been deposed the press had been attacking him viciously, that he was being blamed for all of the empire's ills, and that he was the subject of humiliating articles and caricatures. Even someone as biased as Ali Fethi Bey found these articles exaggerated, unfair, and cruel. The commander was particularly nauseated by those Istanbul journalists who had until recently been palace sycophants and who were now referring to the former sultan as "a drooling, rabid dog." Chief among these new detractors were people whom Abdülhamid had made wealthy, to whom he'd given mansions on the Bosphorus or in Nişantaşı.

He thought of the two cows he'd struggled to load onto the train. A barn was being built for them in a corner of the garden. The sultan ate little and suffered from indigestion, and all his life had been accustomed to drinking fresh milk every day. Along with the chief dairyman Mehmet Ağa, the former sultan's cook, pastry chef, and coffeemaker had also been brought to Thessaloniki. They'd also brought more servants. The ladies were delighted with the furniture, including proper bedsteads, and particularly with the clothing that had been brought from the palace. The commander carried the sultan's carpentry tools to a room off the main hall. It pleased him to see the delight in the man's ravaged face as he touched his tools.

The Alatini mansion was now almost a miniature palace. Meals were served on time, the sultan could once again drink his coffee from two separate cups and resume his accustomed diet of fresh eggs, milk, and yogurt, and the doctor came every day to attend to the medical needs of the household. The sultan continued to oversee his family and the servants in the same manner as he had done in the palace. He rose every morning before dawn, performed his prayers, bathed in cold water, drank his milk and ate his eggs, had his coffee, then spent half an hour walking in the hall at an even pace. He did his best to console his wives and daughters for the predicament they'd fallen into on his account. The parrot's cage was left open, it flew wherever it wanted, perched here and there, then returned to its cage. Hearing the parrot mutter and flap its wings gave the sultan a sense of security and contentment.

He'd always been fond of animals. In Istanbul, he'd spent part of each day with his beloved animals, and when he was distressed by affairs of state he would ride his gray horse Mennan through the palace woods and visit the rare animals he kept in his private zoo. King Menelik II of Abyssinia had sent him priceless gifts. Among these gifts were an ostrich, a civet, a leopard, a tiger, several species of snake, monkeys, and some strange, snake-hunting birds. The sultan was so delighted by these animals that he showered the king of Abyssinia with rare gifts that included jewels, thoroughbred horses, silk Hereke carpets, and Lahori shawls. The sultan loved his Abyssinian zebra so much that he would feed it by hand. However, he never established as much of a rapport with these animals as he had with his parrot, his cat, and his dog. And his horse, his noble horse. Sadly, he would never be reunited with this beloved horse, which had dragged its owner from the battlefield with its teeth. Seeing as he could not ride the horse in the mansion, there had been no point in requesting that it be brought to Thessaloniki.

The only people from the outside world that he could talk to were the commander and the doctor. Of course this isolation weighed heavily on a man who worked an average of sixteen hours a day, who kept careful track of even the smallest developments through a telegraph network that was spread across three continents, who studied photographs to monitor physical changes in his cities, and who was deeply involved in international politics. The one thing he could not adjust to was being unable to access information, to not know what was going on, to live in what seemed to him like complete darkness. He tried to get the commander and the doctor to tell him things, he tried to trick them into letting something slip, to give him some hint, some impression of what was going on, he tried to ingratiate himself with them, he showered them with compliments, he tried to get them to pity him, but none of this worked on either of them.

After weeks of this deep isolation, an order arrived from Istanbul allowing the sultan to see more people and to be involved in certain events. Though in fact this was not an auspicious development for him.

One morning Ali Fethi Bey received an order from the Thessaloniki Third Army Command. All of the former sultan's vast land holdings across the empire, including the oil fields of Mosul and Kirkuk and consisting of more than seven thousand deeds, as well as astounding amounts of money, gold, and jewels, had been seized by the new government, but because they couldn't touch the money he had abroad, they were going to ask him to volunteer to donate it to the army. No matter what they did, they could not get Deutsche Bank and Credit Lyonnaise to give them this money. So they had no choice but to pressure the former sultan.

It would have been naïve to think that Stingy Hamid, who stashed away every penny he made and who had reduced imperial expenditure to a minimum, would willingly surrender his foreign bank accounts. Therefore the new government in Istanbul decreed that this request be conveyed to the sultan as a "final decision" and sent the Third Army two letters that he had to sign. The letters, addressed to the foreign bank directors, stated that he wished to withdraw all of his money and requested that it be delivered to him at the Alatini mansion.

When the commander gave him these letters, the sultan's face turned yellow. "This is my own personal wealth, it has nothing to do with the government, my children have a right to it," he said, but he knew that these words would be of no help to him. The kind-hearted commander told him as politely as he could that this was not possible. The sultan had been giving orders all his life, but he didn't know how to obey one. Reluctantly, the commander implied that his safety and indeed his life depended on this, his superiors had ordered him to do this to break the sultan's resistance. "The empire is facing difficulties and the army is in need of His Excellency's fortune. As you will appreciate, this decision will determine how the government behaves toward you."

However, the sultan was a very clever man, he immediately grasped the implication, and like a nimble prey who smelled danger, he headed for safer ground. "Since such a need exists, I am prepared to sacrifice all I own for the people and the army," he said. The commander heaved a sigh of relief. "I wish there was more," said the former sultan. "But..."

Once again the commander saw the maddening, destructive, darkly delusional fear in the sultan's eyes. *There is only one way for this man to overcome his fear of death,* he thought, *and that is to die.* The sultan wasn't trying to deceive him, he wanted new assurances that his life was not in danger. The commander reminded him that the army had guaranteed his safety, but the sultan asked for a written guarantee from parliament. The commander was on the point of losing patience, but he didn't know how to allay the man's maddening fear.

"Your Majesty," he said, "your request will serve no purpose except to offend the army. It would mean that you don't trust the army's word. Besides, the parliament is always changing, what if a new parliament takes a different position?"

The sultan thought about this for a moment.

"Fine, commander," he said. "Even though I gladly surrender my fortune, there are some things I will request in return. I'll give it all to you in writing tomorrow."

The following day the former sultan presented the commander with his list of requests. He wanted his younger son's education to be provided for, his older son and his three daughters to be allowed to return to Istanbul so they could marry, his servants to be given a degree of freedom, to be paid an allowance sufficient for his needs, and for the Alatini mansion to be purchased in his name. His final request betrayed his anxious state of mind; he asked to be left in peace until he died, and for the army to protect his life.

The commander knew the sultan's concerns about his children; he'd almost begged the doctor to prepare a report that would enable his eldest son and his daughters to return to Istanbul. All three of his daughters were engaged, but their fiancés, who were all from aristocratic families, had remained in Istanbul. He feared that if this situation was prolonged, the fiancés might change their minds about marriage. After all, he was no longer sultan.

The sultan didn't wait for his daughters to be courted, as some fathers did, he chose the grooms himself. In any event, marrying the sultan's daughter was a great honor, and no one could ignore the benefits of being the sultan's son-in-law. But to be the son-in-law of a deposed, exiled sultan... That's where everything became complicated. What he feared most was the danger that his political destiny would affect his daughters' happiness.

These requests struck the commander as reasonable, and he was certain his superiors would accept them. And it turned out he was right, all of the sultan's requests were granted.

One morning the imperial family looked out through the shutters they were now allowed to keep partly open and saw unusual activity in the garden. The officers were wearing civilian clothes and were striding around, smoking cigarettes irritably, whispering among themselves, and casting menacing glances at the mansion. The women in the mansion were terrified. The sultan was kneeling on his prayer rug, praying silently. Not long afterward his fears were allayed when an officer told his chamberlain that the German consul and the bank directors were on their way. The sultan put on his frock coat, sat at the head of the large dining table, and sat his younger son next to him.

When the mansion's front door was opened all the way, the refreshing, flowery scent of a summer morning came flowing in. Bearded senior officers, with so many shiny medals on their chests that they seemed bent over from the weight of them, entered the hall solemnly, accompanied by diffident European gentlemen in frock coats, clean-shaven, their hair carefully combed and their cheeks glowing pink. The four gentlemen were clearly uneasy, and they glanced about warily. The sultan didn't move, he looked at the gentlemen with his large black eyes and seemed to sense their uneasiness. The boy next to him, so little he could barely see over the table, looked on in fear.

The silence dragged on, neither the generals nor the European gentlemen could break it. The parrot became alarmed, fluttered up toward the ceiling, perched on a sill, and started squawking, "Long live the sultan!" As the illustrious generals of the Third Army fidgeted helplessly, one of the European gentlemen solved the problem. A red-faced gentleman who smelled of cologne turned to the generals, who were gazing at the parrot in bewilderment, and said, "Sirs, may we ask you to step outside. Our banks have strict rules that require us to speak to our clients alone."

After the suspicious generals had left, the European gentlemen bowed to the sultan. The gentleman who smelled of cologne addressed His Majesty and introduced himself as the German consul to Thessaloniki. The tall, thin man with the bobbing Adam's apple introduced himself as a representative of Deutsche Bank, and the representatives of Credit Lyonnaise and of the Ottoman Bank introduced themselves in turn. Saddened by the loss of one of their biggest investors, and burdened with the responsibility of conducting this business properly, they asked the sultan if he was having this great fortune brought to the mansion of his own free will. In response, the sultan solemnly stated that he had signed the instructions willingly and that he wished to donate all of his wealth to the nation and the army. Then the bankers gave instructions for the suitcases full of money and shares to be brought from the carriage outside. The crates of gold and jewels would also be turned over to the army. The sultan's treasure was brought in and piled up in the halls, papers were signed, then the European gentlemen got into their carriages and drove off without speaking to the generals in the garden.

The sultan looked at this vast fortune, then called to the officers who were waiting outside to come and take it away. The anxious officers in civilian clothes and their men loaded everything into two landau carriages, and as they were leaving, his daughters, who were watching from a window above, heard Sultan Hamid murmur, "I'm a living corpse now. First they killed me with politics, and now they kill me with perfidy."

The new government had seized millions of acres of his personal property in Mosul, Kirkuk, Egypt, the Hejaz, Greece, Albania, Bulgaria, Macedonia, Lebanon, Syria, Palestine, Iraq, Jerusalem, Mecca, and Libya as well as his money and bonds. If they'd been content with that it would have been bad enough; what the sultan didn't know was that the vast amount of jewels seized from Yıldız Palace had been actioned off in Paris as "the jewels of His Majesty Sultan Abdülhamid II," and that the amount of money they fetched broke all previous records. The Parisians were astounded by this array of Indian diamonds, emerald brooches, pearl necklaces, ivory, gold, and silver jewelry boxes, all of it glistening as if it had fallen from the sky rather than been dug out of the earth. As always, the wealth of the East intoxicated the West.

Now all the sultan had left was the yellow bag of jewels that his daughter had thought was his water bag. He had to hide this small treasure and make sure no one learned of it.

Dreaming of Zarifi—Silent Christmas bells— Istanbul's conquest will not be celebrated

THAT NIGHT HE DREAMED about the Greek money changer Zarifi, who had guided him all his life. He was in the summer house in Maslak, he was still a prince, he had not yet become sultan and had no hopes that this would ever happen. "Did I do the right thing, father?" he asked, and the old man, with a clever smile, said, "You did the best possible thing. You spent your fortune in the best possible manner. You saved yourself and your family." The prince said, "Thank you, father. I feel better now."

The strange thing was that in the dream he wasn't as he was now, he saw himself as a callow, inexperienced young man, athletic, fond of money, trying to become a businessman but not quite succeeding. One day he invited a famous Greek money changer from Tarabya to come and look at his books. After glancing at his accounts, the man said, "This is all wrong. You don't know how to keep your books, and you've made the wrong investments." From that day on he always consulted the money changer, whom he addressed as "father," and who helped him make a fortune; indeed after he became sultan the man helped him delay the payment of the empire's debts and to collect money owed to him so he could make the right investments. He usually ate alone, and Zarifi and his family were among the few people who were granted the honor of being invited to dine with him. Sometimes he would also invite them to his theater to watch opera.

But despite Zarifi, the church bells in the empire were silent for a few years. This was because, for some unknown reason, the oversensitive sultan was offended by his Christian subjects. He wanted both to punish them and to put on a show of force to strengthen his sense of power as an emperor. You don't know you are an emperor until you feel the pleasure of subduing the dangerous tiger beneath you, otherwise your daily life is no different from that of any other person. Shahs and sultans were born naked, died naked, and made love naked; they ate, slept, fell ill, got angry, rejoiced. Then what was the point of being considered God's shadow on earth?

The Greeks were content with Sultan Hamid, both because of his association with Zarifi, who occasionally gave the government loans, and because of the empire's tradition of tolerance.

When some Muslim notables approached him with the idea of holding celebrations to mark the anniversary of his ancestor Sultan Mehmet's conquest of Constantinople, he refused outright, saying that while these celebrations might please his Muslim subjects, it would upset his Greek subjects.

In spite of this, the ban on church bells silenced the Greek population and suffocated them like a black blanket. Then, one Christmas afternoon, he must have been feeling merciful because he lifted the ban. The bells of the Orthodox churches throughout the city began to ring joyfully, and the Greeks, who had been preparing to celebrate Christmas quietly in their homes, felt as if a miracle had occurred. All of them, young and old, flocked to the churches, celebrated Christmas as they'd never celebrated before, and prayed for the sultan's health and success.

That night in his dream, the money changer had consoled the sultan's tired old broken heart. What he didn't understand was why the old man had told the young prince, "Don't worry, it's easy to make money, we can still make more." Fine, but the money changer was dead, were they going to make money in the next world? Was this conversation in the dream a sign that his own death was approaching? Was he going to die, was he already dying, had that moment finally come?

He woke suddenly and began to implore God. He began having difficulty breathing, and as his chest heaved, he reached out to touch his brick, proclaimed his faith, and thought he saw the shadow of the angel of death in the room. That revolutionary doctor was not taking good care of him. Was he prescribing the wrong treatments, the wrong medications? After all, he was an enemy, he'd been brainwashed since childhood to despise the sultanate. This was clear from his treacherous glances and rude demeanor. That bandit was not a gentleman like the commander. The other day he'd said there might be an epidemic and took some vaccines out of his bag. The sultan picked up one of the vials and examined it carefully. The little bottle had been made in Paris, the middle part was rubber, that's where the vaccine would be drawn out with a syringe. It looked completely safe. The doctor said that he, his family, and his staff should all be vaccinated immediately, but the sultan put the vial in his pocket and said, "Let me hold on to this for a few days. Vaccinate everyone else, you can vaccinate me later." The doctor looked at him in amazement for a time, then began vaccinating everyone else.

The sultan's revenge—A young bride's misfortune

WHILE HE WAS THINKING about the doctor, he'd forgotten to listen to himself. He realized that his heartbeat had slowed and that his breathing was now regular. *How strange*, he thought. *Bombs have exploded right next to me, I was able to remain calm as pieces of human and animal flesh flew around me, I had enough self-control to drive the carriage myself and calm the people around me, but when the thought of death descends on me when I'm alone in a dark room I get a tightness in my chest. This in itself may be what ends up killing me. They'll laugh about me when I'm gone, the treacherous doctor will tell everyone that I died of my imperial delusion. This doctor is already looking for an opportunity to poison me, to kill me. Who knows what's in those vaccine vials? After all my years of experience, am I going to fall for that? You can inject anything you want into those vials, it's child's play. Pull yourself together, Hamid, get a grip on yourself, don't give your enemies a reason to laugh at you. Gather your willpower, think about good things, think about nice things, think about beautiful things.*

As he murmured to himself, half asleep, he had a vision of the tall, slender Circassian girl whose long, blond hair swayed as she walked, a girl straight out of a fairy tale. The moment he saw this concubine in the palace garden he was smitten, desire burned like fire in his veins, he had to have her immediately. The magnificent slave who had refused to enter the sultan's bed, who had disdained him even though he had an empire beneath his feet, who made Hamid moan at night as he burned with love for her. After suffering for a long time he summoned her, he stroked his dyed beard and asked her to tell him openly why she didn't want him, was he too old and ugly? The girl prostrated herself on the floor before him and said, "My sultan, it is not my place as a helpless slave to dislike you."

When he asked, "Then why don't you look at my face, why don't you come to my bed?" she answered, "My sultan, I'm willing to sacrifice my life for you, but I've sworn I will be the only wife of the man I marry. I would kill myself before changing my mind about this."

The girl raised her beautiful face as she said these words, and he was so struck by her courage that he said, "Fine, let it be as you wish. But then I'm going to have to marry you off, it will be too painful for me to have to see you every day."

He didn't wait, and immediately arranged her engagement to one of the unmarried chamberlains. The girl moved out of the palace and into the groom's house, but there was a surprise for her. The imam performed the wedding ceremony, they carried out the wedding rituals of eating pilaf and drinking sherbet, then just as the groom was about to go to the marriage bed there was a knock at the door, and the chamberlain was informed that His Imperial Majesty had summoned him to the palace. The man dressed hurriedly, went to the palace with the guards, and sat until morning on a hard, wooden chair. No one came or went. After performing his morning prayers he went to his office for work, in the evening, exhausted from lack of sleep, he made his way home, had a bowl of soup, then, just as he was undressing to get into bed with the Circassian princess who had so miraculously and unexpectedly entered his life, there was a banging on the door: His Imperial Majesty had summoned the chamberlain. Once again the poor man spent the night sitting in a chair at the palace, and the next day and night, and the night after that... This torture continued for fifteen days, then the sultan relented and left the man alone, but he was so exhausted the first night that he slept deeply and didn't even touch his bride. After that, every time he approached his bride he couldn't get past the fear that there would be a knock on the door. From the poor bride's point of view, this had some unfortunate consequences.

Hamid smiled as he remembered this and, pleased that he'd gotten his revenge, fell into a deep sleep. The good memories were generally those that concerned women. Then there was the trip to Europe with his uncle; he cherished the memory of every moment of that trip. In a sense those memories concerned women as well. Accustomed to seeing Ottoman ladies who covered themselves completely, the European ladies were a feast for his eyes, at the receptions their marble-white breasts, accentuated by their corsets, glistened in the light of the crystal chandeliers.

Good commander—Bad doctor

OH, THIS DOCTOR, THIS doctor! Instead of getting a doctor who was a respectful, decent, traditional Muslim like the commander, he'd ended up with this "Westernized, libertarian enemy of the sultanate" who was so hostile to him. With his sandy beard trimmed in the French style, waxed handlebar mustache, wire-frame glasses, and the frock coat and bow tie he wore when he was out of uniform, he looked more like a French physician than an Ottoman.

He had no objection to Western science, and what he'd seen when he was twenty-four had made him an admirer of the West, but he'd learned through years of bitter experience that those great states wanted nothing more than to carve up the Ottoman Empire. What this upstart doctor and his friends didn't know, but that he knew well after his struggles with Queen Victoria, the Prince of Bismarck, Tsar Alexander, Tsar Nicholas, and Emperor Napoleon, was that half of the oil in the world was in Ottoman lands and that the unbelievers wanted nothing more than to carve up this magnificent empire and seize the oil. They would achieve this goal by stirring up the more than thirty ethnic groups in the empire. Indeed they'd already started. The empire was disintegrating, and these young libertarians who thought they were patriots were serving this disintegration. But there was no chance he would be able to explain this to the doctor. The man showed him no respect, he barely even spoke to him. Unfortunately he was the only person from whom he could learn anything about what was going on in the empire. The commander's replacement was a stern soldier, he would only talk to him about practical matters.

(Secret notes: My melancholy has deepened, the good commander whom I'd begun to love like a son has been transferred to Istanbul. This is an enormous loss for me! The most reliable assurance that my life is safe is no longer here. When he came to bid me farewell, his sadness was reflected on his face. He demonstrated his true character when he said, "Although I am politically opposed to you, I cannot stomach the way His Imperial Majesty and his family are being treated." "Don't be upset," I said. "We must accept whatever God wills. The time we spent together in this mansion and the conversations we had here will be among my most treasured memories. I must confess, it was from you that I learned for the first time what the young Ottomans actually want. How bitter it is that you didn't understand me,

and that I didn't understand you. It's a shame."
In a trembling voice he said, "You are right, Your
Excellency. What has happened has happened
to all of us." Then he bowed deeply and walked
away backward. Now I've been left alone with
that cruel doctor. The commander showed me
respect and attempted to console me, but the doctor hates me. He performs his duties impeccably,
I can't complain, I can't fault him, but his cold-
ness and occasional vengeful glances make his
hatred for me clear. He's never addressed me by
my title. Because he's in control of my health, he
plays emperor to me. As if he's the monarch, and
I'm a servant who's accountable to him. It's clear
he enjoys this game of cat and mouse, he doesn't
even attempt to conceal this. But there's nothing
I can do, he holds the power now and that power
increases day by day. I and my poor family have
no choice but to accept this.)

One night he saw a giant shadow of a cat move across
the wall. There was no telling if it was real or imagined. After months of experiencing the terror of death
in this room, his mind could be playing tricks on him.
He thought about the possibility that they'd left a cat
in his room, and he shuddered. When the Abbasids
overthrew the Umayyads, they fed the last caliph's
tongue to a cat. What a horrible way to go, he thought.
The blessed tongue of the Caliph of Islam being fed
to a cat. Both horrible and humiliating. Since he was

also a deposed caliph and surrounded by so many enemies, why wouldn't they do the same thing to him?
He realized that he was holding his mouth shut with
both hands. He got up and searched the room carefully with his lamp. He didn't find anything.

He was already living his life in nearly constant
fear when the doctor cruelly gave him news that
would inflame his delusions. On top of this he showed
him the first foreign newspaper he'd seen for a long
time.

It was an ordinary day, and he was carrying out
his usual treatments. The usual complaints about indigestion and hoarseness...What troubled him most,
however, was his hemorrhoids. As the doctor performed the usual treatment, which was painful and
embarrassing, he reminded himself that he was God's
humble servant, a mortal servant, and that there was
no reason for him to be exempt from such a common
ailment. He comforted himself by remembering that
even the Honorable Prophet had said that he was
human, that he was not a divine being. Had God's
messenger not died after suffering severe headaches
for two weeks? In his efforts to determine what sick-
ness the Prophet had died from, he had talked to doctors and examined all the sources he could find. It may
have been meningitis, which could have been caused
by the sword wound he received during the Battle
of Uhud. This seemed the most likely possibility. If
even the Great Prophet had succumbed to a common
disease, who was he to complain? Of course he could

suffer from any kind of human illness, and he had to face this with patience, maturity, and faith. But to undergo that treatment, with that doctor...It was difficult for him to countenance. Still, he couldn't deny that the doctor's ointments soothed the pain. Occasionally the sultan asked the doctor for various potions, sulfates, spirits, and ointments he believed to be effective, and most of the time the doctor complied.

The doctor and the sultan had to see each other every day. Every day the sultan waited impatiently for the doctor, and the doctor enjoyed his devious persecution of the former sultan. The sultan, shut up in the Alatini mansion, was tormented by curiosity about what was happening in the world, and he tried to get the doctor to give him even the smallest scraps of information. Sometimes he talked about the politics of his own period; he responded to the accusations against him and tried to justify himself. As for the doctor, he had overcome the apprehension of the first days and was enjoying having this old merchant in the palm of his hand. He enjoyed being able to manipulate this delusional old man.

Apart from the fear of being killed, the sultan had few complaints about his life of imprisonment in the mansion. He'd grown accustomed to it. At one time he'd voluntarily imprisoned himself behind the high walls of his palace. For years the princes hadn't enjoyed any freedom, they were never left to their own devices. The only time he'd experienced any sense of freedom was during his travels to Paris, London, and Vienna with his uncle Sultan Aziz when he was twenty-four. He didn't know if it was something in the air or the water or the spirit of freedom in the people he met, but he'd felt as light as a feather, free and independent. He clearly remembered his first impression of Europe: "Nobody interferes with anyone." This was something that an Ottoman could not begin to imagine.

Halley's comet and the approaching apocalypse

ONE DAY JUST AS he was leaving the doctor said, "There's something I have to tell you." His tone was serious and there was a look in his eye that could be interpreted as devious. "I think you have the right to know." Then he took a newspaper out of his pocket, showed it to the sultan, then began reading it aloud. "Halley's comet, which is approaching earth at a high speed, will become visible in the skies above New Caledonia. There are many scientific and religious authorities who claim that the comet, whose tail is estimated to be twenty-three million kilometers long, will collide with the earth and cause an apocalypse."

In alarm, the sultan grabbed the newspaper and read it himself. He asked if this was true. The doctor told him that the whole world was alarmed, that the comet would collide with the earth in a matter of days and destroy everything. He went into detail about how the disaster would unfold, and observed how the sultan went pale, how fear settled into his eyes. He said that scientists from around the world had gathered to study the matter, and had decided that nothing could be done. The Islamic, Christian, Jewish, Buddhist, and Hindu communities had accepted that the world was going to end, and were preparing for this with prayers and ceremonies. The day of judgment that all of the sacred books had foretold was at hand.

After the doctor closed his bag and left, the sultan remained in his armchair for some time. As he entertained visions of the mansion burning and his family being engulfed in the flames, he tried to calm himself, telling himself that scientists could not be trusted and that only God could know when the day of judgment would come. Mankind was weak and did not have the intellectual capacity to understand the divine, but what if this comet did collide with the earth and turn everything to ashes?

He didn't sleep at all that night, he stood by the window smoking cigarettes and looking at the sky, then when the doctor came for his daily visit he said, "No, no, I've given it a great deal of thought, no mortal can understand how our Creator works, no mortal can possibly know when the day of judgment will come. How can we know if this comet will collide with the earth? Does it have a rudder, do the scholars determine its route? Look, in the Holy Quran it says that 'the sun, the moon, and the stars move in their own orbits without colliding.' No mortal can begin to understand how God works. Am I to trust Frankish scholars more than I trust these lines from my sacred book? You'll see, this comet won't collide with the earth. Because there were no omens."

The doctor had brought him the latest French newspapers. Some of them had illustrations of people gazing at the sky in fear and panic. People in London and Paris were waiting in terror for the disaster to occur. These newspapers were enough to fray the sultan's already fragile nerves. Perhaps it was God's will to bring about the end of the world by means of a comet. No one could know that the day of judgment was coming, but by the same token no one could know that it was not coming. No one could question the Almighty Lord's wisdom; perhaps He was punishing the sinful world as He had with the Great Flood, perhaps He would destroy us as He had the peoples of Ad and Samut, perhaps He was sending disaster as He had to Sodom and Gomorrah. The delusions that had haunted him since childhood returned in force, overpowering his logic and intelligence; a look of terror appeared in his eyes and his hands trembled.

The following day the doctor didn't even bother to conceal the pleasure he derived from the state the man was in. "Perhaps it will happen tonight," he said. "Perhaps it will collide with the earth tonight and it will all be over. There's nothing that can be done to prevent this. We will experience a last night of terror as the world burns, as the ground shakes and explodes." The sultan looked him in the eye and asked in a trembling voice, "What is to be done in these circumstances?" He said, "Bid farewell to your family, say your final prayers, and prepare for the hereafter," then left the old man to his agony.

The doctor left the mansion with a smile, and the look of pleasure on his face made the soldiers wonder what had happened. He climbed into the landau, told the driver to take a long route to the hospital, and lit a cigarette. He'd finally been able to make that tyrant squirm in terror. He had not been delinquent in his duties, he had told the truth; yes, he may have exaggerated a bit, but this was a mild punishment for everything the tyrant had done in his life. The thought of "what the tyrant had done" caused him to think about his beloved Melahat, and he felt as if a dagger had pierced his heart and the smile was wiped from his face. He didn't know what to do, how he was going to find that fairy who had enchanted him on that Bosphorus night. When he thought about enchantment, he remembered that beautiful poem.

Oh face of freedom, what a magician you are
We escaped captivity to become slaves to your love

Somehow, it had become his custom to recite Namık Kemal's rousing verses to the young officers every time he left the mansion. The great poet, whose verses about liberty had inspired a generation, had been a victim of the tyrant who was now cowering in fear. Kemal was dead, but after his death his poems had become even more powerful. As the great poet's fame spread, the exiled sultan became irrelevant. At first Abdülhamid had appointed him to a committee to draft a new constitution as well as to other duties, but later exiled him for his talk of liberty.

Thessaloniki was beautiful in the May sunshine, more and more Jews with black hats and Muslims with fezzes were seen on the streets. Considering that half of the city's population was Jewish and a third was Muslim, this was normal. The Greeks, Bulgarians, and other Ottoman minorities gave the city a colorful personality. *Hopefully,* he thought, *I can bring Melahat to this beautiful city as a bride.* At that time neither he, the exiled sultan, nor the Third Army knew that this city, which had been under Ottoman administration for five hundred years, would be lost to them two years later.

While Doctor Atıf Bey and his officer friends found Thessaloniki a beautiful city, it was a source of great pain for Abdülhamid. The rebellion against the throne had sprouted here. Poor Şemsi Pasha, who he'd sent to get the situation under control, had been shot as he left the Thessaloniki post office. The operatives of the Committee for Union and Progress had not been content with that; they'd wounded Lieutenant Colonel Nazim Bey of the Thessaloniki Central Command and had killed Police Superintendent Sami and the regimental mufti Mustafa Şevket Efendi. Every day Istanbul received news of more assassinations. And these high-ranking officers were being killed by young officers of the same army.

Thessaloniki had been a source of deep troubles for the sultan. It was a place full of mischief and the tangled threads of intrigue. In fact, if it wasn't for the young officers, the people of the city would have had no complaint. Indeed, when the Second Constitutional Monarchy was proclaimed, the most spectacular of the celebrations held across the empire was in this city. In the photographs that were examined at the palace and in the moving pictures taken by the Greek Manaki brothers, one could see triumphal arches, flowers, and vast crowds of enthusiastic people. Greek girls dressed in white and wearing laurels tossed flowers to the crowd from decorated carriages; Muslims shouted, "Long live the sultan!" and others carried banners that read *"Vive le sultan"* as waves of joy moved down the streets. Much of this joy stemmed from pride in having forced an absolute monarch to accept a parliament. And the sultan himself saw it this way. From now on they would be like wolves who had scented blood. How was he going to deal with millions of people clamoring for liberty, how was he going to control provinces that were prone to rebellion? Thankfully, apart from Egypt, the eastern provinces were calmer, and for now the sparks had not yet become a fire. The most trouble was in the Ottoman cities of the Balkans, and particularly the Macedonian cities of Thessaloniki, Manastir, and Resne. As if the Bulgarian, Macedonian, and Serbian guerillas in the mountains weren't enough, his own officers were killing their superiors. An officer who was to become known as Niyazi of Resne and his men had gone up into the mountains like bandits and openly challenged the emperor. This

liberty business had gone so far that Niyazi had proclaimed his pet deer to be "the deer of liberty."

Its image had been printed on posters and banners and in newspapers. When the sultan heard about
this, he wondered if they were going to give the deer a
military rank—indeed perhaps it was already a high-
ranking officer. After all, these Young Turks barely had
the intellectual capacity of a deer. He heaved a deep
sigh and wondered how these young people thought
they were going to govern this vast empire. How were
they going to deal with aggressive powers like Russia,
England, and France, who were approaching like hungry jackals? He himself had barely managed to play
them off against each other. It hadn't been enough to
bring the German kaiser over to his side. They dubbed
his empire the Sick Man of Europe as they struggled
to divide it and seize the largest piece.

This was why Napoleon had attacked the province
of Egypt. The English wanted to take over all of the
holy lands, including Mecca, Medina, and Jerusalem,
and they were eager to seize the oil fields of Syria and
Iraq. The Russian tsar had his eye on Istanbul. The Bulgarians also dreamed of taking that city. *These stupid
children*, he moaned, *are going to give away lands that my
ancestors have ruled for hundreds of years, and my brother
on the throne is an idiot, he knows nothing about international politics. If I hadn't used various tactics to prevent the
Greek, Bulgarian, and Serbian churches from uniting, we
could never have put down the uprisings in the Balkans. If
I hadn't put down the Armenian rebellions in Anatolia by*

aligning myself with the Kurdish clans, they would have declared independence by now. Now who's going to govern so deftly? These stupid children, my idiot brother?

These rebels insisted on a parliament, but they were too ignorant to know what this would cost. They thought the Ottoman Empire was like France. But this empire was not like any other nation. All the nationalities and religions of the world were present here. Was it easy to manage so many religions, including Buddhism, and populations as different from one another Arabs and Serbs or Circassians and Africans? Especially now, in this century. Times have changed, everybody wants independence. This was why he had to close the first parliament, whose creation had been a condition for his accession to the throne. Because the Turks were a minority in their own parliament. Those who wanted to bring down the empire had filled parliament with representatives from every ethnic group they could find. Even the Muslim Arabs had been given ideas about independence by the English. It was not a national parliament but a gathering of nationalities. In parliament there were so many different languages spoken, so many different forms of worship were practiced, that no one would think it represented a single state. The assembly hall was swarming with Armenian, Bulgarian, Romanian, Serbian, Greek, Laz, Georgian, Albanian, Turkish, Jewish, Arab, Berber, Pomak, and Circassian representatives. They all read newspapers in different languages. Could an emperor who was already worn out by war trust his fate to a parliament like this? Of course not. But when he closed the parliament they called him a dictator, they nurtured the Young Turk Movement in Paris and directed it to overthrow him. Now they'd forced him to open a second parliament. And even though he'd done what they wanted, they'd overthrown him. *Let's see where this parliament will take the nation without a deft ruler like me, or rather when it will sink.*

As he inhaled deeply from a cigarette he'd rolled from his strong, amber tobacco, it pained him that he had no one to talk to about these things. He definitely couldn't trust that callow doctor. Anyway, he was certain that this man's duties weren't limited to overseeing his health and that he submitted daily reports to his superiors. And that these reports were being sent directly to Istanbul. For years he'd received daily reports about his brother Murad, who was imprisoned in Çırağan Palace, and now he was being watched in the same manner. Not long after his brother was imprisoned, the sultan received news that Murad's mental condition seemed to be improving. The only way to keep the throne was to get men like Mithat out of the way and to convince the public that Murad was still sick. So he ordered his secret service find a man who resembled Murad, dress him in his clothes, and have him wander around on the roof of Çırağan Palace every evening. Those who saw the man in black walking on the palace roof during the evening call to prayer would assume that Murad was completely out of his mind. And that's exactly what happened. The rumors spread, and Murad was remembered as a lunatic who walked around on his roof. When Abdülhamid, a master of intrigue, received news that his plan was working, his confidence in his own cleverness was restored and he felt a deep sense of relief. A clever man does not have to resort to brute force, execution, and war. Only the weak-willed resorted to violence.

When the Armenian bandits raided Ottoman Bank and killed so many people, he'd acted in the same manner. While everyone had expected these raiders to receive harsh punishment, he'd behaved like a mature monarch and sent them abroad on a yacht, but the following day he was content to watch sadly as the burning desire for revenge in Istanbul turned into an uprising that led to the deaths of hundreds of his Armenian subjects. He would never openly challenge his opponents, but he would wait for the right moment, then hit them at a time and in a way they least expected. This was the talent he was proudest of. He'd gone to great lengths to make sure that the various Orthodox churches of the Balkans did not unite. He'd played the same game in the Middle East. The secret of the "Ottoman Peace" that had lasted for centuries in the world's most complicated region was its division into provinces and districts that were designated as either Shiite, Sunni, or Kurdish. For instance the provinces of Basra, Baghdad, and Mosul. That's how the balance was kept. He kept potential enemies apart and set them against each other. In fact it wasn't balance, it was a policy of terror, but he had to do this to hold such a vast empire together. There was no other way. There were palace records that his ancestor Süleyman the Magnificent had secretly sent financial aid to Martin Luther when he challenged the papacy. His blessed ancestor had used the same tactic to divide the church and light a fire right in the heart of Christianity. He was proving himself to be a worthy ruler by practicing what his ancestors had taught him. What need was there to anger the European states by putting down the Armenian rebellions in Anatolia? All he had to do was to approach the Kurdish clans that had been in conflict with the Armenians for years, give their leaders the title of pasha, something they'd never dreamed of attaining, form them into the Hamidiye Regiments, and unleash them on the rebels. The suppression of any rebellion could be passed off as popular reaction. Although it annoyed him that the European press depicted him as the Red Sultan with his hands covered in blood, he could restrict the entry of foreign publications into the empire and strictly censor the Istanbul press.

Once the people were fully convinced of Murad's madness, there was another important matter to attend to. This was to eliminate an influential figure known as Mithat Pasha. His throne was in danger as long as this man was alive. But times had changed. In former times, in England and France as well as in the Ottoman Empire, anyone the monarch wanted to do away with was executed at once. Like Cromwell, or the poor Anne Boleyn. But things weren't done this way anymore. So after thinking about it for nights on end, he found the perfect solution. He would put those who had killed his uncle Abdülaziz on trial, and make sure that Mithat Pasha was named as the leader of the conspiracy. He had tents erected in the palace gardens. He had his judges convict Mithat Pasha and his friends, who had nothing to do with the incident, and sentence them to death. One of the judges was Christos Foridis, a sworn enemy of Mithat Pasha. When he interrupted the pasha while he was making his defense and tried to silence him, the defendant said, "Only the opening blessing and the date of the indictment are correct."

But of what use were these words in a society where orders were followed without question? Abdülhamid's unique style began to emerge after this trial. While Istanbul waited in horror for the execution of the former grand vizier, the great Mithat Pasha, the sultan announced that he had forgiven him and his friends and commuted their sentences to exile and imprisonment. Everyone then admired the sultan's compassion and sense of justice. The pasha was sent to a remote corner of Yemen and left in prison there to be forgotten. But even if everyone else in the world forgot, there was one person who would never forget. And that was the sultan himself. One day Mithat Pasha and his friend Mahmud Celaleddin Pasha were found dead in their cells. Word was put out that this cursed deed had been carried out by the prison warden, but even children didn't believe that a former grand vizier could be killed without a direct order from the sultan.

Abdülhamid never admitted that he'd given the order for this frightful execution. "He'd already been sentenced to death. If I wanted him dead, would I have commuted his sentence? There's something wrong with this story," he insisted. But everyone knew that he'd sent the pasha far away to be strangled to avoid any turmoil in Istanbul.

A dark sky—A dead man's hands

AFTER THAT SINISTER OWL of a doctor had given him the news about Halley's comet, the sultan convinced himself that such a thing could never happen, and he found peace by reading the Quran into the night. But the newspapers the doctor showed him the next day were enough to resurrect his apprehensions. In the evening, after eating some zucchini stew and yogurt, he retired to his room, took out his amber prayer beads, and began reciting the name of God, but he was unable to concentrate, he had terrifying visions of the fires of hell engulfing the mansion. At one point he lay on his bed, pulled the quilt over himself, and tried to find peace. In the darkness, his imagination began to run wild; when he couldn't stand this he got out of bed and went over to the window. He looked out at the night sky and smoked one cigarette after another. His pulse was racing. He searched for any sign that the disaster would occur that night. Perhaps there would be a bright light, perhaps some kind of aurora. That enormous comet would have to give off some kind of light. But the sky was completely dark. There was nothing visible but a few stars. He suddenly realized he was perspiring; his undershirt, his hair, and his neck were completely wet. This was one of the things that frightened him most. God forbid, but if his sweat got cold he would get ill, so ill that he would be confined to bed. He'd seen many men die from colds. At times like this he would have his butler rub the willow-and-yogurt mixture on his body. For a moment he thought of summoning his servant. Then he changed his mind because he couldn't tear himself away from watching the sky. Was he going to worry about catching cold on judgment day? Who could catch a cold while fire was raining from the sky? He thought about the tens of thousands of hands that would cling to him on judgment day, denouncing him and beseeching God for justice. He began to feel these hands closing around his neck. These severed hands began to move around the room. Like the thousands of hands that had been sent to the King of Belgium to reassure him that a rebellion had been put down.

He was barely able to breathe. He rubbed his congested chest and tried to mutter a prayer but found himself unable to speak. He could sense the hands moving around in the dark. The room was completely filled with these hands. White hands, black hands, children's hands, peasants' hands, clerks' hands, viziers' hands, innocent hands, pashas' hands, pashas' hands, pashas' hands, elegant hands with slender fingers, long fingers wearing a grand vizier's ring. Suddenly the rustling of the hands he sensed moving in the dark stopped. There was a deep and unsettling silence. The sultan tried to calm himself and slow his breathing. He tried to slow his pulse by thinking of happier times. Rowing on the cool waters of the Bosphorus, racing the wind on the back of a thoroughbred, the harems, the beautiful girls who had been given to the palace. He had almost managed to calm down when he was startled to feel two hands around his throat. They squeezed so hard he could no longer breathe. As he struggled to free himself from these hands he fell out of bed and onto his back. He tried to pull the hands away from his neck. The hands were so cold they could have been made of ice or cold iron. He pulled at them as hard as he could but he couldn't move them at all. What do you want from me? Who are you, whose hands are you? He kept asking these questions but the words wouldn't come out of his mouth. It was as if the hands heard what he was thinking. *These are the hands of a dead person. These hands have come from the grave. From a grave far, far away, in the desert of Yemen. Mithat*, he thought, *Mithat, these are Mithat's hands, they've come from the grave to strangle me.* He pulled with all his strength to free himself from these iron hands, but to no avail. It was impossible to move them a millimeter. *I'm dying*, he thought, *so I'm going to die by Mithat's hand.* As a devout Muslim and the Caliph of Islam, it broke his heart that he could not profess his faith aloud before surrendering his soul. He started reciting prayers silently. Just then there was a knock at the door and he heard his chamberlain calling to ask if anything was wrong. Then the man opened the door, saw him lying on the floor with his hands around his neck, and asked in a panicked voice, "What happened, Your Majesty? Did you fall?" He took the sultan by the arm and helped him up. He sat him in the armchair and brought him a glass of water. Then he asked permission to call the doctor. After the sultan had calmed down a bit, he asked the man what had happened and why he'd come. When the chamberlain explained that he'd heard a noise, followed by the sultan professing his faith three times, he slowly began to understand. He sent the chamberlain away and lit a cigarette. He paced the room a bit, then turned out the light and sat in the armchair by the window. He began watching the sky. He calmed himself by taking refuge in his faith, he repeated to himself that Halley's comet would not collide with the earth, that the very idea contradicted the Quran, but he continued to watch the sky until morning, just in case. In the morning, after he'd bathed and performed his prayers, he felt better. When the doctor arrived he said, "Your scholars appear to have been mistaken, doctor. It is God who created the heavens, the earth, the stars, and the moon, judgment day belongs to Him and nothing can happen until He gives the word. Look, by the grace of God, the world is still intact."

He felt pleased at having defeated the doctor for the first time; he lit a cigarette, squinted his eyes, and looked at his adversary in satisfaction.

The palace ladies' frayed nerves

THE SULTAN'S ROUTINES IN the mansion had now become fixed. He got up early in the morning, bathed in cold water, performed his prayers, drank his coffee from two different cups, then started walking up and down the main hall; every day he walked for half an hour to try to free himself from the dark thoughts that swarmed through his mind. A respectful silence reigned in the mansion, as it had at the palace. His family and staff tried to be as quiet as possible; if they wanted an audience they informed him in advance, and when they spoke to him they addressed him by one of his many elaborate titles. Even though he had been dethroned, he was still the sultan in the mansion. No one prostrated themselves on the floor before him anymore, but the men bowed and the women curtseyed.

One day as the sultan was pacing the hall and agonizing over his plans to write his memoirs, he was startled by an unexpected noise. There was a crash on the top floor, followed by the sound running feet and women shouting, then the noise stopped abruptly and the mansion was once again silent. The sultan was curious and called to the chamberlain to go find out what had happened. The chamberlain rushed off, and when he returned he told the sultan that his youngest son, Abid Efendi, had bumped into a chair and knocked it over, but hadn't been injured in any way. His Majesty could be assured that there was nothing to worry about. The sultan listened to the chamberlain with an expression of doubt, then asked that his son be brought to his room. He never believed anything the first time he heard it. Abid came to his room and kissed his hand, and the sultan asked him what had happened and if he'd been hurt.

His son said, "No, father. I'm fine, nothing happened."

It was clear from the boy's expression and demeanor that he was reluctantly telling a lie he'd been forced into, so the sultan interrogated the prince until he told the truth. Şadiye Sultan and Ayşe Sultan had never gotten along. In the freedom of the palace, where they had so many activities, it had never come to a head, but in the confinement of the mansion, where they shared the same sleeping quarters and couldn't avoid each other, they'd reached the point of a nervous breakdown and, despite the sedatives the doctor prescribed them, they were constantly at each other, and this time Ayşe Sultan had grabbed a plate from a nightstand and smashed it on the floor, then the other ladies had all rushed to get the situation under control.

After he heard this, the sultan remained alone in his room to think. He'd been aware of this tension for some time, and had guessed that it would come to a head sooner or later. It wasn't just his daughters; the other ladies, who used to have their own palaces and woods they could retreat to, were on the verge of a nervous breakdown after spending nearly a year in such cramped quarters. They weren't even allowed onto the balcony, let alone into the garden, and all of their jealousies, resentments, and hatreds came out into the open. His daughters were in a particularly bad state. They missed their fiancés in Istanbul; they feared that their dreams of establishing homes with them might never come true, that their fiancés would abandon them because their father had been deposed, and they had frequent crying fits that they did their best to conceal from their father.

He had to solve these problems within his family in the same manner that he had once solved important matters of state. Because, even if he has been deposed, a sultan must always behave like a sultan.

After thinking and blowing smoke rings for a long time, he called for his chamberlain and asked him to send word to the commander that he wished to speak to him if possible. When he received word that the commander was busy that day but would drop by the following day, he laughed bitterly. Rasim Bey, the new commander, wasn't understanding, tolerant, and compassionate like the former commander. He wasn't like that strange doctor either. He was faultlessly respectful, but he was a stern soldier. When the commander came the following day he refused the offer of coffee and a cigarette and asked the sultan what he wanted. In a persuasive tone, the sultan reiterated his devotion to his brother Sultan Reşad and the new government, said that he prayed every day for their success, but that he wished for the granting of a small request that had now become urgent. He had already asked that his daughters be allowed to return to Istanbul so they could marry, but he had received no reply. He requested that the commander take the matter up with his superiors. It was also known that his son Abid, who was of school age, needed to attend a school in Thessaloniki. He would be grateful if a solution could be found. After all, his daughters and sons were His Majesty Sultan Reşad's nieces and nephews. He was certain his brother would want to be merciful to them. Then he said, "Commander, will you allow me to make one final request for myself? We've been closed up in this house for almost a year. I can understand why I'm not allowed into the garden, but if I could at least be allowed onto the balcony that overlooks the garden so my aging body can get some sun and fresh air."

Rasim Bey replied in a respectful but serious manner. "Fine," he said, "I will inform the highest authorities of your requests." Then he gave him a military salute and left.

That evening the sultan asked that his family gather for a meeting on the ground floor. Only family members were to be present. His wives, daughters, and sons kissed his hand respectfully.

The sultan was sitting in his armchair fingering his worry beads. His family stood waiting in front of him.

"It gives me great joy to see you all in such good health and spirits," he began, then continued in a sonorous voice: "We may have lost the sultanate, we may have been removed from the throne, our dignity and happiness may have suffered. All of this is the will of Almighty God. We know that everything comes from Him, we consent to our destiny with resignation. However, we are members of one of the most important dynasties in the history of the world, indeed perhaps the most important. No family but the Ottoman dynasty can boast of six centuries of uninterrupted rule. Rome and Byzantium were ruled by several different families, and the same is true of France and England. The Ottomans have ruled longer than any other family. God willing, it will continue to rule for centuries. Even if we are no longer on the throne, the responsibility of being members of this glorious family rests on our shoulders. Together we must show the world that we can carry this burden with dignity. I am not incapable of understanding the state of mind our young people are in after being confined to this mansion for so long. I am doing my best to resolve this issue as quickly as I can. Until that moment comes, I want you to accept the situation with patience and fortitude, and to avoid rebellious behavior. Remember that judgment belongs to God."

Ayşe Sultan and Şadiye Sultan listened with their heads bowed. Although they were aware of what their father was speaking of they felt it incumbent on them to remain silent, and when the sultan said, "May God comfort you all," they backed away bashfully.

The joy of returning to Istanbul—A shadow falls across the joy—The socialist prince

THE GOOD NEWS THEY awaited arrived ten days later. The government, either because it had become merciful or because it no longer perceived the former sultan as a threat, had decided to allow some family members and their servants to return to Istanbul. On the ground floor of the Alatini mansion this news was received with cautious satisfaction, and on the top floor with joy and excitement. The destiny of at least part of the family had been altered. The children would get married, and they would be able to give Abdülhamid grandchildren who would continue his lineage forever.

His three daughters, his eldest son, and three of his wives began preparing to return to Istanbul, but his wives Müşfika and Naciye had decided they could not bring themselves to leave the sultan there by himself. Indeed Müşfika Hanım couldn't even imagine living apart from her husband. She would not part from him until death. His wives were much younger than him, they were Circassian beauties with blue or green eyes. They had been specially selected for the palace, and had received extensive education in poetry, music, and foreign languages. The aging sultan loved all of his wives, but Müşfika had a special place in his heart. He wanted to draw his last breath in her arms. She stayed with him throughout the years he spent at the Alatini mansion.

The ladies who wanted to return to Istanbul made it clear that they wanted to take their children with them. And the sultan agreed to this. In fact Müşfika's daughter was among those returning to Istanbul. Despite this, and even though she was still young, Müşfika had decided to sacrifice her chance to witness her daughter's success in order to stay in Thessaloniki with her aging husband. She was perhaps the only one of the many women who'd entered the harem who fell in love with the sultan. She'd been born in an Abkhaz village in the Caucasus; when her father was killed in battle she was given to the palace as a concubine, and at the age of fourteen she married the sultan, who'd developed an infatuation for her. Her original name was Ayşe, which had been changed in accordance with palace customs, but the name lived on with her daughter, Ayşe Sultan. Because she herself had originally been a concubine and her daughter was the sultan's child, she was extremely respectful to her daughter and stood whenever she entered the room. This was how she had been trained at the palace. When they received permission to return to Istanbul, Ayşe begged her mother, insisted that she come with her, but Müşfika couldn't bring herself to leave her husband after he'd suffered so much misfortune. All she would say was, "He needs me." Everyone in the palace knew that the sultan was deeply attached to her. Once, Abdülhamid became convinced that all of his doctors were conspiring to kill him, and even though he was ill he refused to take the medicine they'd given him. Indeed he fired all the doctors. The only person who was able to calm him down and get him to take the medication was Müşfika Hanım. There was a deep bond of trust and tenderness between them.

The news that they'd been given permission to return to Istanbul was celebrated on the top floor of the mansion. The princesses clapped their hands, danced, played cheerful pieces on the piano, hugged each other, and danced the rondo despite the tensions among them. They prayed for their uncle Sultan Reşad for granting them permission to return. They were going to leave this prison in Thessaloniki, be reunited with their fiancés, and establish their own families. They were already dreaming of the palace weddings their compassionate uncle would hold for them. It did not even occur to them that the main reason these handsome gentlemen and high-raking officers wanted to marry them when their omnipotent father was on the throne was for the opportunity to gain power and wealth. The young men had fallen in love with the princesses, there was no other explanation. But now, poisonous doubts began to gnaw at them. "What if he

doesn't want to marry the daughter of a man everyone curses?" Questions like this planted themselves
in their minds, causing them to lose their appetites
and weep silently into their handkerchiefs at night. It
would soon be clear that the poor princesses' doubts
were not unfounded.

The big day finally arrived, and the girls set off
with their mothers and servants to catch the train to
Istanbul. The princesses were barely able to contain
themselves, they felt both the sadness of knowing they
might never see their father again as well as the excitement of beginning a completely new life. They wept as
they kissed his hand at the door of the mansion, and
the sultan, unable to bear this farewell, rushed to his
room and closed the door.

The fresh air and sweet breezes in the garden filled
the princesses with a zest for life. They were going
outside for the first time in a year. The soldiers and
officers gave them hostile glances, but this didn't spoil
their mood. At one point the commander came up to
them and said, "We're going to take you into a room.
You will be searched from head to toe. It will be our
wives who search you. You'll be given new clothes.
You are to put them on and leave your old clothes
here." The princesses and their mothers flushed at
this impudent suggestion, a burning rebellion and a
desire to protest began to rise within them, but the
commander's stern, expressionless face broke their
courage. They had no choice but to submit to this final
torture. It was even worse than they'd expected. The

women who had gathered in the barracks took the palace ladies one by one into a small room and stripped them naked. The palace ladies were mortified by this intimate and humiliating search. The hostile women moved their cold hands all over their bodies. Their long hair was searched thoroughly. When the young women came back out into the garden they couldn't look at each other, or for that matter at anyone else. Nothing could have been more devastating for them. All of them, including the servants, felt as if they'd been raped. They held themselves together until their carriages passed the gate, but once they were outside the mansion walls, the tears they'd been holding back began to flow down their cheeks. They sobbed without uttering a single word until they reached the train station. After they'd boarded the train with an army of guards, Refia Sultan turned to her sisters and said, "The shame does not belong to us but to those revolutionary bandits. I seek refuge in God from their evil."

Ayşe Sultan said, "Yes, you're right. And there's one more thing. Despite the position our father is in, they're so frightened of him they're willing to commit these sins in order to try to find some message scribbled on a scrap of paper. They're much more frightened than we are."

Then, to the monotonous rattle of the train, they sighed as their young hearts filled with dreams of the dashing, handsome young aristocrats who would welcome them back to Istanbul. These gentlemen and other relatives would be waiting for them at Sirkeci

Station. Of course they would come, they had to come. But even as they thought this, doubts began to take shape in their minds. Would they really come? Would they come rushing to meet the daughters of a former sultan whom everyone cursed? And what of their brother? Even if everyone else came, they were certain that Abdülkadir wouldn't. The prince who had proclaimed himself to be a socialist had little to do with the family or the palace.

To this rebellious boy, the palace, the throne, and the sultanate counted for nothing. His life was centered around the violin and socialism. He made it clear that he had no respect for his father's outdated ideas, and had been admonished for this for years. The sultan would bang his cane on the floor and say, "Forget about this nonsense, you're a prince. What business do you have dabbling in this depravity called communism? Can any good come from the philosophy of the rabble? This is the work of Russian hooligans."

When the Russian tsar couldn't cope with the mutinous battleship *Potemkin*, the sultan had even issued orders for it to be watched. He'd placed cannons on the shores of the Bosphorus and had the entrance mined in case the ship attempted to sail into Istanbul. A mutiny on a warship was one of Abdülhamid's greatest fears. Incidents like that could ignite sparks that quickly turned into conflagrations. It could easily spread to Ottoman territory. If a warship on the Bosphorus shelled his palace, there was nothing he could do. Everything could be ruined in a moment.

Fortunately the ship didn't come to Istanbul, and when the crew surrendered in Constanta, the sultan heaved a sigh of relief. Then, when he began to fear that some of the mutinous officers had come to Istanbul, he ordered a thorough search for them in every corner of the city. Throughout this period, he rebuked Abdülkadir constantly: "Look what your communist hooligans are up to. Are these the people you want to emulate?" But the prince, who secretly read censored newspapers and banned foreign publications, had seen his father described as a "sultan who is terrified by a single ship, who trembles day and night in fear that the *Potemkin* might come and shell his palace." During his uncle's time, the Ottoman navy had been the second largest in the world, but out of paranoia his father had left the fleet to rot in the Golden Horn, leaving the Ottoman seas defenseless. He sent the minister of the navy to the Black Sea with instructions to give the rebels whatever they wanted, to meet all of their conditions so long as they left Istanbul alone. According to these journalists, the sultan had reduced the great empire to a deplorable state. Indeed according to some writers, after the *Potemkin* incident his father had said, "Look, don't you see that I was right to neglect the navy," and that he had called back two warships that had been sent to frighten the rebels in Yemen. But he was surprised one day when his father called him in, gave him some newspaper clippings, and with a proud smile said, "Here, read these." Both Vladimir Lenin and Leon Trotsky, who were in exile in Europe, had said on different occasions that they found his father to be cleverer than Tsar Nicholas. The prince was amazed by this, but after thinking about it for a long time he concluded that they'd only said this because they didn't know his father, then resumed playing a concerto on his Stradivarius violin. He couldn't imagine a life without music or his violin, and had no ambitions whatsoever regarding the sultanate. But he couldn't compete with his father concerning music. Pieces by famous composers all over the world were sent to the palace to be presented to the sultan. When Johann Strauss's "Tales from the Orient," which he'd dedicated to the sultan, was performed in Vienna, one of the posters that were put up all over the city was sent to the palace. He had devoted his life to music, but he would never be as famous in the world of music as his father was. Because his father the sultan was a strange man. He prayed five times a day and showed great respect for Islam. At the same time, he allowed the establishment of breweries and distilleries, and had seen no reason to object to the opening of the first legal brothel. The increasing number of translations from foreign languages, the transition to European time standards, and the banning of veils for women were all his doing.

Assassination attempt

THE SULTAN, FREED FROM his terror of Halley's comet and constant worries about his daughters, was sitting by the window that opened onto the balcony, inhaling deeply from his strong cigarette and looking out at the now familiar trees and flower beds, watching the leaves flutter in the breeze, when suddenly he heard a gunshot and a bullet whizzing past his ear. When he was alone at night he was nearly undone by fear, but when faced with actual danger he kept his composure. He didn't move but simply held his breath and waited. There was a great deal of running around and shouting, both inside and outside the mansion. There was a knock at the door and his chamberlain asked anxiously if he was all right. He said he was fine, and told the man not to come in. He was listening to what was going on, and at the same time he was trying to get his thoughts in order. There'd been only one shot fired. If an order had come from Istanbul for his execution, this was not how it would have happened. The commander would come and read the order to him, allow him to perform his ablutions and prayers, and then carry out the execution.

So this was not an execution. It could be an attempted assassination by one of the officers. It would be best to stay away from the windows from now on. There was another knock on the door, and this time it opened. Müşfika came rushing in with a look of terror on her face, shouting, "My monarch, my monarch, have they murdered you?" When she saw that her husband was alive and unharmed, she prostrated herself, threw her arms around his knees, and wept without restraint. The sultan held her by her shoulders and raised her to her feet, then held her chin and looked into her eyes and said, "I'm fine, my dear, I'm fine. There's nothing to worry about." The young woman kept sobbing and said, "If any harm came to your blessed body I couldn't live." The sultan gently kissed her wet cheeks, then embraced her tightly. The thin body in his arms trembled like a leaf. Just then there was a knock on the door, and the chamberlain informed him that the commander would like to speak to His Majesty. After stroking his wife's hair, the sultan went to the hall, saw the commander waiting for him, and said, "Commander, what's going on? What happened?" The commander looked distressed, his swarthy face seemed even darker than usual. "Sir, there's been a mishap," he said. "I hope you're not hurt." The sultan said, "No, as you can see, I'm fine. What happened?"

The commander said, "One of the officers committed an injudicious act. He fired a shot toward the mansion. We caught him right away and put him in a cell; we'll send him to headquarters for interrogation."

"Good God!" said the sultan. "Who committed this criminal act?"

In embarrassment, the commander said, "Lieutenant Salim."

"The one they call Salim the Kurd?"

"Yes, sir."

The sultan remained silent for a time, stroking his beard, then said, "So it's true."

"What's true, sir?"

"A good deed had evil consequences. I helped Salim a great deal. He came from a poor family. He wanted to become a soldier. One day he waited on the road to the palace, he implored Ismet Pasha, the pasha told me. I sent the boy to military school. So he's a lieutenant now, what does he want from me? Did he say anything?"

The commander was ashamed, he bowed his head and murmured, "When we first questioned him he said his gun had gone off by accident, but when we pressured him a bit more we realized that he saw this assassination attempt as a heroic act."

Abdülhamid laughed bitterly and said, "I suppose that's the latest fashion. To kill Sultan Hamid, to insult Sultan Hamid, to blame every evil on Sultan Hamid. What did this Hamid do to you? What did he do except serve the state? Commander, the state only survived because of the diplomatic measures I took. Is this how I'm to be rewarded?"

He got carried away and continued complaining, then remembered the situation he was in and stopped talking. Perhaps for the first time in his long life he'd dropped his vigilance and had come dangerously close to angering the commander by revealing his emotions. He lowered his voice and said, "Of course, everything comes from God. So this is what the Creator decreed. I was already exhausted. I intended to give the throne to my brother and free myself of these great responsibilities. May God bless our sultan, he's providing a comfortable life for me."

The commander smiled slightly, gave a military salute, then left.

After the commander left, the sultan inhaled deeply from his cigarette and contemplated the dust particles that danced in the beams of sunlight that reached in through the window. Even though he received no news from the outside, he could guess that he was being slandered, that false stories were being told about him, and that newspaper columnists were heaping insults on him. He was helpless to do anything about this, but still, he should have had some recourse. After all he'd done to serve the nation, they shouldn't allow his name to be blackened like this. His maker would be calling him soon, and once he sloughed off his mortal coil he would not be able to respond to this slander. The best thing to do would be to tell his side of the story. So the truth would not be covered up.

That evening he summoned his clerk Ali Muhsin Bey to his room. At the palace the clerk had been a busy man, he seldom got a chance to look up from his work, but at the mansion there was nothing for him to do but count flies, so when he received the summons he rushed to the room eagerly, hoping for something to do, and listened attentively as the sultan whispered to him, "Ali Muhsin Efendi, I'm going to give you a very secret duty. It's so secret that no one but you will know about it, and you are to forget it as soon as you've performed it. Ask them to give you a notebook in which to keep your accounts. Come here at a different time every day and write what I tell you in that notebook. Don't hold the notebook when you enter and leave the room, hide it under your jacket, under no circumstances should anyone see it."

As he left the room, Ali Muhsin Bey trembled with excitement at having been entrusted with an important duty. He realized that he was going to be the deposed sultan's privy secretary, that he was going to write what could be an earthshaking memoir. His heart trembled at the thought that one day these memoirs would be published and he would become famous; the title of the book would be *Abdülhamid's Memoirs, As Told to Ali Muhsin Bey.* Indeed these memoirs could make him a lot of money. Unfortunately for the clerk, his request for a notebook aroused suspicion, three days later it was seized in a raid, and the clerk was imprisoned in the mansion's dark cellar.

The sultan was so distressed by this that he closed himself in his carpentry workshop for days, and kept busy with his saws, his spirit level, and all of his carving and boring tools. He felt he had suffered a great injustice. As he dexterously fashioned boxes and cabinets with secret compartments, he thought about what was going to happen to the empire. Despite the stern measures taken by his grandfather Mahmud II, this long-lived empire seemed on the verge of dissolution. The unfortunate War of '93 that had been thrust upon him when he first came to power had been like a nail in the empire's coffin. He knew well what he'd done to keep the state afloat, and what the English had done to take the oil fields away from him. He both admired and feared the English. While he sanded a board with a cigarette dangling from his mouth, he sighed as he realized that he feared both the English and rats. He'd seen many people whose ears or noses had been gnawed by rats as they slept. Rats could do this without the victim feeling a thing. Rats were able to numb the flesh. The English were the same; when they were determined to seize territory, they used methods that wouldn't even occur to the devil, they'd get what they wanted at any expense. And meanwhile, the victim wouldn't feel anything. Until it was too late. His lethargic brother knew nothing of these things. The sultan didn't know who was serving in the new government, but he was sure it contained no true statesmen. Indeed if those rebellious officers in the Balkans took power, the empire for which his ancestors had sacrificed their blood for centuries would be gone within ten years. He was certain of this. The Jews were buying land in the vicinity of Jerusalem and wanted to establish a state there. And Mecca and Medina had been in danger since the Wahhabi uprising.

Müşfika Hanım—The Jewish State

FOR THE MOST PART the doctor was happy with his life, but going to the mansion every day to treat the family and the servants was a bore, and he found the sultan's strange medical opinions particularly irritating. The women complained of diarrhea, itching, or boils, and were constantly catching cold. The strange thing was that he didn't hear these complaints from the women themselves but from the sultan. "Doctor," he would say, "could you make a syrup for my third wife, using a bit of aloe, a dash of senna, and some cinnamon." When the doctor asked in an irritated tone why this was necessary, he learned the third wife had a touch of neuralgia. Everyone had their own minor complaints. The sultan had chronic digestive problems; he ate like a bird because he couldn't digest anything. His favorite foods were zucchini and yogurt. Even though he never left the house, he constantly caught colds. But his biggest problem was his hemorrhoids. They would bleed from time to time. He would bring the subject up when he couldn't stand the pain. One day the doctor told him that he would have to research the matter thoroughly because it was clear it was causing him a great deal of discomfort, and the instrument he took out of his bag the next day was enough to terrify the sultan. It was metal, with two hooks at the end. When he asked what it was, the doctor said it was a speculum.

The sultan's face went completely white. "You mean this huge thing is going... pardon me... is going to go in there?"

The doctor said, *Yes, Your Majesty* to himself, then thought of a strange joke. Then he realized this would be a tasteless joke, and erased it from his mind. No matter what, he had to perform his duties in the best possible manner, and to not do even the slightest thing wrong.

The proud sultan adamantly refused to allow him to use the speculum. "I would rather die."

Every day the doctor filled his bag with ether, quinine, tincture of thuja, laudanum; tinctures of mint, cinnamon, black cumin, and cloves; cantharidin and various elixirs and laxatives to treat the imperial family and their servants. The sultan was certain that he knew more about medicine than anyone else, and irritated the doctor by objecting to his conclusions and even trying to teach him. Even though the two men had seen each other every day for a long time, their relationship did not become deeper, yet they developed a strange, distant intimacy. The doctor was slowly beginning to forget the man's political identity. He was faced with a sickly, delusional old man who

didn't quite know how to behave toward him; sometimes he adopted a fatherly manner, at other times he
was gracious, arrogant, or overly respectful. However,
he seemed more relaxed than he had been during his
first days at the mansion, and for the moment, at any
rate, he no longer feared execution.

Of all the members of the household, the doctor
found Müşfika Hanım to be the most interesting. Although she was the sultan's favorite wife and Ayşe
Sultan's mother, she was a quiet, polite, respectful
young lady; the doctor could not help but admire her
beauty, her almost transparent skin, and the look of
refined distance in her hazel eyes. Unlike the other
family members, who invented illnesses out of boredom and behaved like spoiled children, she seemed
to him like an angel who radiated light and kindness.
What surprised and astonished him most about this
remarkable woman was the inexplicable love she felt
for her elderly husband. She frequently said, "Doctor,
I'm very concerned about our monarch's health. Forget about us and take care of him. Those who don't
know him well are not aware of what an exceptional
person our monarch is, how sensitive, compassionate,
and altruistic he is. If our patron is well, then all of us
are well. I beseech you to make sure nothing happens
to him. Because that would mean the end of my life
as well."

The doctor admired the deep love that made this
young woman's heart soar, the way she blushed when
she spoke of her husband, the way she talked excitedly

like a girl, and he was almost jealous because no one had ever loved him the way she loved this old man. Even though she'd been given permission to return to Istanbul with her daughter, she'd refused to leave her husband. "My place is by his side," she said. "No force is strong enough to pry me away from him."

Every evening when he returned home, the doctor conscientiously wrote a letter to the lover he was no longer sure was real, sealed it in an envelope, and placed it in the drawer. Then he took out one of the notebooks the pharmaceutical companies gave out and recorded what he'd talked about with the sultan that day. He didn't keep the hundreds of pages he'd written in his desk for fear they might be found; he hid them in a space under the stove. He didn't share his secret with anyone, not even his closest friends. He could not forget that what he perceived as his daily conversations with an elderly patient were the views of a deposed emperor. The new government was very sensitive about this. After giving it a great deal of thought, he'd come to the conclusion that the new era was no different from the old era, the new order cast a shadow that frightened everyone and brutally crushed any opposition. So why did they bother to overthrow the Red Sultan? Why turn everything upside down if nothing was going to change?

The deposed sultan was obsessively curious about the state of the empire and what the great powers were up to. What was happening in the volatile Balkans, what kind of relationship had developed between Italy and Tripoli, had it been possible to protect the oil fields of Mosul and Kirkuk, and of course Palestine...Were the Jews still trying to establish a state in Palestine? These were questions that nagged him from morning till late at night. It was his job to protect the empire by knowing everything that was going on, but now he couldn't get even the smallest tidbit of information. The doctor was aware that the sultan was always trying to get him to let something slip. The truth was that the situation was disastrous, the Balkans were out of control, the Orthodox states had overcome their differences and were declaring independence one after the other on the urging of Russia. Millions of refugees fleeing these territories were trying to reach Istanbul on foot. They were being massacred by bandits and rebels. The English were doing their utmost to seize the oil fields in the Middle East, they were encouraging the Arabs to rebel against Istanbul. In short, as the old man fussed about with his elixirs, balms, and hot iron, and rubbed his hands constantly with Atkinson cologne out of fear of germs, his vast empire was slipping away from beneath his feet. It was just as well he didn't know what was going on, it would be too much for him. European magazines depicted the empire as a wild beast being torn apart by predators.

WHEN THE DOCTOR ARRIVED at the sultan's mansion one day, the rain was pouring down like a storm. He got completely soaked as he climbed the stairs. When he entered the hall, the former sultan was looking out the window, watching the rain.

"Ah, you're so beautifully drenched," he said. "Believe me, I've missed getting wet. No matter how intense the rain was, I used to run around the palace gardens. God's mercy is healing."

Perhaps it was the melancholic atmosphere created by the rain, but that day the doctor had the opportunity to understand a bit more about what was going on in the old man's mind. He revisited the past, the victories and the devastating defeats that never left his thoughts, and most importantly, the regrets he replayed over and over again.

Starting with a tired and difficult-to-hear voice, which blended into the monotonous patter of raindrops on the palace windows, the old man complained about his discomfort. He mentioned how his intestines had been tormenting him all night, despite his only having had a bit of zucchini and yogurt for dinner. He wondered why medicine couldn't solve such a simple problem and why he couldn't devise a remedy himself. After the doctor assured him he would provide immediate relief and gave him a calming syrup from his bag, he watched as the elderly man with trembling and partly bluish lips drank the brown liquid. Then he said, "Of course, all the aching discomforts worsen in rainy weather."

"No, no," the sultan said. "It's not the illnesses; it's the painful memories that come alive, and the worst part is that the rain never stops."

He chuckled lightly. "There are so many of those memories. They sleep during the day like vampires, and when darkness falls, they pounce on me."

Then suddenly, he said, "I know you can't provide information from the outside, but please, at least help me in one matter." He mentioned that the previous night his thoughts had been focused on the Palestine issue. According to his account, Zionists, concerned about the increasing anti-Semitism in Russia and European countries, had once approached his government in an attempt to establish a Jewish settlement in the Holy Land, and had even tried reaching out to him directly.

Who hadn't intervened in this matter? Polish nobles, French diplomats, English lords, and even the world's richest families, like the Rothschilds? The Jews wanted to own land in Jerusalem and Haifa.

"It's quite strange, you know," he said. "My great ancestor Sultan Bayezid II welcomed hundreds of thousands of Jews fleeing Spain in 1492, saving them from the persecution of Ferdinand and Isabella. Since then, Jews in our domain have lived comfortably. There are many Jews in high positions in the government. In truth, our Jews have never made such a land claim because there was no need. But the Jews in Europe approached us to buy land in the place they believed God had promised them."

"Why don't they come to places like this city?" the doctor asked. "Wouldn't it be easier for them?"

"I told you," the sultan said. "They want to return to the land of David and Solomon. The reason behind their attempt to overthrow me lies in my refusal to grant this request."

The doctor exclaimed in surprise, as this was the first time the former sultan had accused the revolutionaries. His regretful expression, which appeared as soon as he spoke these words, revealed that he had grasped the magnitude of the tree he had cut down. His dark eyes grew even darker, and his rapid movements, indicative of his fear, suggested he was searching for a solution in vain.

"Oh, no!" he exclaimed. He looked as if he were about to faint. "May God grant long life to my brother the sultan. Surely, our heroic army must know something. I'm just . . . well, I'm just wondering if the Palestine issue has any influence on this situation."

"Okay," the doctor insisted. "Since the topic has come up, what led you to think like this?"

The sultan pleaded. "Doctor, my son, can we please close this unpleasant subject?"

"No," the doctor persisted. "Now that you've started, please continue. Don't worry; I'm not an informant. You can trust that what you say will stay between us."

The skeptical old man fixed his gaze on the doctor, unable to decide what to do, writhing in discomfort. He lit a cigarette with trembling hands, took deep drags, and then asked, "Can I trust your word?"

"You absolutely can trust my word!" the doctor affirmed.

After much contemplation and deep drags on his cigarette, as if realizing that there was no turning back, the old man began by explaining that Baron Edmond Rothschild, the head of the Rothschild family, had come to visit him.

"The baron asked for permission to purchase property in the Promised Land," the old man said. "I treated him well, and I even gifted him a thousand of my specially made cigars. While I didn't grant full permission for them to own the land, I did relax the rules. Gradually, they expanded their holdings. So much so that ten years later, fifty percent of the coastal strip between Gaza and Jaffa belonged to the Jews. But..."

He took a deep drag from his cigarette and then continued. "Have you heard of Theodor Herzl?"

"No," the doctor replied.

"His name is important," the old man said. "He convened a Zionist congress in Switzerland, advocating the idea of Zionism to achieve a state for the world's Jews. He first presented his demands to our government. My councilors and I rejected his requests. But he didn't give up. After years of effort, I became curious about who this man was and agreed to see him. He spoke tirelessly, and I can't remember everything he said, but his main point was that they were willing to pay off our external debts in exchange for permission to settle in the Holy Land. At that time, our debts had increased significantly, and such an offer could have been quite appealing. But how could I give away Jerusalem, the Al-Aqsa Mosque, and the rest of the Holy Land to the Jews? How would my people accept that? I not only rejected Herzl's proposals, but after he left, I issued an order to make the holy sites in Jerusalem my personal property by reimbursing the expenses."

"Why did you do such a thing?"

"I knew that the Zionists would not give up on this ideal. If those lands remained my personal property, I could prevent the establishment of a Jewish state in Jerusalem in the future. But now . . ."

"Now?"

"You know, they confiscated my personal property. I don't know what they'll do next. That's why I'm curious about the developments."

Then, as he gazed at the smoke rings rising toward the ceiling, speaking as if to himself, he said, "It was the wealth in the territories my state controlled that led me to this situation. Just think about it—Jerusalem, Mecca, Medina, the legacy of Greek civilization, Constantinople, and, perhaps most importantly, oil. None of these brought me happiness."

The doctor thought, *This man may be a tyrant, but what he's saying is true. They won't leave all this wealth to a single dynasty.*

A cholera epidemic in Thessaloniki—Monsieur Pasteur—The Imperial School of Bacteriology

BECAUSE HE'D CLOSED HIMSELF up in his palace for so many years, the former sultan didn't find his imprisonment in the mansion to be difficult. He had fewer distractions, and he no longer had his translation team, his opera, or his theater, but what was most difficult for him was not being allowed out into the garden. He missed the spring, the rain, the cold, and the snow. If they gave him permission, he would spend hours in the mansion's large garden, examining all of the plants. Unfortunately, no matter how many times he brought the matter up, they always refused, so he had to be content with a pair of binoculars, through which he could look at the neighboring streets and houses, and ships passing in the distance.

One day he noticed unusual movement in the streets beyond the mansion walls. People were loading tattered furniture onto carts and moving out of the city. From their clothing, it was clear these were poor people. When he looked more closely, he saw that these were the lower classes of Thessaloniki's Jewish community, and he became deeply curious about what was going on. Where were these people going, and why? Early the next morning when he saw lime being poured in several places in the neighborhood, he realized there was a cholera epidemic. His heart skipped a beat. He'd worked hard to contain many epidemics, and they terrified him. His experience had taught him how difficult it was to contain an epidemic, you had to take precautions beforehand and use vaccinations to get the situation under control.

The use of vaccinations was widespread in the Ottoman Empire. They would collect smallpox scabs, place them in a walnut shell, dip a pin into the shell, and scratch the skin, then cover the scratch with rose petals. Europe learned the smallpox vaccination from the Ottomans.

The person Abdülhamid most admired in the field of microbes was Pasteur. He'd sent a delegation led by Aleksander Pasha to Paris to meet him. The delegation brought him the sultan's greetings, presented him with the Order of the Mecidiye, and donated ten thousand franks to the newly established Pasteur Institute. This was the largest donation ever made to the institute. Aleksander spent six months learning from Pasteur.

The sultan knew all too well what a disaster cholera could be. The disease had once descended on Istanbul like a leaden cloud of death. In every neighborhood women and children wept silently as coffins were carried through the streets, and people were frightened by even the slightest sound. He was proud to remember that on account of the precautions he'd taken, this scourge had lasted only eight months. He set up clinics on every pier and at every intersection, patients' clothes and belongings were burned immediately, water was purified, doctors from the Imperial School of Bacteriology, which he had founded, followed the latest developments in the field. Everything collected from affected neighborhoods was disinfected with water vapor at one hundred and ten degrees. He followed these measures personally, and was able to get the epidemic under control in eight months. But now it had come to Thessaloniki, where there were no such measures in place. His brother would never be able to handle the situation. He was lethargic and ineffective. Which meant that everyone was in grave danger.

When the doctor arrived toward noon, he shared his thoughts with him. At first the doctor tried to conceal the situation, but when he saw that the old man knew what was going on, he gave up. Yes, there was a cholera epidemic in Thessaloniki, they were doing everything, including expulsion from the city, to contain it.

The sultan said, "I have a great deal of experience. You don't know how many disasters I've managed, how many epidemics I've contained. Benefit from my experience."

Even as he said this he knew there was no hope, he knew that no one was going to consult him about anything. So as soon as the doctor left he went around the mansion to implement protective measures. He decreed that everyone would drink and wash with boiled water, everyone was to wear clean clothes and pile their old clothes outside their doors. He sent word to the commander that these clothes were not to be touched and that they should be burned immediately.

He ordered the servants to clean every surface in the house, the floors, windows, banisters, doorknobs, as thoroughly as possible. Then he placed the mansion under quarantine. No one but the commander and the doctor was to enter the mansion, they would keep their distance, there would be no handshakes, and nobody at all would be allowed to touch him. This order applied to everyone in the household. All fruit and vegetables that came to the house were to be washed in vinegar. As he issued these commands, his back seemed to become a bit less hunched, his pale skin seemed to take on color, and his voice had a more decisive tone.

The doctor's curiosity becomes more important than his love letters

WHEN THE DOCTOR RETURNED home he took the little notebooks from their hiding place, sat at his desk, and began writing; the writing was so small that he could barely read it himself. There were two reasons for this. One was to keep the number of notebooks at a minimum so they would be easier to hide, and the second was to make them difficult to read. That evening he was struck once again by the importance of what he was doing. He was writing down the memories of an exiled monarch; this wasn't easy. If the government found out what he was doing, he would immediately be court-martialed and then face a firing squad. Just recently they'd imprisoned the sultan's clerk. What he was doing was dangerous, but it also had an appeal. As far as he knew, Abdülhamid II had not published any memoirs, so this would be the only record of his own words. It would be the only authentic document for future generations. Chance had given him a duty, a historical duty. It also gave meaning to his monotonous life as a doctor in Thessaloniki, traveling between the hospital and the mansion.

As he recorded that day's conversation, he glanced at the decorative writing paper and envelopes. He realized he hadn't written to Melahat Hanım for some time. His yearning and love had not diminished, but his letter writing had been replaced by these secret notes. In any event, he never mailed the letters, and when things calmed down a bit he could begin writing to her again.

Of course there had been some excitement when the sultan arrived, but everyone had grown accustomed to his presence. Nobody found it interesting that an old man who had imprisoned himself in Yılıdız Palace for years was now imprisoned in the city.

The doctor was tired of this sick man's suspicions and of listening to his bizarre medical opinions. It occurred to him from time to time to ask his commanding officer to relieve him of this duty and replace him with someone else.

But now everything had suddenly changed. The man was going to talk, and he was going to listen and then write it all down. He sensed that he and the sultan had reached an unspoken agreement. From now on he wouldn't interrupt, he wouldn't be in a hurry to leave the mansion, he would listen attentively, and indeed would even ask questions. He would ask him about Namık Kemal, about the Young Turks, his brother Murad's madness, his uncle's murder, the strangling of Mithat Pasha, then he would ask him about foreign monarchs, about Kaiser Wilhelm, Queen Victoria, Napoleon III, whether it was true that his uncle had a love affair with Eugénie, what he had experienced in Europe, why he hadn't used Europe as a model for developing the empire, about the March uprising, he would ask about whatever came to mind.

That evening the doctor smoked one cigarette after another; he even brought out his bottle of tsipouro and took an occasional sip, something he rarely did.

The interrogation of a monarch

THE FOLLOWING DAY, THE old wolf didn't fail to notice that the doctor had arrived earlier than usual, and that he was talkative and full of questions. As usual, he listed what he'd eaten and what herbal medications he was taking, then he said, "Curiosity is good, but if it's unsatisfied it can make you sick." Then, as the doctor looked at him in surprise, he continued, "For several days I've noticed you have some questions for me but you hesitate to ask. Please ask!"

"Everything?" asked the doctor.

"Yes," said the sultan. "I'm prepared to tell you everything."

Thus the doctor and the former sultan entered an unspoken agreement. His memories would become history. The sultan cheerfully ordered three coffees, two for himself and one for his new privy secretary.

Then he began the conversation with the following question: "What does delusion mean?"

When the doctor answered, "Imagining something that's not real, suspicion, fear," he realized why the sultan had asked this question.

"Something that's not real, you say. So if a suspicion or fear is grounded in reality, it cannot be considered a delusion." Then he inhaled deeply from his cigarette and said, "There are various periods in history, my boy. It's impossible to live outside the period in which you find yourself. I was given the throne at a time when all empires were falling apart and emperors were being killed. I've known so many monarchs who were killed." He took another deep drag from his cigarette, then exhaled slowly through his nose. "Some were assassinated, some were killed in battle, and some were executed. I'll never forget the horrible death of Shah Naser al-Din of the Qajar dynasty. I knew most of them, they were decent people. Unfortunately they were killed. Monarchs are probably still being killed today, but as you know, I receive no news of the world. They cut my uncle Abdülaziz's wrists and held him down while he bled to death. They tried to pretend it was suicide, but there were witnesses. Besides, how could someone cut both wrists with a pair of nail scissors? I tried the perpetrators, I set up a court in the palace gardens. All of them, including Mithat Pasha, were sentenced to death, but I commuted these sentences and sent them to Yemen."

The doctor's pulse began to quicken, they were touching on an important point in recent history. "Would you allow me to ask a question? Mithat Pasha was strangled in Taif prison. How did this happen?"

"I swear I had nothing to do with that. If I'd wanted him dead I wouldn't have commuted his sentence, I would have ordered he be executed. No one could have stopped me."

At this point the doctor decided to try an experiment to set the tone for future conversations. Would the sultan allow him to object, would he be willing to argue about the matter? Otherwise these notes would be nothing more than dreary self-justification.

"Excuse me," he said. "May I ask some questions that occurred to me while you were speaking? Do you have any objection?"

The sultan gestured for him to go ahead.

"Could the warden of Taif prison kill an illustrious former grand vizier without orders from you?"

"It seems that he did."

"How could he dare to kill someone so important?"

"I keep wondering the same thing. How could they carry out this execution without me being aware? Who could have given this order?"

The doctor smiled. "His Majesty the sultan is omnipotent. No one else could have given that order. You know this yourself."

When the sultan didn't answer, the doctor asked another question. "So was the warden punished for these murders?"

"I don't remember," said the sultan. It was clear from his expression that he didn't like the direction this conversation was taking.

"Don't bother, we know the answer," said the doctor. "He received no punishment whatsoever. Wasn't it Mithat Pasha who put you on the throne, wasn't it he who paved the way for you to take power?"

"Yes," murmured the sultan.

"On the condition that you accept constitutional monarchy and open the parliament?"

"I did open the parliament."

"Yes, but you closed it within a year and began exercising absolute authority," said the doctor in an accusatory tone.

"Yes, but I had my reasons," said the sultan. "I was obliged to do this." Then he began telling the story slowly. "As soon I ascended to the throne, I found the Russo-Ottoman war in my lap. I hate war. Whether you win or lose, it breaks the nation's back. That's why I try to solve everything through negotiations. But this war had already started. Throughout history, we've fought the Russians more than we've fought anyone else. And we weren't in such a good position. The empire no longer had enough resources. I had some ideas in mind about how to bring the war to an end. But there was no way I could implement these plans with that disaster of a parliament."

"Why?" asked the doctor. "After all it was your parliament."

The sultan laughed bitterly, stroked his beard, and seemed to be struggling to find a way to explain something so complicated.

"Look," he said, "let me tell you about this ensemble they called the Ottoman parliament: The deputies were Greek, Armenian, Turkish, Arab, Kurdish, Laz, Wallachian, Albanian, Bosnian, Bulgarian, and Jewish. Serbia, Montenegro, Romania, Egypt, and Tunisia also sent deputies. The majority of the deputies were from minorities who wanted to break away from the empire. They were working to bring down the Ottoman state. What government can survive a situation like that? Especially in wartime... Can you imagine a national parliament in which Turks are a minority? That's why I had no choice but to close it. Excuse me, but this is a reality that the Young Ottomans have somehow failed to understand. They go to Europe, fall under the influence of their ideas and wonder why we can't do that too. Every race and religion there is exists within our borders. Now they come and clamor about liberty. Let's see what comes of this."

The doctor stopped and thought. The Balkan War was eating away at Ottoman territory. Entire districts and regions had been lost, and now the enemy forces were marching on Thessaloniki. The poor old man had never even imagined a situation like this, and if he heard about it he would probably have a heart attack.

That evening, the doctor once again wrote excitedly in his little notebook, smoking cigarettes and swigging tsipouro as he did so. He was now certain that he and the former sultan had reached a new agreement. It was as if he was the judge and the sultan was the defendant. One was interrogating, and the other was being interrogated. The doctor laughed aloud at the sense of power he felt, then began coughing from the cigarette smoke he'd just inhaled. After he got his coughing under control, he thought to himself, *Having power is a wonderful thing.*

The doctor took a sheet of decorative letter paper and began writing carefully.

Light of my eye, joy of my heart, you conquered me with a single glance.

I've been longing for you for years, and each day I spend without you is torment. I don't know where you are, or whether you've returned to Istanbul. I hope that your father's exile came to an end when Hamid was overthrown. After all, it would be easier for me to see you in Istanbul, and to visit your father in order to make a proposal.

I no longer have much to do except visit the mansion every day to treat the former sultan and his family. I feel as if my life in Thessaloniki is suddenly going to change, that a miracle will occur and my longing will come to an end. I wish you could hear the things the former sultan told me, and see how polite and ingratiating he is to me. It's not just him, his entire retinue is like that. Sometimes I wonder if we were misinformed about these people, if we were misled by false rumors, but then I immediately remember all of their cruelty. I think that people behave one way when they have

*power and another way when they don't. He might
seem like an innocent old man who has retreated
into a corner, but there are many who have deep
grievances against him. Sometimes when he's
sitting there with his eyes half closed, looking
tired and worn out, I wonder to myself, could this
really be the descendant of Mehmet the Conqueror,
Selim the Grim, and Süleyman the Magnificent?
This is a sultan who never led a campaign, who
never stepped foot on a battlefield, he's not like his
ancestors.*

*He loves to talk, he's always talking about his
memories, and I don't know why but he seems
to try to ingratiate himself and gain my trust.
Perhaps it's because he's worried about his and his
family's health, perhaps it's because he wants me
to speak well of him, to show him in a good light.
I have to confess that this sultan I used to see as a
tyrant with no conscience now seems to me like a
melancholy patient who suffers pain and loves his
family, a delusional, fearful old man.*

When the doctor read the letter again, he didn't
like the last paragraph. He hadn't been able to express
this complicated matter the way he'd wanted. If anyone got hold of this letter it could land him in a lot of
trouble. He tore the letter into small pieces and threw
them in the stove.

The following day began in the usual manner. The
sultan sat three yards away from him, complained that

he hadn't slept because of the pain of his hemorrhoids, he'd made the mistake of eating three meatballs at dinner and this had upset his stomach and given him gas, and he'd rubbed camphor on his belly; Zülfet, the chief housekeeper, was in a lot of pain so he'd given her some syrup; he'd started giving brewer's yeast to Abid Efendi; he mentioned that their sheets and clothing had been burned in a corner of the garden and asked about the cholera epidemic. "These epidemics always hit poor people the hardest," he said. "I imagine that's the case in Thessaloniki as well."

The doctor put him at ease by telling him the cholera was under control and the number of deaths was decreasing every day. Then he asked, "Shall we continue our conversation?"

"Yes," said the sultan. "Let me order coffee."

The doctor asked a question that had been bothering him all night. "There's been a lot of discussion about why you gave Cyprus to the English," he said. "Why did you give away such a large island you'd inherited from your ancestors?"

The sultan laughed bitterly. "Doctor, if you'd been on the throne instead of me you would have done the same thing. I had no other choice. Our archenemies the Russians had come down through the Balkans and were practically at the gates of Istanbul. They set up their headquarters in Yeşilköy. There was nothing we could do to keep the city from falling. We had to sign a harsh and unfavorable agreement with the Russians. It was humiliating for me, as sultan of the great

Ottoman Empire, to negotiate with Archduke Nicholas, commander of the Russian army. In that difficult period, I thought about playing the great powers off against each other. I knew that the English were unhappy about this agreement. English warships sailed into the Marmara. I said that I would grant them the administration of Cyprus for a hundred years in order to establish a balance against the Russians. I didn't give them the territory, I allowed them to administrate it. It still belonged to us, but oh, those English. Once they get hold of something they never let go."

What am I going to do with this man, thought the doctor in distress. *He has an answer for everything. He turns everything around to make it seem as if the opposition was at fault. But that's the man's profession. He's conducted so many negotiations over the years. He's used to it.*

He decided to change the subject a bit. "You've had so many interesting experiences," he said. "You've met all the kings and emperors in the world. Would you like to tell me a little about them?"

The sultan was pleased by this suggestion, a smile spread across his face, he always enjoyed talking about world leaders and his relationships with them.

"Tomorrow I'll start telling you about my trip to Europe," he said. "Perhaps the strangest experience of my life occurred during that trip."

PART
TWO

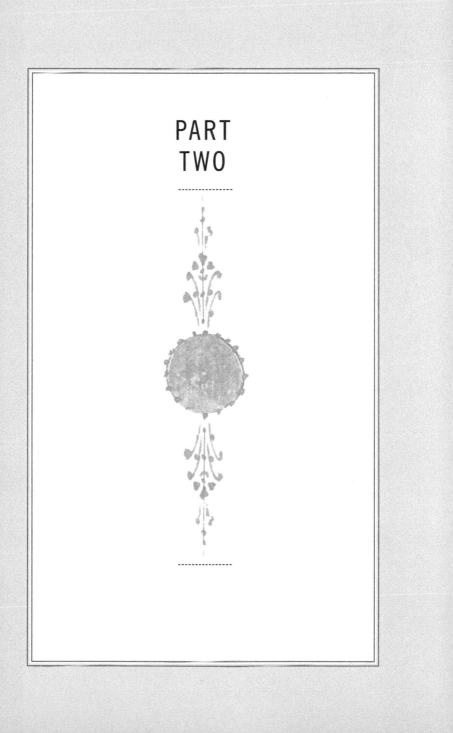

A young prince

A HAPPY PRINCE WHO experienced the pleasures of life to the fullest, whose every breath made him feel alive. A young man who enjoyed fishing for bluefish on the silvery waters of the Bosphorus, hunting in the forests of Strandzha, swimming every day summer and winter, running, riding horses, playing the piano…

The doctor didn't quite believe what he was hearing, but the apprehensive, imperious wreck of a man kept going on about this, trying to convince him that this was what he had been like as a youth. The doctor could not reconcile these conflicting images. Sultan Abdülhamid bore no resemblance to the youth he was describing, but despite this he insisted: This was what I was like, as God is my witness that's the kind of young man I was.

His happiest year was 1867. The other princes had expectations of ascending to the throne, but nothing could have been farther from his mind. It was clear that his brother Murad, who was two years older than him, took the idea very seriously. At that time he was making investments according to Zarifi the money

changer's advice, and he was making a great deal
of money. So much so that when he ascended to the
throne, he possessed a large fortune. He was able to
pay his expenses out of his own pocket, without being
a burden to the state.

His uncle Sultan Abdülaziz was on the throne. He
was a large, gray-eyed man, quick to anger, fond of
wrestling, but he had a good heart. He treated his nephews well and didn't lock them up in remote palaces,
but left them to their own devices as long as they didn't
get up to any mischief. He was not as handsome and
elegant as his late father, but he had a strong presence.
When he frowned and rolled his eyes, his staff would
be terrified. He often called in wrestlers to wrestle with
him in the palace gardens. He was fond of hunting and
throwing the javelin, he was a born sportsman, but he
was also an unexpectedly graceful musician, and composed enchanting barcaroles for the piano and lute.
His late father, on the other hand, had been an elegant
man who was quite fond of women and seldom left his
harem. He had nearly forty children he acknowledged,
and more he didn't. But he didn't come close to the record set by his ancestor Murad III, who had a hundred
and thirty-five children.

At this point the doctor had to keep from laughing. Because he couldn't explain everything that came
to mind. When the rakish Abdülmecid fell ill, they
brought a doctor from Europe. Through the chief interpreter, the doctor asked the sultan to undress. At one
point he looked at the sultan's private parts and said

something. The sultan asked what he'd said. The interpreter replied, "He said everything seems to be fine in this department, Your Majesty." The sultan roared, "Tell this infidel he should have said magnificent, tell him to say magnificent!" He couldn't tell the old man this story that had been going around for years, so instead of laughing he pretended to cough. The sultan thought the doctor was sick and grew alarmed and started to leave the room. The doctor assured him he was fine, and the sultan sat back down.

"My father started building a palace in Dolmabahçe. Previously, sultans had lived in more modest places, but my father wanted to build a palace that would match the splendor of European palaces. My uncle spent even more money, and built another palace on top of it. I couldn't digest this. Because I understand what money is. The state treasury was depleted. So they just kept printing money. My uncle closed himself up in this enormous palace with his six thousand servants and his harem. Everyone was aware that he was spending enormous amounts of money on the palace and that the people were getting poorer. The people began to resent my uncle. Fortunately he was blessed by the presence of the last two great statesmen: Ali Pasha and Fuad Pasha. They were excellent men. They tried to make up for the sultan's shortcomings and to correct his mistakes. After all, the state is not run by the sultan but by statesmen. If they're good, they call you good; if they're bad, they call you bad.

"My father embraced the European style, but my uncle was exactly the opposite. So when I heard he planned to go to Europe I didn't believe it. For centuries, no Ottoman sultan had stepped foot outside the empire. They only ever went west to conquer it with enormous armies. When my brother Murad, who'd been raised in a Western manner, told me about this he laughed and said, 'How would you like to go to Paris and sit cross-legged on the floor and eat with your hands.' He didn't like my uncle's Oriental manners."

When the doctor left the mansion that day, he struggled to believe that this old man had been so different when he was young. Why did he insist so much, why did he speak so passionately about the distant past, why did he defend that young prince with so much enthusiasm? What need was there for this? Also, what he said couldn't possibly be true.

However, the sultan's efforts made him curious, and when he left the mansion that day he went straight to the library. He started browsing through old newspapers and books. Until 1909 the Istanbul press had been full of praise for him and referred to him as "God's shadow on earth, our gracious lord, and His Imperial Majesty," but after that they changed their tune and began to refer to the former sultan as "cursed devil and dishonorable demon." The doctor decided he couldn't learn anything from this kind of newspaper, so he started looking at books. A lot of books had been written about Sultan Hamid. There were two books that caught his attention, so he took them home and began reading them. He read straight through till morning. The doctor was surprised to encounter a man so different from the former sultan he knew. Some of the foreign commentaries were enough to make him wonder if they were talking about the same man. The American ambassador had described him to *The New York Times* as "the most intellectual man I encountered in Europe," and the Russian tsar described him as "completely Western."

The Ottomans in Europe

"IT WAS 1867, AND as princes under my uncle's absolute authority, we were grateful to be alive, that none of us had been killed. Even though in our family the killing of princes to preserve 'the order of the world' was lawful. My ancestor Sultan Mehmet enacted this law not out of cruelty but so that the empire wouldn't be torn apart by rival heirs, as had happened when Genghis Khan died. To tell the truth, I have difficulty understanding the sultan who had nineteen of his infant brothers strangled, but I suppose things were done differently then. But we were approaching the twentieth century, we couldn't do things like that anymore. Europe would not look kindly on such acts.

"We used to look down on Europe, but it had gained strength and substance. We began to follow developments there more closely, and we were astounded by what we heard. For the first time in history, what they thought of us began to matter. In the old days, we didn't pay any attention to the infidels' ideas, and we laughed when they called us barbarians. Everyone knew that the real barbarians were the

Crusaders who had come to the East. The Latin barbarians had even ransacked Constantinople. My late
ancestor spent years rebuilding the city. However, as
we followed recent developments, we realized that
Europe had become a completely different place, and
we grew curious.

"It was at just about this time that my uncle received an invitation from Napoleon III. His Majesty the
emperor had invited the Ottoman sultan Abdülaziz
to Paris to attend the opening of a world fair. I can't
even begin to tell you how much excitement this invitation caused. Foreign ambassadors filled the palace
corridors and waiting rooms and whispered among
themselves. The Russian tsar was more opposed to
this trip than anyone, but it was assumed my uncle
wouldn't go to Paris. It had been centuries since an
Ottoman sultan had stepped foot outside the empire.
Indeed they hadn't even visited Jerusalem or taken the
hajj to Mecca, both of which were imperial territories.
Therefore no one believed my uncle would break this
tradition and go to Paris. But then the impossible happened. Whether Ali Pasha and Fuad Pasha convinced
him or whether he wanted to see the wonders he'd
heard about for himself, news that His Imperial Majesty would visit France fell like a bomb on the Ottoman Empire. When my brother Murad heard the news
he said, 'Oh, what is the wrestler going to do there,
what kind of gaffes will he commit?'

"We were both certain our uncle would not take
us and we were saddened that we would not see

Europe, but we were in for a surprise. The next day we received the good news from the palace that we were to be included. Murat, myself, and my uncle's son Yusuf Izzeddin were to accompany my uncle. We were thrilled and surprised. It was only later that we learned Ali Pasha had convinced my uncle to bring us along, and we prayed for him. To tell the truth, it would never have occurred to us to replace our uncle on the throne. After centuries of sultans being overthrown or killed, no one trusted anyone. Sometimes when my brother and I talked about our family's bloody history we would say, 'Who needs the throne and all the trouble that comes with it. Let's just enjoy life…'

"We thought we should live as modern, secular people according to the changing mentality of the nineteenth century. As two princes who knew that in the past our destinies would be either the throne or the silk cord, we were honest with each other and spoke our minds. We both felt that the throne was dangerous.

"I was twenty-four years old and I had the opportunity to see Europe; it was unbelievable, it was a miracle. As I said before, Europe had been seen as 'the land of the infidels,' their economy was seen as weak and their currency worthless. Sultans would frequently wage war against 'the heathens'; they conquered vast territories as far as Vienna and returned to Istanbul in glory. An envoy once left his post in Europe and returned to Istanbul in anger at how he had been treated. This ill treatment consisted of making the envoy listen to a chamber orchestra and serving him seafood. The envoy was offended and called his hosts impudent. 'They shamelessly serve me bugs and sweepings, they make me listen to this infidel fiddle, I'm going to go home, eat lamb and listen to proper music.' However, everything changed over time, news from Europe and the sumptuous illustrations in publications such as *The Illustrated London News* and *Le Monde illustré* began to shake Ottoman confidence and European fashion became an irresistible wind. French fashion reigned supreme, particularly in Istanbul. And the ladies of the palace were more impressed than anyone by the new fashion.

"When the journey was announced, there was a great deal of excitement in both Europe and Istanbul. A number of large companies competed to benefit as much as they could from this trip, taking advantage of lobbying opportunities and receiving contracts for the lavish receptions that would be held in Paris. The only reception my uncle agreed to honor with his presence was the Valle de Cristal. Ambassadors and religious leaders prayed for the sultan to have a safe journey and return. The Greek patriarch expressed sadness that the sultan would be absent, but found solace in the thought of the benefits of this trip, which he had no doubt would be successful. The chief rabbi of the Jewish community, who was very attached to the sultan, consulted the stars and predicted that everything would be well as long as the monarch didn't eat from the forbidden fruit during his visit to Europe. This prediction led the sultan's mother to worry. Fortunately Fuad Pasha was able to reassure her; he told her that forbidden fruit referred to political matters that might upset the sultan, but that she should not worry because he would always be by His Excellency's side.

"The Ministry of Foreign Affairs announced that His Imperial Majesty would set out on June 21 and disembark at Toulon on June 28. I'll never forget that day. Friday prayers were held at the beautiful mosque on the shore in Ortaköy. My uncle arrived on a gray horse, medals glistening on his chest, greeted the throngs of people who'd come to see him, then returned to the palace after the prayers were concluded. We were ready and impatient to board the ship. But my uncle was late. The Russian tsar's son Alexei had arrived in Istanbul on the steamship *Olga*. The sultan was meeting him and General Ignatiev, and the meeting dragged on longer than expected.

"Finally, at four o'clock, cannon salutes were heard on both sides of the Bosphorus. This cannon fire from the frigates anchored off the palace announced that His Imperial Majesty had boarded the imperial caique and was about to leave Istanbul. We had long since settled into our cabins. My uncle arrived on the gilded imperial caique and boarded the magnificent yacht *Sultaniye*. The *Sultaniye*, which swayed gently in the breeze on the dark blue waters of the Bosphorus, would host the sultan and his retinue. The yacht *Pertevniyal* would house the servants and the provisions.

The convoy also included two steam frigates, the *Osmaniye* and the *Orhaniye*, and the yacht *Fobin*, which would carry the French ambassador Monsieur Bure.

"But now I have to tell you about another aspect of this. It may or may not seem strange to you. My uncle hadn't wanted to be the first sultan to set foot in unconquered territories. He'd had no intention of doing any such thing. But there was increasing unrest in territories such as the Balkans, Egypt, and Crete, which were struggling for independence. And he had received reliable intelligence that the great powers were stirring up this turbulence. Under these circumstances, it made sense to use Napoleon III's invitation as an excuse to visit France and England, reach new agreements with them, and seek their help against Russia. However the ulema, who stuck their noses into everything and were quick to issue judgments, insisted that the sultan could not step foot in what they called 'the house of war.' If this obstacle were not overcome, the public would be adversely affected. In the end, the crafty chamberlains at the palace found a solution. Another layer would be added to the soles of his boots, creating a compartment that would be filled with the soil of Istanbul. Thus the great empire avoided a serious problem. The sultan would not step foot on infidel soil. There would always be Ottoman soil beneath his feet. Murad just laughed at this nonsense. The things they concerned themselves with!

"I can't begin to describe the sound of the crowds cheering on both sides of the Bosphorus and the deafening roar of the cannons firing from the frigates and the castles as the convoy left Istanbul. I knew my uncle was worried about undertaking this adventure, but he didn't let this show, and like a great sultan saluted the people.

"There was another loud celebration as we passed through the Dardanelles. Then, within two days, a storm blew up. Gamiz Hasan Bey, the captain of the *Sultaniye*, had failed to convince the palace that they should set sail before the Mediterranean storms began. And the poor captain's fears proved correct, the convoy was caught in a storm. The *Sultaniye* was being tossed about like a walnut shell, waves were washing over the deck, everyone was seasick, some were vomiting and others were hanging on to the rails. We saw my uncle stride out onto the deck, walk up to the captain, and look him in the eye. Then we heard him say, 'Stop this at once! Stop this rocking immediately. Or else!'

"The poor captain turned completely white and collapsed on the deck in terror. Just then a large wave crashed and everyone, including the sultan, got wet; my uncle was holding on to the captain and we feared he might throw him into the sea. Then our cleverest statesman, Foreign Minister Fuad Pasha, convinced him to return to the imperial cabin. The palace doctors gave the sultan an elixir to calm his nerves and it put him to sleep for quite some time. When my uncle woke the next morning, the storm had passed and the sea was completely still. The danger was past and the sultan, believing that the captain had obeyed his order, decided to spare his life.

"The rest of the trip passed without incident. We stopped in Naples for three days, but we didn't go ashore.

"When we reached Toulon a week later, there was an incident that would put Fuad Pasha in a difficult position. At the port of Toulon, the French held a magnificent ceremony to welcome the sultan. All of the noble men and women in the city had put on their finest clothes and gathered at the harbor. The women came with colorful umbrellas to protect themselves from the sun. We were surprised to see men and women mingling, but we'd heard that Europe was like this and didn't give it much thought. A large triumphal arch had been erected in the harbor, and it made our hearts swell with pride to see Ottoman flags flying everywhere. A hundred ships came to greet my uncle. There was one cannon salute after another. The infernal roar of a hundred ships firing cannons created a sense of doomsday horror, it was enough to wake the dead. My uncle waited for the cannon fire to end before disembarking, and we lined up behind him. The cannon fire didn't end, my uncle waited and waited, then frowned and looked at Fuad Pasha. None of us had expected anything like this. My uncle was already suspicious of Europe and expected something bad might happen at any moment, he got it into his head that he was being mocked, his face turned red with anger and he ordered Fuad Pasha to sail the convoy back to Istanbul. Everyone on deck froze. Murad and I looked at each other anxiously. My brother was biting his lip. How could they snub such a magnificent welcome and sail away? But the sultan was trembling in anger. Fuad Pasha was facing the second crisis of the journey. The poor man already had a weak heart. Thankfully he was a clever and cultured man, and he found a solution right away. He told the sultan that Toulon held a very special place in our history, and that's why the welcoming ceremony was at the highest level. We didn't know this. According to what Fuad Pasha said on the deck and the details he related to us later, when King Francis I of France lost his wars against the Holy Roman Empire, Charles V imprisoned him in Madrid. Francis found a way to contact our illustrious ancestor Sultan Süleyman and ask him for help and protection. He accepted this request and sent a fleet under the command of Barbaros Hayreddin Pasha. When our fleet rescued Francis and brought him to Toulon, it was greeted with great fanfare, and the thirty thousand men of the fleet spent the winter there. Toulon cathedral was converted into a mosque, and the city began using Ottoman currency. This was why there was so much excitement in Toulon at seeing Ottoman ships after three hundred and twenty-four years. After listening to Fuad Pasha, the sultan calmed down a bit, meanwhile the cannon fire ended and an orchestra on the shore began playing pieces my uncle had composed. This was a pleasant surprise for all of us, but I think my uncle was more pleased than anyone. Because when his ten-year-old son Yusuf Izzeddin turned and asked, 'Father, aren't these your compositions?' he said, 'Yes, my son' and a big smile spread across his face.

"Everyone was clean, stylish, and well cared for. The people who had gathered seemed to be the city's most prominent citizens. My uncle was wearing his large uniform. We were behind him. Fuad Pasha spoke fluent French and was interpreting. I was pleased by this because it meant I wasn't obliged to speak French. Murad's French was much better than mine. At Toulon we boarded the imperial train, which had been decorated with laurel branches and red and white flowers. We traveled to Paris through beautiful plains, vineyards, and cities and towns with interesting architecture and splendid cathedrals. Throughout the journey, crowds of people lined the tracks to greet us.

"The Gare de Lyon was completely packed, if you threw a needle into the crowd it wouldn't fall to the ground. My uncle stepped off the train, and Napoleon III rushed to greet him. The sultan of the East and caliph of all Muslims shook hands with the emperor. The dream that was to last forty-seven days began at that moment. The two emperors boarded an open carriage. All of Paris was out in the streets, shouting '*Vive le sultan!*' The whole city had come out to see us. They were curious to see what Ottomans looked like. There was a constant cheering. We didn't know where to look. The tall buildings, broad avenues, double lines of chestnut trees, and men and women mingling together in cafés made us feel as if we were in a fairy-tale world. Our convoy reached the Tuileries, where we were greeted by Empress Eugénie. She was a beautiful young woman, and she was wearing an elegant dress that accentuated her figure. We'd seen illustrations in French magazines of her wearing outfits that were more daring, that indeed to us seemed defiant, but she'd chosen to dress more modestly for the occasion. She greeted my uncle with an elegant courtesy and we were all enchanted by her. Then my uncle amazed us by bringing her hand to his lips like a French gentleman. He didn't actually kiss the empress's hand, but he came very close. Indeed among the infidels this was how it was done. But we had different customs and didn't know this. Or rather Murad would have known, but in any event he was more like a European prince than an Ottoman prince.

"What was I saying. Hmm. We were going to have lunch at the palace, then we would go to Élysée Palace, where we would be staying. We were invited to a long table where butlers in frock coats stood waiting, and as we made our way my uncle said something to Fuad Pasha, who then translated the comment for the emperor and empress. The emperor was clearly surprised, but we heard him say, *'Bien sûr, bien sûr, absolument.'* My uncle nodded his head, and the chief muezzin of the palace, dressed in robes and a turban, stepped forward and began reciting the call to prayer. Everyone stood. The call to prayer echoed off thc walls of palace. After the call to prayer the chamberlains spread prayer rugs to face Mecca and we all performed our prayers. As we prayed, we could feel the French dignitaries watching us. Since we were traveling, my uncle could have skipped the prayers, but I think he did this as a diplomatic show of force, and the French imperial family and all the dignitaries saw fit to remain standing during the prayers.

"Excuse me, this cough just won't go away. I get frequent fits of coughing. Just like this one. No, no, there's no blood. Could I ask you to prescribe a new medication? Müşfika Hanım suffers a great deal of pain at night. How can I explain, she's the best woman in the world. I would be pleased if you could treat her. Would you be able to see her today as well? But under no circumstances are you to give her morphine, I'm terrified of morphine, the doctors gave morphine to one of my wives and the poor thing died that night.

"Anyway, what was I saying, we were in France, but now I want to tell you about something else. It will be important in helping you to understand me. As you know, nine years after the trip to France they dethroned the mighty sultan, locked him in a room, and insulted him. Two courtiers even had a picture taken of themselves with their elbows on his broad shoulders and vengeful grins on their faces. Then they killed him by cutting his wrists. That's how the throne is, the people who prostate themselves before you and swear to die for you won't hesitate to take revenge the moment they can. That day, as he left the Tuileries as a proud Oriental sultan, the poor man would never have imagined his life would end like this.

"Power brings death, and absolute power brings absolute death. Particularly in these parts. You know that only seventeen people attended our Prophet's funeral prayers, only the people from his household were present. Because the struggle for succession had already begun. Those who had come with him from Mecca insisted that one of them should be the caliph. The men of Medina insisted the caliph should be one of them. The sword of Umar cut through Islam's first knot. Umar, who was as tall as two men, pulled out his sword and said, 'I swear allegiance to Abu Bakr.' No one could say anything. When Abu Bakr died one year later, Umar took over from him and ended up being killed. He was replaced by Osman, who was also killed. Then his successor, Ali, was wounded by a poisoned sword in the mosque. He died not by the sword but of poison. Don't ask me to tell you what happened after that, doctor. The Prophet's descendants were killed, and very few of the caliphs who came after them died in their beds. The caliphs from whom I am descended were killed in Istanbul. Do you understand now, doctor? To be on the throne and to be the caliph is to face death at every moment. Day and night you wonder where death will come from, how you'll be attacked, will it be a dagger, poison, a bullet, or the silk cord? There's no knowing. Which seemingly faithful grand vizier is a traitor, which minister has been bought, which janitor is secretly working for whom? What is being talked about in the palace corridors, what murder plots are being whispered, when I go to bed at night will I be able to get up in the morning, who's going to try to bomb me when I go to Friday prayers? I was haunted by this for thirty-three years and it has worn me out.

"Do you know what people forget when they talk about me? They forget that I too am human. I'm a father, I laugh, I cry, I get sick, I have moments of cheer. They didn't see the person, they only saw the power. I'm at ease being in exile in Thessaloniki. At first I feared for my life, but in time I realized my brother has no intention of killing me. I'm more comfortable, I'm calmer. Of course even now, if, God forbid, there should be some conspiracy to kidnap me and put me back on the throne, the government would get rid of me immediately. Indeed even a rumor about anything like that could result in a death sentence for me. God forbid that anyone put my life at risk by committing such a mad, foolish act. Yes, we were talking about power and death.

"It's no different in other countries. For instance, when I went to Paris all of the royal families were in mourning. Two days before we arrived they'd received news of the execution of Emperor Maximilian in Mexico. He was Franz Joseph's brother. Napoleon III also lost wars, was deposed and taken prisoner, and died in misery in London. I received a report that after giving him an heir, Eugénie had no further contact with him. The man had a great many mistresses, but I received intelligence that he lost his manhood at forty due to prostate inflammation and kidney stones. What instructive stories. All emperors know about each other's health and private lives. How? By giving their doctors plenty of gold. I'm certain that my doctors were reporting to someone about me.

"You're different, of course. You give your reports directly to the government. God bless you, doctor."

The doctor had considerable trouble writing these last paragraphs. It was difficult to remember the sultan's exact words and also to keep his writing so small. But it was worth it. He was learning some very interesting things. "To become acquainted with a person is to become acquainted with an empire," he murmured. He thought of the strange fate of this former sultan who received no news from the outside world. He thought that the empire had remained as it was when he left it. He didn't know that the last Ottoman territories in Africa had been lost, or that, with Russian support, Balkan countries were declaring independence one after the other. The Arab provinces were in turmoil, and the Kurdish and Armenian insurrections were escalating. Everyone knew that after six centuries, the empire was on the point of collapse. The only person who didn't know was the former monarch. He had become fully accustomed to his life in exile; he spent his days making furniture, praying, and telling the doctor the details of his trip to Europe and the most enjoyable period of his life. He was like the captain of a sinking ship who was unaware of the rising waters because he had been confined to his cabin.

Strauss's waltz

AS THE DOCTOR ENTERED the mansion he heard a pleasant waltz. It was from a gramophone that had been allowed into the mansion. The sultan was sitting in his usual seat, his head tilted back and his eyes closed, listening to the music reverently. When the doctor coughed slightly to announce his presence, he put his finger to his lips and gestured for him to sit. The doctor and the sultan sat in complete silence, almost without breathing, until the record finished. When the piece was finished he said, "Doctor, did you know that this piece was composed for me? A Viennese composer named Johann dedicated it to me. He was a very famous man. The piece was performed at the opera in Vienna. When I heard about this I gave him a medal and an amount of gold. Now this record has taken me back to those days."

Of course the doctor knew Johann Strauss, but he didn't know he had composed a piece for the sultan. *How strange*, he thought, *you never hear anything positive about this man. It was all concealed behind a dark curtain of fear and hatred. It was also strange that a piece had been composed for him in Vienna, which his ancestors had besieged twice.*

He knew that the sultan valued music and carpentry, but he seemed to have no interest in the many wonderful historical artifacts in the territories he ruled. He hadn't hesitated to give ancient Bergama and other ruins to the Germans. Foreigners wishing to excavate were told to hand over any gold or jewelry they found but that they could take the stones, and cartloads of artifacts were sent to Europe. Statues were looted from the temples of the ancient cities of Pergamon, Troy, and Aphrodisias. He was aware of the increasing importance of the oil fields of Mosul and Kirkuk. Therefore he was not content to allow the oil fields to remain the property of his own state but made them his personal property. However, he did not regard the masterpieces of Rome, Ionia, Caria, Phrygia, and a host of other civilizations as wealth. His ancestor Mehmet the Conqueror had read Homer and had gone to Troy to try to find the tombs of Hector and Achilles, but few of his descendants had taken any interest in history.

"Welcome, doctor. I didn't sleep well last night. There was a burning in my throat, it's still there, perhaps I've caught cold. I don't know if it's because of the cold baths I take, but I've been doing that all my life. Is there a draft in this mansion that's making me sick? It's not just me, my wives and some of the servants are sick. I think that I need sulfate, but you prescribe whatever medications you think are necessary. It's not just the sore throat and the cough that keep me awake at night. After our talk yesterday, I had so many vivid memories that I almost felt I was twenty-four again. I could even smell the particular smell Paris has. I can never forget it. I remember as if it were yesterday. After our lunch at the Tuileries, we went to the Élysée, where we would be staying. Oh, I almost forgot, at lunch at the palace there were thin, reddish, jewellike glasses on the table. They were engraved with stars and crescents. We were amazed by their elegance. We were surprised when we were told that these glasses had been made especially for the sultan's visit to Paris. They were made by the famous Baccarat company. The silverware had also been made especially for the visit by the Christofle company. We were immediately impressed by how delicate the French were. My uncle maintained his proud demeanor, but we could see from his face that he was beginning to appreciate this magnificent welcome. I don't know how to describe Élysée Palace. Gilded halls and rooms, jewellike chandeliers, our magnificent bedrooms, knowledgeable, well-dressed, polite servants. This was where the Empress Josephine had lived with her husband, Napoleon. Amid all of this, what I admired most was a dark hall hung with black cloth. This was where Napoleon had signed his abdication as emperor. Here he experienced the bitter ending that awaits so many monarchs.

"Speaking of Josephine, there's another interesting thing I have to tell you: In the following days, Napoleon III gave my uncle a book. It was by a French writer named Ubicini, and it had been printed in France in 1855. As Napoleon was presenting the book, he said, 'We are relatives. Because your grandmother was a French countess from our family.'

"My uncle found this claim so interesting that he ordered the short book to be translated in a single night. Fuad Pasha and his men stayed up all night to translate it, and the following day we were able to read it. According to the story, Josephine's relative Aimée de Rivéry was captured by pirates on her return to France from Martinique. The pirates either gave or sold this beautiful young noblewoman to the Ottoman palace. The next part is still a bit confusing. My ancestor Abdülhamid I made her one of his wives, changed her name to Nakşıdıl Sultan, and she bore his children. One of these children became Sultan Mahmud. Consequently, Napoleon's family was related to the Ottoman dynasty. My uncle ordered Fuad Pasha to research the matter, and it turned out that his grandmother's relatives lived in the city of Orléans. Indeed the emperor offered to present the family to my uncle, but he declined because time was so short. Later, when I ascended to the throne, I had our ambassador in Paris secretly investigate the matter. The ambassador met our grandmother's relative Baron de Gonse and learned some more details from him. While she was alive, Nakşıdıl Sultan remained in contact with her relatives and sent them gifts. Indeed my uncle sent the family a miniature of Nakşıdıl Sultan. They were excited to see that in middle age, Aimée looked exactly

as she had when she was young, but they were saddened that a French countess had converted to Islam
and entered the sultan's harem. As you know, it was
rare for a Turkish woman to give birth to a sultan. Even
as far back as 1300, our dynasty's founder Osman's
son Orhan married the Byzantine emperor's daughter.
Ever since then, the women of the harem have come
from a variety of backgrounds. There were Russians,
French, Italians, Jews, Serbs, Hungarians, and a host of
other nationalities. My mother was Circassian, and so
are most of my wives.

"Anyway, let's get back to the Paris visit. Our retinue included several Italian and Greek valets. They
dressed us with care and struggled to make sure we
were presentable to the French. There was also Ömer
Faiz Efendi, the mayor of Istanbul, who was a superb conversationalist and always spoke his mind. I
enjoyed talking to him, and often asked him for his
impressions of the trip and about what the rest of
the delegation was up to. Despite his advanced age,
Ömer Faiz Efendi liked to enjoy life, he loved Paris
and said he found French women more intoxicating
than champagne.

"I think that this was the thing that amazed us
most. Women weren't covered up or kept in cages,
and they went wherever men went. This reminded
me of what Sultan Mahmud's brother-in-law Admi-
ral Halil Pasha said about Russia. The sultan had sent
his brother-in- law to Russia to find out how they had
advanced so quickly and left us behind. In the report

that Halil Pasha presented to the sultan on his return, he said clearly that the greatest difference was the position of women. 'In Russia, as in Europe, women are valued and are involved in all aspects of life. They formed the nation together with men. Our women, on the other hand, are kept in cages. That is, we only have half of our population. This is the most important issue we have to address.'

"Of course the pasha was right, we saw this with our own eyes on our trip to Europe, but now you're going to ask me why, after ruling the empire for thirty-three years, women have still not been set free. You're right, but in this country it's not easy to get past sharia. The shaykh-al Islams, hodjas, religious scholars, sects, and sheikhs are so powerful that the sultan can't do what he wants. Please remember that they stabbed my ancestor Selim to death over the issue of Europeanization, my ancestor Mahmud barely survived, they called him the Infidel Sultan. Tell me what you would have been able to do if you were in that position. It's not true that a sultan can do whatever he wants. It just seems that way. If you don't keep the right balance, they either kill you or send you into exile. You yourself have seen what a sincere Muslim I am, but didn't they label me an enemy of Islam when they deposed me?

"My uncle and my brother and I weren't blind. We saw with our own eyes how much Europe had advanced, and how far behind we'd fallen. And don't think I'm exaggerating when I say this was enough to make us weep. They brought Louis IV's carriage out of a museum to take my uncle to the International Exposition in Paris. The rest of us rode in six-horse carriages. By God, what an exposition it was, I can't begin to describe it. What machines they'd invented, what innovations they'd created. Everything we saw seemed unbelievable, we couldn't fathom it all. There were twenty thousand people there. My uncle sat with the emperor and gave out some awards. When a thousand-piece orchestra played the Ottoman anthem, our hearts swelled with pride. They were doing everything they could to please us, but there was no way they could understand the sadness in our hearts. It was painfully clear to us that it would be impossible for us to catch up to them, that we'd missed the scientific age. At the Ottoman pavilion there were carpets, candlesticks, silks, embroidery, weapons, and prayer rugs, and they'd set up an Ottoman coffeehouse where young Turkish men in national costumes invited passersby to have coffee. People drank coffee and smoked pipes. We had no machines, inventions, or techniques, all we had to offer were the pleasures of the Orient."

As the doctor waited while the sultan lit a cigarette, he thought to himself, *Ah, our sluggish, mystical Oriental realm, bearing the weariness of the ages, ignorant of the rest of the world and fond of pleasure.* These were precisely the reasons that the revolt that had begun in Thessaloniki had overthrown the man he was talking to, but the strange thing was that he was complaining about the same thing. They'd overthrown the sultan they thought was defending the old order and had replaced him with his idiot brother, they'd thought the movement to Westernize would gain momentum, but in fact things were now much worse. That meant that the sultan had been powerless to do what he wanted. He'd been aware of the distance between the Ottoman Empire and Europe, indeed he'd been more aware than anyone. Ever since Selim the dynasty had been struggling to Westernize, and had even given lives for this. Sultan Hamid had been aware that these efforts could cost him his life, he'd had no choice but to dress Westernizing reforms as Islamist and had modernized schools, encouraged the translation of foreign books, opened schools for girls, and built railroads. So then why did this revolt occur? These Young Turks had been speaking against the sultanate in Paris for years, they'd managed to gain Western support. Why had they changed as soon as they came to power? The doctor was unable to bring himself to say this, but everything was worse now and the empire was disintegrating rapidly. At first the Young Turks had accused the sultan of massacring Armenians and had proclaimed a desire to unite all of the religious and ethnic minorities, but now they were oppressing these people.

"May I ask you something?" said the doctor.

The sultan seemed pleased and said, "Of course. These are interesting matters."

"As you know," said the doctor, "there was a movement opposed to your uncle, and most of these intellectuals had gathered in Paris. Indeed they even printed newspapers there. What happened during your visit to Paris, was there any contact?"

The sultan drew on his strong cigarette and blew out smoke rings. "No," he said. "We knew those people. They were all decent, worthy people. Our ambassador in Paris reported that dissidents, including Namık Kemal Bey, Şinasi Bey, and Ali Suavi Efendi, had gone to the Paris police chief and said, 'We have reached the conclusion that it is not appropriate for us to be present in this city during our sultan's visit. We want to go to London.' The police chief replied, 'We were going to ask you to do this. We thank you for your sensitivity.' So we had no contact with these gentlemen of the opposition. But I know them. Namık Kemal Bey in particular, we worked together. He was a worthy individual, but he got caught up in these strange ideas about liberty. And he's the one who got my brother Murad to start drinking."

The doctor was moved by the gentle manner of this man who had smothered dissent with his thousands of spies. *I wonder if they always misrepresented this man.* He was so convincing when he spoke, and his manner was so polite, it was difficult to believe that this man and that tyrant were the same person. He decided to talk this over with his friends.

The sultan continued to talk about Paris. It was clear that the level of civilization they'd seen there had a tremendous impact on them, and indeed left them a bit confused. When they saw the Palais de la Cité, the first building in the world to be illuminated at night, they were amazed that these people had managed to turn night into day. But the trip was not without difficulties. The Ottoman sultan had never known any rules, he'd never had to be anywhere on time, it was incredibly difficult to wake him, dress him, and get him to his appointments with the emperor. At the palace his word was law, it was difficult to remind him of his obligations because this made him angry. This led to situations in which Fuad Pasha nearly had a heart attack. Indeed after this trip, the pasha went to Nice to treat his heart condition and ended up dying there.

One day the emperor came to Élysée Palace for a visit, but no one had had the courage to wake Sultan Aziz. The man paced irritably in the hall muttering, "These barbarians are a constant headache. They don't keep track of time, they don't understand appointments." Then he noticed Fuad Pasha waiting by the door and said, "Please pretend you didn't hear that, don't pass it on to your sultan." The pasha responded, "Don't worry, Your Majesty. I don't tell you what he says about you and I won't tell him what you say about him."

The doctor enjoyed listening to these stories, they were like adventure tales set in a distant land, but he was also becoming increasingly confused. After being bombarded with stories about emperors, world politics, and recent history, he would go home and write what he'd heard, then he'd sit and think, sometimes staying up till morning. He was neglecting his love letters and rarely went out with his friends in the evening. But he'd promised to meet them that evening.

His friends wanted to know what was going on in the mansion, what the "demon" was telling him, and was he about to "drop dead." Mehmet Akif, the Islamist, a nationalist conservative poet who had dubbed the sultan a "demon," said that once he'd seen him pass in his horse carriage and had been unable to resist the urge to vomit. The hatred ran deep. The doctor's mind had been full of questions for the past few days, and he was pensive as he walked slowly toward the Olympos. What a strange fate it was that led a monarch who lived like a shadow behind his high palace walls and pulled strings all over the world to have daily conversations with a young man who was born in Kumkapı as the son of Hüseyin Efendi and who had struggled to make it through Military Medical School. Had Abdülhamid and the other sultans really thought about these issues as much as he said they had, had they really tried to find solutions and develop the empire? Because only a Young Turk intellectual would make the kind of comparisons between East and West that he had been making over the past few days.

It was growing dark, the shops were closing, and people were making their way home. Life was proceeding as it had for centuries. The doctor was surprised by this calm. Because there were uprisings everywhere, Ottoman regions were declaring independence and there was constant news of disaster.

The Olympos was the same as always, it hadn't changed at all in the three years he'd been going there. His friends seemed strangely anxious. These Young

Turk officers of the Third Army seemed quiet, daunted, and weary. Their conversation wasn't as excited and focused as it used to be. The hope that had been kindled when the sultan was overthrown, hope that the empire would remain intact despite the loss of territory and that there would be a campaign of Westernization, was being replaced by doubt, fear, and pessimism. They didn't confess this to one another, but they all felt that their colleagues who were controlling the government through the puppet sultan weren't making things better. There was a constant stream of bad news from Istanbul. Journalists were being killed and dissident intellectuals and the Armenian and Arab communities were being oppressed...It was clear that the new government was becoming a dictatorship. Why had the tyrannical sultan been overthrown, what purpose had it served? The empire was still the sick man of Europe, the economy was in shambles, much of the army had been demobilized, and, worst of all, there was tension in the army between pro-government and anti-government officers. That evening they spoke of the rapid Slavicization of the Balkans. The former Ottoman provinces of Montenegro, Serbia, Bosnia and Herzegovina, Bulgaria, Romania, and Albania were about to unite against their former rulers. The army was in no state to counter this Russian-backed onslaught.

Major Saffet, who was no longer as enthusiastic as he used to be, asked, "What's the old man doing, is he sick all the time? Does he have any idea what's happening in the world? That the Italians have taken Libya, that Albania has declared independence, that Crete has united with Greece?"

"No," said the doctor. A young Greek girl was singing with an orchestra on the stage, but somehow the music that had once enchanted him had lost its magic, and indeed was giving him a headache. It wasn't just their table, everyone in the place seemed cheerless.

"He has no idea about anything," continued the doctor. "He's dying of curiosity, but he doesn't know who's in the new government, he doesn't even know who's grand vizier."

"So what do you talk about. Is it only about his health?"

"He's been telling me all about his trip to Europe with his uncle Abdülaziz. They were all terribly impressed by the developments in Europe. Steam engines, factories, high technology, they were also struck by the way men and women mingled."

"Don't tell me you believed him."

"Why would I lie?" replied the doctor. "Don't be surprised if I say I do believe him. He sounds so sincere when he talks, and his analyses are so good it surprises me. It's as if I'm not talking to that tyrannical, reactionary sultan but to an Ottoman intellectual. An intellectual who's aware of the poor state of the country and is sincerely saddened by this, and who knows that Europeanization is the only course. Yes, yes, you're right to be astounded, sometimes I can't believe what I'm hearing. Sometimes I wonder if he's just pretending, if he's trying to trick me, but to be honest, I can't refute many of the things he says. He really seems to believe what he's saying..."

"So why didn't he put his ideas into practice?"

"That's the real problem. He says the fundamentalists wouldn't let him do anything."

"Is there anyone in this country who's more fundamentalist than he is?"

"Well, the man said we're not a single nation the way European countries are. We base our ideas on the French Revolution, but are we really like the French or the English?"

The two officers thought about this for a time. Then Saffet said, "Unfortunately he's right about this. We're seventy-two nationalities trying to coexist. Everyone has a different language, religion, and identity. The Muslims take Friday off, the Jews take Saturday off, and the Christians take Sunday off. Is there any country in the world as strange as we are?"

Nihat chimed in: "If all these people have been living together for six hundred years, why haven't they been able to come together, why haven't they been able to unite?"

"First of all, we're spread out across a huge area," said the doctor. "Is it easy to unite North Africa with the Caucasus or the Arabian Peninsula with the Balkans? They have nothing in common. They don't even look alike."

"That's right," said Nihat. "Even the three of us are different. The doctor is blond, Saffet has slanted eyes, and I'm a bit like a monkey."

The three of them laughed.

Nihat said, "It looks as if you're warming to this man. At least you don't hate him as much as you used to."

"I'm just passing on what he said to me," said the doctor. "He always seems to be trying to justify himself. When he talks about the Armenian issue or the other issues, he insists that he didn't kill anyone, he tries to make out that he's compassionate, that he was kind to his subjects."

"Of course," said Nihat. "He didn't kill anyone with his own hands, perhaps he didn't even give his men direct orders, but who can deny that he always turned people against each other? Who established the Hamidiye Regiments, who set the Kurds against the Armenians? Who shed all that blood? The man is trying to fool you, Atıf."

"Why would he try to fool me? What would he gain from it?"

"What will he gain? You told me yourself that they wouldn't allow him to write his memoirs."

"Yes, that's true."

"Don't you see he wants to use you to get his side of the story into the historical record? You're his notebook. He wants to use you to justify himself to future generations."

The drunken captain smiled when he said this, but when he poked the doctor mockingly in the forehead, the atmosphere suddenly became tense.

The doctor went completely red. "Me? Are you calling me a fool? How dare you? I'm an officer just like you, and on top of that I'm a doctor. How can you say this to me?"

When they raised their voices, people at the other tables glanced at them anxiously. In the current climate of rebellion and assassinations, it was not unknown for arguments between officers to end in gunfire.

Nihat backed down. "You misunderstood, and perhaps I didn't express myself well. I was talking about the man's intentions. He's always loved intrigue."

"Do you think I'm naïve enough to fall for that and allow myself to be used? Do you think I don't understand his intentions? Or are you suggesting that I secretly work for the sultan and that I defend him?"

Saffet came to Nihat's rescue. "Of course not. Doesn't the damned man know that Atıf hates him and would never speak for him? Of course he does. He's a crafty man. He's trying to befriend the doctor who holds his life in his hands. Because he's terrified."

"Excuse me, Atıf," said Nihat. "I suppose I got overexcited. Who could doubt your integrity?" Then he tried to change the subject. "Have you heard that the Albanian church is using Albanian in its liturgy? It wasn't long ago that the patriarch said that God doesn't understand Albanian. What a stupid thing to say. As if God only knows one language."

Saffet said, "Fine, but don't we pray in Arabic? I suppose that means God doesn't know Turkish."

Nihat laughed and said, "But you're right. People just can't see themselves. But it's not good that the Balkan churches are uniting. I'm afraid they'll come together and attack us."

"You're afraid?" said Atıf. "That's naïve, it's worse than naïve. That war is about to start. And this time we won't be fighting guerillas, we'll be fighting regular armies supported by Russia."

"Do you think our colleagues don't know this?" asked Saffet. "Do you think they don't see it?"

"Of course they see it," said Nihat. "Enver sees it, Niyazi and Talat Bey and most of the senior officers in the region see it. They know these mountains like the backs of their hands, but they don't have complete power. They're doing everything they can to influence the government and the sultan. And don't forget the liberals."

Saffet raised his glass and said, "Then be ready for a new party. I know that Enver would never countenance a situation like this and will do everything to take complete control."

The three officers raised their glasses and then drank. The doctor no longer had confidence in the new government, but at the same time he was upset by this. As he walked home he realized he was still angry at Nihat. *What an idiot*, he thought, *he doesn't know anything but he acts as if he knows everything. It's really hard to take. I'm not going to sit with this man and*

let him annoy me again. Saffet wasn't so bright either.
"These men live small lives in their small worlds," he
murmured to himself. For better or for worse, the old
man in the mansion talked about important things,
he'd known the emperors of the world, he knew their
secrets, he'd been an actor in world politics for thirty-
four years. He listened carefully during their conversations, he paid attention. His officer friends weren't
the least bit curious about him, they didn't ask about
him, they didn't want to learn anything. *Perhaps I
overreacted to Nihat,* he thought, *perhaps there was no
need for me to get so annoyed.* Perhaps he'd gotten so
angry because he thought they were implying he'd
become close to the sultan. He wasn't close to that
dictator at all, he still hated him. Was it possible for
him to feel sympathy for a man who had caused so
much misery? Was it? Perhaps it was possible. The
doctor began to feel doubt. Was he still as angry as
he'd been on the first day? As he reached his door he
decided that he was, that there was no change in his
feelings toward that demon. *I'm only carrying out my
duties as a physician, that's all.* He was just as angry
as he'd been on the first day, he was certain of that.
When he stumbled a bit as he was taking off his uniform, he realized he'd had a bit too much to drink
that evening. After his altercation with Nihat he'd
started drinking too quickly. But he wasn't drunk,
he was just tipsy. He liked that word: tipsy, tipsy, he
enjoyed saying it. He took his notebook from its hiding place and recorded that day's conversation. When

he'd finished he read poetry for a while, then allowed his mind to wander.

The doctor realized that over the past three years he'd become calmer, more relaxed. His relationship with the man and his family was complicated. But he felt differently about Müşfika Hanım. He respected her the most.

I wonder if what Captain Mustafa Kemal said at the secret party conference three years ago was correct, he asked himself. This rebellious and independent young officer, whom the party officials disliked, had taken the floor during a night session and had issued a courageous warning about the involvement of the military in politics. He said it was dangerous for soldiers to act like politicians. It would disrupt the order of the military, undermine the administration, and weaken the state. He proposed that the party leadership, which had achieved tremendous success in overthrowing Abdülhamid, resign from the military and carry on as civilian politicians. As he spoke, the party leadership became visibly tense, they twirled their mustaches, and Enver in particular was like a tightly wound spring; it felt as if they could reach for their guns at any moment. Atıf didn't know Kemal Bey well but he sympathized with him, he knew that he was disliked in military circles for his lifestyle, behavior, and "lone wolf" attitude, but he'd never stirred things up the way he did that night. Like all party members, he knew that gunmen were sent after anyone who fell into disfavor. It was practically impossible to escape these gunmen. These men were deadly, prepared to kill or die at any moment, and Mustafa Kemal was taking a great risk. All that the doctor knew about him was that he had studied at the Manastir Military Academy, that his father had died when he was young, and that his mother was a religious woman known as Zübeyde Molla. He was a thin, blond, blue-eyed officer with a handlebar mustache. His mustache was in the same style as Enver's, but the two men didn't resemble each other at all. Enver looked more Ottoman, and Kemal looked more European. But one thing was for sure, they didn't like each other. There were rumors that after the congress, a gunman was sent after Mustafa Kemal, but that he skillfully evaded assassination. The doctor didn't know if the story was true, Thessaloniki was always full of rumors, but it was said that Kemal knew what was happening the moment the gunman entered the room. When the gunman asked him why he was defying Enver, he convinced him to sit and have a coffee with him and listen. The man reluctantly sat and had a coffee and a cigarette, and they began conversing. Kemal explained at length why it was dangerous for soldiers to get involved in politics. The empire was already falling apart, imagine a colonel in the government and a general in the field, in wartime who's going to follow whose orders? Will the general follow the colonel's orders or will the colonel obey the general's orders? A situation like that would cause confusion in the military and weaken us. After he'd spoken for some time, the gunman, who was a lieutenant, said, "You explained it well. After listening to your ideas I've decided you're right. I have to confess something to you. I was sent here to shoot you. If we hadn't had this conversation you'd be dead by now." Mustafa Kemal laughed and showed him the gun he was holding under the table and said, "In fact it is you who was saved from certain death. I've had my gun trained on you from the moment you entered the room. If you'd reached for your gun instead of accepting my offer to talk, you would have gotten a bullet right between the eyes."

I don't know if the story is true, thought the doctor, *but this young officer is certainly becoming a legend. A strange, proud, lonely officer. And his lifestyle isn't that of a Muslim, Ottoman officer. People like him usually don't live long.*

England—Queen Victoria

"THE EMPEROR AWARDED MY uncle the Legion of Honor. This is the highest award in France. It's something like our Mecidiye. Despite their grief over poor Maximilian, they continued to honor us with feasts and celebrations. One evening at a banquet, I saw Baron Haussmann, the mayor of Paris, ask Ömer Faiz Bey something, and I wondered what they were talking about. Later Ömer Faiz Bey told my brother and I that he'd asked how the streets of Istanbul are cleaned. The streets of Paris were cleaned with sprinklers every evening. Was it possible that we did something similar? The witty Ömer Faiz Efendi said he gave the following answer: 'The municipality doesn't sprinkle the streets. That duty falls to the shopkeepers. They throw their wastewater into the streets and that's how they're cleaned.' I realized this was why an expression of amazement had appeared on the baron's face. We laughed bitterly about this for the rest of the trip. My brother Murad said, 'If I had the authority, I would bring this baron to Istanbul and put him in charge of public works. Civilized life can only emerge in beautiful cities like this.' Then he told Ömer Faiz Efendi to tell the sultan about this if he found the opportunity. My uncle was usually acutely aware of everything that was going on around him, but during these Paris evenings I noticed he was growing increasingly distracted, sometimes he toyed with his handkerchief and seemed lost in thought. I also noticed the way he glanced furtively at Eugénie. Indeed on three occasions I saw them glance at each other, and when their eyes met Eugénie bowed her head slightly. It was clear that something was going on between them. Later developments proved me right, but I'll save this interesting love story for another time. But I do promise I'll tell you.

"The following day we all boarded the *Queen Hortense* in Boulogne and sailed for England. The huge ship was tossed about like a walnut shell in the English Channel. My uncle sat, then gestured for us to sit as well, fortunately the sea calmed down after a while and we were spared a scolding.

"Our welcome in Dover was at least as impressive as that we'd received in Toulon. The Prince of Wales and the Duke of Cambridge boarded the ship to greet His Imperial Majesty. Musurus Pasha, our ambassador to London, was also there. Later I'll tell you about the disasters that befell this worthy man, who was the most distinguished representative of the empire.

"After lunch in Dover we boarded the train to London, and I'll never forget what I saw on that trip. I was struck by the factory chimneys and the industrial manufacturing plants. There was a smell of coal smoke in the air, and the sky was covered with coal-colored clouds. Everywhere I looked it seemed as if people were hard at work. They'd brought King George III's carriage out of the museum to take my uncle to Buckingham Palace, where we would be staying. London may not have been as radiant as Paris, but it was clear they were more advanced in industry, technology, and science. We saw how they built those huge ships in the shipyards, we saw the miracles they produced in their factories. Suffice it to say that we were amazed.

"Queen Victoria spent most of her time at Balmoral Castle in Scotland. After her husband, Albert, passed away she became reclusive. She met my uncle at Windsor Castle. The great queen was worn out, she was only in her fifties but she was never the same after her husband's death. She looked ill and tired.

"The English are a very clever people. They managed to rule the whole world from that rainy, foggy island. No one has ever frightened me as much as the English. I'm going to be honest, doctor: I'm afraid of the English and of rats. No, no, don't laugh, I swear I'm not joking. I've seen many men who've had their ears and noses eaten by rats. They come to you at night, numb your ear or your nose or wherever, then eat it. You wake up and see that your nose is missing. You'll ask what this has to do with the English. If the English want to seize territory, they numb the place in a way nobody notices, they make it stupid, and then they own it. When it's being taken away from you, you don't even feel a thing. I truly am frightened of them. Throughout my reign, I always kept careful track of what the English were doing. They not only conquer the world, they make the world serve their country. They founded a great civilization. When we saw all of this it broke our hearts. Even my proud, defiant uncle was saddened. We saw how much they'd advanced, and how far behind we'd fallen. We never spoke of it, but we all had the same question: Where did we go wrong?"

After saying this, the old man remained silent for a time, smoking his cigarette, and the doctor could feel his deep sadness. The man was truly sad, even after all these years he was sincerely sad. But if he'd seen all this when he was only twenty-four, why hadn't he done something while he had the chance, why hadn't he brought the empire to the level of those countries? He knew the answer he would get if he asked. He would say he hadn't been allowed to do anything. He would explain how he couldn't do what he wanted, that a monarch's authority only extends so far, the grand viziers were at fault, and that the ulema always put pressure on him and his government.

Perhaps he was right. He was amazed that, as he got to know the sultan better, he'd reached the point where he could say, *Perhaps he was right.*

One day the old man was practically in tears as he spoke about how he had to go to the tsar's uncle Grand Duke Nicholas to sue for peace. It was impossible to describe what had happened that day and that night.

The mighty Ottoman sultan got into the imperial caique and went to Beylerbeyi to talk to the monstrously
large and beribboned grand duke, who behaved like
a proud and victorious commander. If his army had
given him a victory, he would of course have been as
haughty as his ancestors had been. But the Russians
had been victorious in the Caucasus and the Balkans,
seizing the Danube valley and reaching Yeşilköy, right
outside the walls of Istanbul. What could a sultan
whose army had been defeated do but go to the feet of
this grand duke, who wasn't even his equal. His heart
was already heavy when he arrived at Beylerbeyi, but
after agreeing to humiliating terms in the presence of
that gigantic Russian general, he felt he no longer possessed the greatness of an emperor, that he was just an
ordinary person.

He cursed the pashas and statesmen who'd thrust
this war upon him the moment he'd ascended to the
throne. They'd ruined the state over problems that
could have been solved diplomatically. That treacherous institution, that nest of mischief called parliament where most of the deputies were not Turkish,
had supported this great evil enthusiastically. He had
to take revenge on those who had put the ancestor of
the great conqueror in such a shameful position, he
had to change the government and close that vipers'
nest of a parliament. He realized that it was only by
doing this that he could become a true ruler. He didn't
like the death penalty so he wasn't going to have anyone killed, but he was going to exile the ringleaders of

the opposition to the remotest corners of the empire. He planned all of this on his return from those painful hours with the grand duke, but this only partly calmed his shaken spirit.

He got tired of trying to figure out who was a spy, so he hired tens of thousands of his own spies, who sent him millions of denunciations. He no longer had to think about this or do any research, because he knew that everyone was a spy and an enemy. The doctor, the commanders, even his own men. Everyone was busy writing reports, they reported every detail of his life, how he was breathing, how many cigarettes he smoked, how often he went to the toilet, how often he coughed, his relations with his wives and children, what time he went to bed and what time he got up. He heaved a deep sigh. Now, toward the end of his life, he'd finally relaxed. Everyone was a spy, everyone was an enemy. What could be more soothing than this? He rolled a cigarette of his strong, amber-colored tobacco and smoked it with pleasure.

The Order of the Garter—Madame Müzürüs's sad end

"IN LONDON WE HAD both amusing experiences and sad experiences. At that time, the English had the largest fleet in the world, and we had the second largest. The queen had planned a magnificent show to dazzle us with the power of their navy, but the day before, a terrible storm blew in and they even considered canceling the event. Indeed they would have canceled had the queen not given them strict orders. In that weather, we went to Portsmouth on the *Osborn*. We were greeted with cannon salutes. A little later the queen arrived, and we went to the *Victoria and Albert* yacht. Meanwhile the storm had become so fierce that it was nearly impossible to steer. The fog and the smoke had made the warships invisible. If they did not remain at anchor, they would begin to collide. An order was issued for them to do nothing but fire their cannons. Two groups of ships fired at each other for almost an hour.

"The royal families aboard the *Prince Albert* didn't think they would survive this storm. Despite this, Queen Victoria planned to give my uncle the Order of the Garter that day, and she never changed her mind once she'd made a decision. They had difficulty dissuading her. The noblewomen's skirts were being blown, and hats were flying off their heads. Anyway, we survived that adventure. At first we were pleased by the news that my uncle would be given England's most prestigious award. After the Legion of Honor, this would be a great honor for us. This news, along with other details of our trip, appeared in Istanbul newspapers. The public was delighted. Because of my disposition, I looked into this award. I learned that it didn't have a very honorable origin, but I kept this information to myself. There was no need to stir things up. The Order of the Garter had first been awarded by King Edward. And this is how it happened. One evening when His Royal Highness was dancing with his mistress the Countess of Salisbury, who everyone mocked, the woman's garter snapped and her stocking fell. The noblewomen laughed behind their fans and glanced maliciously at one another, so Edward picked up the garter, held it in the air, and said, 'From now on this will be England's highest award. Whoever mocks it should be ashamed.' All of those who had mocked the mistress now bowed respectfully to this garter. I don't think about these things much, doctor. I don't understand why people do the things they do. At one time, governors and pashas would kiss the tassel of a gold cord that extended from my throne. And this didn't even seem strange to me. Because that was the custom. Now when I think about it, it seems strange."

The doctor said, "You were looking at everything from a different perspective then, but now you're just an ordinary person like the rest of us, Your Majesty." He hadn't been able to resist saying this.

The sultan laughed bitterly at this. "You're right," he said. "I'm even lower than an ordinary person, I'm a miserable prisoner who's had all of his rights taken away."

The doctor thought, *Pray that you don't end up like your grand vizier, that they don't strangle you with a greasy rope, that they don't break your neck*, but he didn't say it aloud. If he did, the man would say, "I didn't kill him," he would swear to this, but of course everyone knew who'd had the reformist grand vizier killed.

As the doctor was thinking about this, the old man, who'd clearly thought a lot about the matter, said, "Reverence for the king isn't worldly, it's otherworldly. This dependency can't be explained by fear or a desire to advance oneself."

"That's true," said the doctor. "Before Anne Boleyn was beheaded she prayed for the king's health. Why would someone about to be executed pray for the king who was having her killed?"

"To assure her place in the afterlife," said the sultan.

"I suppose that's the case. Since the monarch rules in the name of God, everyone accepts him as an extension of the Creator. This is the case in Europe as much as it is here."

"That's true, but I'm the same person. Since the Almighty bestowed this authority on me, I was the shadow of God on earth, so what's changed? God did not curse me for mortals to remove me from that position."

"Perhaps you were cursed, Your Majesty," said the doctor. "Perhaps God removed you from that position."

"I've thought about this too," replied the sultan. "I praise God every day for protecting me from a worse fate. I'm content not to be involved in affairs of state. I pray for my brother, our new sultan. May God protect our monarch."

At that moment the doctor realized that their sincere conversation had come to an end, and that the man had retreated into his shell to make his delicate plans. It was impossible to guess what he was thinking.

"EARLIER I MENTIONED MUSURUS Pasha, our envoy to London. The Ottoman Greek Musurus family had rendered many services to the state. Musurus was given the title of pasha and was an excellent ambassador. This distinguished man represented the Ottoman Empire in London for thirty-five years. He knew seven languages. He translated Dante's *Divine Comedy* into Turkish and Greek. His wife, Madame Musurus, was held in high regard in London society. I heard that she was close to Queen Victoria, that the queen would come to her house and sit her children on her lap.

"One day they held a banquet at India House in my uncle's honor. As we were climbing the marble stairs I noticed a fat woman who was having difficulty climbing. Her face was red and she was having trouble breathing. I remember thinking that someone should help her. It turned out she was Madame Musurus. We finally reached the hall. And what a hall it was. Wonderful decor, waiters serving champagne, an orchestra, aristocrats. The orchestra was playing dances. I can't quite remember, I think it was the Prince of Wales who went over to her to ask her to dance. He'd given this honorable and well-liked woman the honor of the opening dance. But the woman wasn't well, her face was bright red and her chest was heaving. No one else seemed to notice, but I'm always curious about what's going on around me. They started to dance, the prince turned her this way and that, and the woman struggled to keep up with him. And she had to do this under the stern gaze of the Ottoman sultan. They'd been dancing less than a minute when the woman started to faint. The prince was unable to hold up her large body, and she fell to the floor. Court doctors and footmen rushed to help her; they took her away on a stretcher. This unfortunate incident was forgotten within two minutes. Everyone carried on.

"Let me tell you an amusing story. My brother Murad was standing next to me at the ball. Of course we were young. We couldn't take our eyes off the beautiful, scantily dressed women. We noticed a lovely girl playing a piano nearby. We started commenting on how beautiful she was. I asked Murad if he would like to sleep with her that night, and just as he was saying, 'By God, I would,' a man came up to us and said, 'Your Majesties, the young lady playing the piano is my daughter. I am from Chios. My Turkish is very good. I request that you not continue speaking of her this way.' We moved away from there at once. Fortunately my ill-tempered uncle didn't hear about this incident.

"As the ball was ending, we received news that Madame Musurus had passed away. This death saddened us, but it also saddened London society, and the newspapers announced it as 'the sudden passing of Madame Musurus.' The queen attended her funeral. Despite all of this, Musurus Pasha did not neglect his duties for the remainder of our stay. He buried his pain and grief and continued to serve the sultan. He was a very loyal man. While he was serving as the ambassador to Athens, some Greek nationalists, who could not countenance a Cretan Greek serving the Ottoman Empire, planned an assassination and fired five shots at him. Fortunately he was agile, and only one of the bullets hit him in the left arm. The man served as the ambassador in London for thirty-five years. In my time he was one of the best ambassadors.

"Queen Victoria did not want to be bothered with 'Oriental' visitors such as ourselves. 'I am ill. Don't disturb my quiet life at Balmoral,' she said, but the state felt it had to outdo the lavish welcome the French had offered, and the poor woman was obliged to come to Windsor Castle. To me she always seemed sullen, mournful, and downcast. One day she pointed to her diamond earring and said that the stone had come from a necklace my uncle had sent her. My uncle laughed and said, 'I am pleased. I will remain on your ear as an earring. And so will the issues of Crete and Montenegro.'

"Then we understood why my self-indulgent, 'Oriental' uncle had gone to so much trouble to take this trip he hadn't wanted to take. He wanted to win over the great powers and seek their help in solving the empire's problems. After all, he was the only sultan to step foot in Egypt, and that was centuries after our ancestors had conquered it.

"Meanwhile, Victoria had taken a shine to Murad. Young women were fascinated by his European manners, his lithe and graceful waltzes, and his perfect French. When Victoria glanced at Murad, I could tell that she was thinking, 'How nice it would be to have a European like this ruling the Ottoman Empire.' As a matter of fact, it was said that one day the queen proposed the incredible idea of Murad marrying a member of the British dynasty. I don't know if it was true or if it was just a rumor, but it's possible the queen had something like this in mind. Having the caliph's son as a son-in-law was a perfect way to gain favor with the Muslims of the world.

"I've always had suspicions that the English played a role in my uncle being assassinated and Murad succeeding him. There was no marriage, but during that trip they made Murad a Mason. I had nothing to do with this, I'm not even interested in Freemasonry. In the end they succeeded in putting Murad on the throne. If he hadn't gone mad and been deposed ninety days later, who knows how long his reign may have lasted?

"Perhaps it would have been better for me as well. I would have carried on with my commerce and been free to go wherever I wished. I wouldn't have had to shoulder so much weight, and I wouldn't have been in constant fear of death. It was fate. I've had a lot of time to think in this mansion. I keep wondering what I am. Am I a servant chosen by God to be an extension of His will, or am I just an ordinary person? When I was in power, I knew the answer to this question. Of course I had been selected as God's representative, I was our Prophet's caliph. But now questions swarm through my mind. If I was chosen by God, how could my authority be taken away by a decision of parliament? Or was it just a dream, something we were all made to believe? Please don't misunderstand me. I'm content with my current situation, because power is more about responsibility than it is about authority. The state governs an empire spread across three continents, there's the grand vizier, the ministers, the directors, the provincial governors, and the shaykh al-Islams... There are thousands of people running the state, but if even the smallest thing goes wrong, only one person is held responsible. This is a load that's impossible to carry. Everything I did for the empire has been forgotten now. All of the empire's problems are being blamed on me, I bear the weight of centuries on my shoulders, I'm cursed everywhere."

EVEN THOUGH THE DOCTOR was interested in these matters, he would get bored if the session went on too long. Yes, the details of the trip were interesting, and the story of Madame Musurus falling dead in front of everyone was quite dramatic. It was clear that the woman's weak heart hadn't been able to stand so much excitement. To dance a Western dance in front of the sultan, with everyone watching her... *May she rest in peace*, he said to himself.

To draw the sultan out of the world of memories into which he'd sunk, he said, "The foreign press didn't say only negative things about you. For instance the American ambassador Terell praised you highly."

"Ahh," said the old man, "I remember he was a particularly nice person. I always had good relations with the United States. My late father did too. In our archives we have letters of thanks to him from Abraham Lincoln. We supported Washington during their Civil War. Like all of their other ambassadors, Terell was a polite man. He gave me guns that were made especially for me at the Colt factory, as well as some beautiful saddles. And this will seem strange, but he also gave me Native American costumes."

"Really?"

"Yes, yes, he knew I was curious about the natives."

The doctor was going to ask if he'd ever worn these costumes, but when he pictured Abdülhamid running around with feathers on his head, he changed his mind.

"LOOK, LET ME TELL you an interesting story about camels," said the sultan with a laugh. "It's a nice story. During the American Civil War, an officer thought that camels might be useful, and wrote an advisory report to this effect. The American government accepted this and asked my late father for camels. Anyway, let me get to the point. Camels and camel drivers from the vicinity of Izmir were sent to America. From what I heard, the camels didn't do well in that climate and weren't of much use, but the American people were fond of them. Indeed a company that made cigarettes from Turkish tobacco started producing a cigarette called Camel."

WHEN I RETURNED THE following morning, he was in a state of panic. "Müşfika Hanım is ill. She never complains, but I know. She's my favorite. Look, even when her daughter went to Istanbul she wouldn't leave me. But please, doctor, don't give her morphine."

"I know," the doctor said. "You told me. One of your wives died from morphine."

"Yes, yes," he said.

The doctor sent a servant to tell Müşfika Hanım he was coming to see her. When he entered her room on the upper floor, she wasn't in bed but in an armchair, and she was dressed. Her delicate face seemed more strained than usual, and there were rings under her eyes. It was clear she was uneasy about the situation.

"What's the matter, ma'am?"

"I'm putting you to a lot of trouble, please excuse me."

"Please, this is my job."

"I can't sleep at night."

"Why is that?"

She showed me her left arm. In a faint voice she said, "It hurts a lot, I can't get any sleep."

"Did you injure your arm in any way?"

She thought for a moment. "No, I didn't injure my arm, I didn't fall or anything. It aches from the inside."

"I'm going to give you some pain medication. Take one dose now, and another before you go to bed. Then we'll see."

He took an analgesic from his bag and gave it to her. Then he said, "Let me give you some of this just in case. Take it before you go to bed, but don't take it during the day."

"What is this medication called?"

"It's a new invention. A German doctor discovered it. It's a panacea. It's called heroin."

"God bless you," said Müşfika Hanım.

Heroin was in fact a derivative of morphine, but it was being used all over the world and it wasn't at all dangerous. This elegant young woman was going to feel much better. The doctor didn't think it necessary to tell the sultan he'd given her a derivative of morphine. The man was even suspicious of the water he drank. He also had a tendency to want to treat himself. He acted as if he didn't believe in medical science. Most of the time he would tell the doctor what elixirs or balms he wanted him to prepare. Apart from his mental state, the old man suffered from indigestion, hemorrhoids, and chronic bronchitis.

The doctor wondered who this man loved apart from himself. Or rather, was he capable of love?

The doctor couldn't answer this question, because for the first time he couldn't fully see his patient. Even though he was completely familiar with his physical condition, the man only allowed him to see so much of his psyche. At a certain depth there was a turbid undercurrent, and after that nothing was visible. It was either a personality trait or this was how emperors were raised. The doctor laughed to himself. He didn't know any other emperors, so he couldn't make a comparison.

He was much busier at the hospital now; there were soldiers with shredded arms or legs; there was tuberculosis, dysentery, and cholera; sick and malnourished children; there were sick refugees and babies that had been abandoned by the roadside; civilians with ears cut off or eyes gouged by Balkan guerillas...It was unbearable. So this was how an empire collapsed. As if the nation's stitches were coming loose. First the Italians had taken Tripoli, Benghazi, and the Dodecanese islands, then the Bulgarian, Greek, and Serbian armies had united to bring an end to five hundred years of Ottoman rule in the Balkans. Of course Russia was backing them. The empire's arch enemy Russia. For some reason the Third Army had become complacent. There was tension between the reactionary older officers, proud sullen men with long beards and dozens of medals, and the fiery young officers who dreamed of revolution and reform. As a result, mistakes were made and strategic positions were abandoned to the enemy. The situation was heading toward catastrophe, the helpless puppet sultan in Istanbul and his revolutionary masters, who were already fighting among themselves, were going to sink the Ottoman Empire. *It seems as if nothing is changing, but the ground beneath us is slipping away.*

First they'd seized the old man's personal fortune, now they were seizing his family's property bit by bit but the unfortunate—*Did I say unfortunate?* He was startled by a thought that seemed strange to him: *Is he unfortunate, did I just call him unfortunate?* He was spending his last years in a mansion whose garden he could not step foot in, and he was completely ignorant of what was happening in the world. It fact this was the best possible situation for him.

Müşfika Hanım—Heroine

THE OLD MAN SEEMED quite preoccupied that day. As if his body was present but his mind was far away. He was both there and not there. He didn't even notice the doctor's arrival. The doctor wondered if he'd drifted off to sleep. His eyes were half closed and it was impossible to tell. He sat in an armchair without saying anything. He squinted his eyes and took a strange pleasure in examining the old man, who seemed as if he was in a trance and looked vulnerable, his skin covered with brown blotches, patches of white in his beard, and his mustache stained by nicotine. Because he was a doctor, he knew that all human beings were bound by the same biological rules. The fundamental rules applied not just to people but to animals as well. Yet one mortal among them was worshipped as if he had divine powers. And it was this man, thought the doctor, this old man on the verge of death who writhed from the pain of his hemorrhoids. What was there about this poor man now that was divine? He thought about smoking a cigarette, but he didn't want to wake the man.

Just then he saw the man's lips move and heard him murmur something, but he couldn't make out the words. He got up and moved closer to him, taking care not to let the floorboards creak. The man was saying something that sounded like "flor." Was flor some kind of medication? *Floralis*? Flower elixir? Cologne? He listened more carefully to the word he kept repeating. The man was saying "Flora" over and over again. Who could Flora be? Was she from the harem? Was she someone he'd met on his trip to France? He himself had never met anyone named Flora. He was tiptoeing out of the hall when he saw Abid Efendi. He put his finger to his lips, and the boy nodded his head. He was a well-behaved boy. He was calm, he didn't have temper tantrums like his sisters. Perhaps this was a factor in his being allowed into the garden, and to go to school. Sometimes he would draw happily with the colored pencils he was allowed to bring home, and sometimes, dressed in his prince outfit, he would look in the mirror as if he was wondering about his identity. There was a touching sadness in his eyes. His tiny brocade jacket, gray pants, and long boots didn't match the frightened, childish expression in his eyes. At the palace he would have been wearing a small sword, but that wasn't possible here. The doctor was interested in psychology, and he wondered, *What does this child feel? Does he remember the palace, or is prison all he knows? He doesn't know what it was to be an emperor, to be deposed, he has no concept of power or exile. Does he see his own father like other fathers? He can't even make that comparison because he doesn't know any other families, any other fathers. The child is growing up in this mansion without any idea about the world. Does he have any chance to be happy? He doesn't know enough about life to know what he wants from it.*

He saw the shadow of a lifetime of imprisonment on the boy's pale face, and this saddened him. Then he thought about his own childhood, and of the unhappy life in the dark, heavy shadow of the dictator. He thought about their modest house in Unkapanı, about how his father, like all civil servants, lived in constant fear of exile; about how people had denounced each other, how fear had been palpable; about the clouds of suspicion that had emanated from Yıldız Palace, the anxious whispers and fearful glances. Had this helpless old man, snoozing in a tattered armchair and murmuring the name Flora, been responsible for this atmosphere of terror?

The doctor patted the melancholy boy on the head and was heading out the front door when he stopped suddenly. Perhaps he wasn't sleeping. He'd never seen the sultan like this before. He couldn't just leave him like this. His and his family's lives had been entrusted to him. He went back, the old man was still in the same state. The doctor called the chamberlains and told them the sultan should be brought to bed. In a panic they grabbed him by the arms and tried to drag him, but this seemed disrespectful, so they sat him back in his chair and carried it to his room. Then they gently stretched him face up on the bed. It was strange that the man still hadn't woken. This wasn't normal, it was a good thing he hadn't left, that he'd come back. The man's pulse and breathing were regular. His blood pressure was a bit low, but that far from explained the situation. The doctor asked the chamberlain about Müşfika Kadınefendi's condition. Would they ask her to honor him with her presence?

The doctor heard hurried footsteps on the stairs, then the woman rushed into the room in a panic, asking what was wrong. She was perhaps the most beautiful young woman he had ever seen. She went to the bed, stroked the old man's head, and said, "What happened, sir, what happened my sultan? Please don't frighten me like this." There were tears in her eyes. The doctor looked on in amazement, and perhaps with a bit of envy as well. She may have been the only person who loved the deposed sultan with this much passion. The man was old enough to be her father, but she wept as she kissed his bony, blotchy hands, and she kept asking the doctor what was the matter.

"Could it be something he ate?" asked the doctor. "What did he eat last night and this morning?"

"He ate what he always eats, he didn't have anything different. Let me see... Last night he had a little zucchini, some yogurt, and some stewed apples. In the morning he had cheese, bread, coffee, and a little rose petal jam. Nothing different."

"Try to remember if anything out of the usual happened."

"He didn't eat anything else, but during the night his arm was hurting a lot, he called me, he was in a lot of pain, at one point I even thought of calling you."

"I wish you had. What happened after that?" The doctor noticed a faint look of confusion on Müşfika Hanım's face. "Tell me what happened. Did you give him any medication?"

Müşfika Kadınefendi approached him with a bashful look and said, "His pain was so unbearable that I thought of the medications you gave me. His Imperial Highness would rather have died than accept the medication, but I couldn't bear to see him suffer like that. Toward morning I mixed one of the medications in hot milk and gave it to him. It's a good thing I did, his pain diminished after a while and he fell into a deep sleep. I went to my room and said a prayer of gratitude. But now he's like this... Did I do something wrong? Did I cause this?"

"Calm down, ma'am, please calm down. There's nothing wrong with your sultan. Could you show me which medication you gave him?"

The young woman murmured, "Oh my God!," rushed upstairs, and returned at once. The doctor carefully examined the medications she brought. "I gave you four pills in a vial. There are three of them left. Did you take this medication?"

"I gave it to him in the hope that it would ease his pain. Was this the wrong thing to do?"

The doctor laughed and said, "No, no. I wouldn't have given it to you if it was a bad thing, madame sultan, I told you to only take it in the evening, and you gave it to him toward morning. Don't worry. Your monarch will be fine in a few hours."

There were still tears in her eyes. "God bless you, doctor, I'm so relieved. You know that we have complete confidence in you. The sultan is very happy with you. He prays for you every day."

The doctor thanked her and said, "With your permission, I'd like to stay with him a little longer."

As she was going out the door she stopped and turned around. "I thank you again, doctor. But please don't address me as sultan. I'm not from the dynasty. My daughter is sultan. Ayşe Sultan."

The palace has some strange customs, thought the doctor, *titles are very important in that world.*

He'd been able to put her at ease and convince her she hadn't done anything wrong, but he didn't tell her she'd given her husband a narcotic. The sultan didn't drink much, he never had more than a beer or some rum, the heroin had overpowered him and he'd drifted off into the land of dreams. Now he was sleeping quietly. *Good*, thought the doctor, *we were able to make the poor man happy. He prays for me, and I was able to repay him by introducing him to this miracle drug.*

Toward noon the sultan woke coughing, looked around, saw the doctor, and asked what had happened. The doctor chose not to tell him the truth because he was so frightened of morphine, it would just cause a lot of problems.

"You weren't able to sleep last night, the painkiller made you feel a bit better and you slept for a while, there's nothing to worry about."

"But I woke up in time for morning prayers, and then...I don't remember whether or not I actually prayed. How strange. Is it some kind of memory loss?"

"No, no, sir. It's a temporary thing. It happens to everyone."

"Are you certain? Please tell me the truth. Is it neuralgia, is it psychasthenia? Ah, it's a cerebral hemorrhage, isn't it."

The delusional sultan was trembling as if he were having a seizure and listing every illness that came to mind. The doctor decided he could not leave his patient alone in this condition, especially as he had indirectly caused it. He would spend the day with him and try to calm him down. He did his best to convince him he wasn't sick.

He had him stretch his arms in front of him, bring them up above his head, touch his index fingers together, had him touch his nose, then asked him to follow his own index finger. He tapped his knees to test his reflexes.

Finally he said, "There's nothing wrong with you. There's nothing for you to worry about."

"But," objected his patient, "you found me sitting in my armchair in the hall. I have no memory of getting dressed and going down there."

"You told the chamberlains you wanted to go downstairs, they dressed you and helped you down. This kind of thing happens, there's nothing to worry about."

The sultan seemed a bit more at ease. "So I drifted off into some kind of fugue."

"Yes, sir. And you kept repeating the word 'flora.' Is that some kind of medication?"

The sultan muttered the name Flora several times, then suddenly seemed tired. As he drifted off to sleep again, the doctor noticed a single tear roll down his cheek. He tiptoed out of the room, then told the anxious chamberlains that the patient should be left alone for a time. "When he wakes and calls for you, bring him something light to eat. Soup or vegetables. Nothing heavy."

The sultan's greatest secret: Flora Cordier

THE YOUNG PRINCE LOVED to go horseback riding, but that day he got into his fancy two-horse landau and set out for Pera. It was refreshing to be on what the infidels called the Grand Rue de Pera, which was lined with classy restaurants, music halls, theaters, and shops that sold the latest fashions from Paris. It was a civilized avenue, you never saw even a single person who was badly dressed. There were ladies wearing what seemed an infinite variety of hats and carrying colorful, frilled umbrellas. As he made his way down the avenue past the shopwindows, the colorful awnings, and elegant people, he did not know that he was about to meet one of the most beautiful of these ladies. The prince preferred to go about without his liveried guards. He felt freer this way. At the lower end of the avenue, he entered a shop that he didn't know would play a role in his destiny. He noticed some leather gloves that he guessed came from France. As he was looking at them, he sensed one of the clerks approaching, and when he raised his head he found himself looking into a pair of blue-green eyes. Enchanting, he thought, enchanting. He was dumbstruck. As she said something to him in broken Turkish, he became aware of her long blond hair, her white skin, and her lips.

"*Bonjur matmazel*," he said.

The young woman smiled to show she was pleased this customer spoke French, and the prince thought, *Her smile is like the sun, it chases away the clouds.*

"*Bonjour, monsieur*," said the girl. "*En quoi puis-je vous aider? Intéressé par les gants?*"

Oh my God, thought the prince, *oh my God*, and at that moment he knew that he was capable of any kind of madness in order to be with her. It was as if there were wrestlers pushing him toward the girl behind the counter. His head was spinning. He went pale, and his breathing became more rapid. The girl asked him if he was all right, and gestured for him to sit in a nearby chair.

Then he remembered who he was, took a deep breath, and said he was fine.

"Yes, yes, I want to buy gloves, they look very nice."

He bought two pairs of the soft gloves the girl recommended, one gray and the other beige.

"May I ask your name?"

"Flora. Flora Cordier."

"*Êtes-vous français?*"

"*Non, monsieur, je viens de Belgique.*"

When he got into his carriage, he could still feel the warmth of the hand that had brushed against his as she was helping him try on the gloves, that soft, silky, youthful skin, he forgot that he was a prince, he forgot the palace, his uncle the emperor, he forgot the sultanate and his dreams of making money, he rode all the way to Tarabya in a kind of ecstasy, unaware of his surroundings, and from that day on he could think of nothing but Flora.

He went back to the shop the next day to buy a silk scarf, the day after to buy a frock coat, then an Istanbuline, then a pair of shoes. He went to the shop every day, he thought about her all the time. The owner of the shop was pleased, of course, and rubbed his hands together every time he came. But the girl didn't seem to have any idea who he was. She treated the prince as a good customer. She didn't seem to be aware of how infatuated he was.

One day he asked if the gray suit he'd bought could be delivered to his home.

"Of course sir," said the girl. "Let me write down your address." She picked up a notebook and a pencil.

"There's no need to write it down. It's very short. Çirağan Palace."

The girl didn't understand, and gave him a puzzled look.

"*Palais de Çırağan*," he said to her. "*Palais imperial*."

The owner of the shop went over to her and whispered into her ear. The girl gave him an elegant curtsy and said, "Excuse me, Your Majesty, excuse me."

That night, as he thought about her, Hamid wondered if revealing his identity had been the right thing to do. *What if I scared her off?*

The following day he didn't go to the shop. In the evening, at closing time, he waited in his carriage on the corner. The staff came out one by one. Then there she was, the Belgian miracle. She was wearing a coat with a fur collar and a pair of elegant gloves. She parted from the others and began walking toward Galatasaray. The young Hamid began running after her. "Oh," he said. "Did I get here too late, is the shop closed?"

The young woman looked at him in surprise. "Yes, Your Majesty, but if you like I can open it for you right away." She turned and took two steps toward the shop.

"No, no, there's no need, I can come back tomorrow."

"But you came all this way."

"Well, at least I had the pleasure of seeing you."

The young woman seemed to blush slightly.

"But I would like to ask something of you. My carriage is waiting right here. Might I drop you home?"

He saw her hesitate.

"Don't disappoint me. For a long time I've been looking for an opportunity to converse with you on matters other than shopping."

She smiled and said, "*D'accord, majeste.*"

What followed was like a dream for Hamid. Listening to the young woman's voice as the carriage rattled over the cobblestones to Pangaltı made him happier than he'd ever been.

He brought her home again the following day. And the day after that, and so on.

Meanwhile he spent a lot of time brooding. Being a prince was a great obstacle to his being with this woman. No heir to the throne could marry a Christian woman who had not converted to Islam. He could not have children with her. If, God forbid, his uncle should hear about it he'd get angry and send him to Fezzan, deep in the desert of Libya. The prince would be happy to forgo the throne for Flora, in any event he had no ambitions in that direction, but they still would never allow their union.

One evening he gathered all his courage and invited her to dinner at his home.

"Don't disappoint me, mademoiselle, please."

Lying in his bed in Thessaloniki under the influence of heroin, he felt the touch of Flora's skin on his old body, flames rose up within him as he felt her lips on his. "Flora," he moaned.

His time with Flora flashed before his eyes, their secret marriage, how he kept her hidden like a treasure in his mansion in Tarabya, showing her to no one, being with her day and night, skin to skin, together, it was as if he had come across a spring in the desert, he tried to drink his fill from it but still couldn't quench his thirst, that beautiful year, that beautiful woman, that beautiful lovemaking, those burning vows...

The sultan's dry, bony hands moved as if he were putting on a pair of gloves, and as he remembered those times, a soft, tender smile spread across his face. It was perhaps the first time he'd smiled since being brought to the mansion.

Unfortunately, as the effects of the heroin wore off he had to come back to the bitterness of his reality, and he was unable to return to his "eternal bliss" with Flora.

He had to make the most difficult decision of his life when Mithat Pasha and his friends came, saw that Murad V had indeed gone mad, decided to depose him, and offered him the sultanate on the condition that he proclaim constitutional monarchy. On one side was the imperial crown, which he'd thought he didn't want but which excited him when it became a real possibility, and on the other was the deep love that still turned his head. He couldn't have both. If his secret marriage became known, it could be an obstacle to his dreams of the sultanate. Perhaps the only solution was for Flora to convert to Islam and enter the harem, but this was a very strange solution. She was a free woman, she would never accept this. The young prince writhed in turmoil. His ancestor Mehmet the Conqueror's mother and wife never converted to Islam, but that had been a different age.

The adventure ended with broken hearts and tears, with him ascending to the throne and her getting out of a carriage in front of the Belgian embassy and telling the guards at the door, "My name is Flora Cordier, I'm a Belgian citizen. I want to go home."

The marriage that Abdülhamid thought he'd managed to keep secret had long been common knowledge among foreign intelligence services; indeed in a report to Lord Salisbury, Benjamin Disraeli had referred to

Flora as the new Roxelana. Just as Roxelana guided Süleyman the Magnificent, Hamid's sultanate would be guided by Flora. But this remained an unfulfilled dream. Because hundreds of years had passed and Hamid wasn't Süleyman, nor was Flora Roxelana.

Thus Hamid's monogamous life came to an end, and he began living like an Oriental sultan with the women in his harem. He had many wives and hundreds of concubines. And as he grew older, the girls he summoned were younger.

The doctor's anxieties increase

THE DOCTOR WAS QUITE anxious as he returned home through the deserted, cobblestone streets of the Muslim quarter. The newspapers didn't mention it, indeed they said the opposite, but from what he heard at the hospital and the news he received from the front, the war was going badly.

He sat at his desk, took out a sheet of writing paper, and began writing a love letter.

> It's difficult to believe, but the great empire we thought would last as long as the world is melting before our eyes like a sputtering candle. There's terrible news from the front. After Eastern Romelia, it seems as if we're completely withdrawing from the Balkans. We fear they may even take Thessaloniki. The Greek and Bulgarian armies are headed this way.

For the first time, he didn't feel like writing words of love to Melahat, and he left the letter unfinished. The visible collapse of the empire distressed him day and night. He even had trouble breathing. It was clear that these young, inexperienced committee members, who were becoming more thuggish, oppressive, and quick to shed blood, weren't up to the job of governing. He was angry at Enver, but he didn't have the courage to say this to anyone. His life would be in danger. If the sultan was telling the truth, he'd only had four or five people executed during his thirty-three year reign, and they were all monstrous murderers, but the number of people his friends were killing was much higher. They didn't question what they were doing. Unfortunately they were behaving like a gang of assassins. Since the old man had been overthrown, political factions had been tearing the empire apart. Governments could not hold together. The uprisings in the Balkans had caught them unprepared. Now the government of Gazi Muhtar Pasha had resigned. The liberal party, which opposed the committee, had won the elections, but the two parties continued to clash. Each saw the other party as a greater threat than the enemy. The army was also divided in two.

Perhaps more than two. The committee, the liberals, and the conservative officers, and the older and younger officers who tried to undermine each other. There's so much hatred in this country, everyone hates each other, everyone is trying to cut each other's throats. It was delusional to think that one man was responsible for this mess. But that wasn't the truth. The problems that raged after the man was overthrown revealed that perhaps hatred of him was the only thing these factions had in common.

The doctor was taken aback. Did this mean he was starting to think favorably about the dictator? Had his close contact at the Alatini mansion brought him to the point where his opinions were changing? If this was the case, he should be ashamed of having such a weak character. What about March 31, he thought. Hadn't the crafty old man organized the revolt of the reactionary soldiers that drenched Istanbul in blood? Every time he brought the subject up, the man would swear on everything sacred that he had no hand in this. The incident got out of hand because of the incompetence of the pashas. Otherwise, why would a rebellion be organized in the capital, and why would it be allowed to proceed? Was there any logic in this, for God's sake?

The doctor finished a cigarette and lit another one, then poured himself a healthy measure of Bulgarian brandy in the hope that it might ease his heartache. He heaved a deep sigh.

What was going to happen to the attractive, fascinating, cosmopolitan people of Thessaloniki?

A festival of severed hands—Islam learns from the West

WHEN THE DOCTOR WENT to the mansion the following day, he found the former sultan rested and carefully dressed. He was far from the state he'd been in the day before. Neither of them mentioned what had happened. It seemed best to forget it.

As they were drinking their coffee, the old man suddenly asked, "Are we at war? Doctor, please tell me the truth. Are we at war? I think I have the right to know at least this much."

The doctor said, "No. Where did you get this idea? Did someone say something?"

"No," said the sultan, "no one has said anything, but for some time now I've been sensing something. When I look out the window, I see the officers having heated discussions. The other day I saw one of them pointing to something on a map. And there's also...well..."

"Go ahead. There's also?"

"I don't know if I should tell you this. The other day, the pencils they brought for my son were wrapped in a scrap of newspaper. It was torn and crumbled, I couldn't make out much, but there was something about the state of the army, and the lack of weapons and ammunition. Then it occurred to me, perhaps we're at war."

"No, no, we're not at war. And even if we were, you know I don't have the authority to tell you. And we have a twenty-five-thousand-man army in Thessaloniki."

"Yes, I'm sure we do," said the sultan. He thought for a time. "Do you know, I'm terrified of war. Whether you win or lose, it wearies the people, drags the nation into misery, war is a terrible thing. Many have criticized me for taking this position, but none of them know what a disaster war is. I'm in favor of solving international problems through diplomacy. God help us if the new government goes to war..."

The sultan offered the doctor a cigarette. As they smoked, the old man leaned forward, looked into the doctor's eyes, and asked an unexpected question.

"Do you think I'm a murderer?"

The doctor was taken aback. "Excuse me, I don't understand."

"Am I the Red Sultan that was described in the foreign press, do I have blood on my hands? I see that even you hesitate to answer this. Among the countless slanders about me, two of them bother me a great deal. The first is the shaykh al-Islam's fatwa that I harmed

Islam and the Quran. Was I the kind of sultan to be deposed for this reason? They wouldn't have done this if they feared God."

The doctor fidgeted uneasily in his seat, he tried to interrupt what was turning into a monologue, but the old man raised his hand to silence him.

"Do you know the King of Belgium? Leopold II. Isn't he a civilized, European king? But do you know what this man did in the Congo? Of course not. The European press was busy depicting me covered in blood, but they said nothing about what this king did to the people of the Congo. Ten million people were killed in the Congo on the king's orders. Can you imagine that, ten million people, including women and children. Do you know what else they did? They cut off millions of people's hands. I've seen photographs. It's an unbelievable scene, it's heartbreaking to see children with no hands. I always avoided war and killing, but they called me the Red Sultan and they said Leopold was civilized. And what should we call the Russian tsar? He sent countless people to Siberia to die. But they tolerated this because he's Christian. I'm the only guilty one because I caused problems for the powers that were trying to tear the empire apart."

At this point the doctor raised his hand. "I understand you, but please allow me," he said. The sultan was not accustomed to being interrupted, and he gave the doctor a look of amazement, but he stopped talking.

"Excuse me, but you sent a great many people into exile, you broke up families. Some of them died in the wilderness. They never saw their homes again."

"Stop, stop for a moment. Yes, what you say is true. To deal with threats against myself and the state, I had to send a lot of people into exile. But I didn't seize their property or take their lives. Indeed, I paid salaries to people in exile, so they could live comfortably. Can this be compared to cutting off heads or hands? Please, answer me, are they the same thing?"

"Of course not," said the doctor in surprise. "Ten million people, you said. That's unimaginable."

"Of course, of course," said the sultan. "And he had thousands of severed hands brought to Belgium, to his palace. It seems he enjoyed looking at them."

"It really is unbelievable," said the doctor. "How could anyone do something like that?"

"Did I do anything even close to this? Did I?"

"No, you didn't."

"Then write this, tell people, for the love of God, I don't want people to have a false picture of me, tell them about what happens in foreign countries. I'm an old man on the verge of death. Before I surrender my soul, I need the truth to be known and to be remembered well."

"Please calm yourself, sir. This much excitement is not good for you."

"How can I be calm, doctor? How can I be calm? Do you think it's easy to be called a murderer when you haven't committed any crime? The Armenians call me a killer."

The doctor remembered an episode from his youth in Istanbul. Yes, as the man said, he'd pardoned the Armenian terrorists, but the next day Muslims, including Turks, Kurds, and Bosnians, broke down their Armenian neighbors' doors and killed everyone they found. It was a massacre.

But the doctor didn't want to bring this up and get into an argument with the man. It was clear he wanted to influence him and get him to write his defense.

"Look," continued the sultan, "I always treated my subjects well. I treated everyone equally, the way a father treats his children. I made a lot of Armenian families wealthy, all of our palaces and mansions were built by the Balyan family, there were Armenian ministers in my governments. The same goes for the Greeks. I loved Zarifi the money changer enough to address him as 'father,' Karatodori Pasha represented me at the Berlin Conference, and you already know about Musurus Pasha. There were many others. Ask the chief rabbi how I treated the Jews. Didn't I build a hospital for them on the Golden Horn? You're a doctor, you must know about it. I did this, but what did the European monarchs do? They exploited every corner of the world and traded in slaves."

The doctor was overwhelmed, the old man was acting as if he were defending himself in court, and it was getting to be too much. He waited for the man to pause to inhale from his cigarette, then jumped to his feet and hurriedly said, "Excuse me. I have to go; they're waiting for me at the hospital."

Reluctantly, the sultan said, "Fine. Good luck. I'll see you tomorrow."

The doctor had just reached the door when the man called out after him. "There's something I should say in order to be fair. Franz Joseph was different from the others. When I got sick in Vienna, he cared for me in his palace like a tender father for three weeks. I have to give him his due. Wait, wait a moment. It occurred to me a little while ago when I was talking about the hands. I can tell killers from their hands. Their hands are different. People whose thumb knuckles are longer than their index finger knuckles are prone to commit murder. That's why I always look at people's hands first."

The doctor heaved a deep sigh as soon as he was out in the garden. He was bored by so much talk about emperors, tsars, kings, and queens. The hospital was full of wounded soldiers, dark clouds were approaching Thessaloniki from the horizon.

Involuntarily he looked at his thumb. He hadn't committed murder himself, but he felt complicit in the murders he knew had been committed by committee members, and sometimes this weighed heavily on his conscience. No, this wasn't the thumb of a murderer.

He'd spent his childhood and youth in Istanbul under this man's rule. In the streets Albanians sold liver, Greeks sold fish, and Serbs sold milk and yogurt.

And the Armenian neighbors were always subjected to persecution.

There was a lot of movement on the streets of Thessaloniki. Military vehicles were coming and going, long-faced officers strode by without even noticing the soldiers who saluted them. There were so many wounded men in the hospital garden he could barely get through. Istanbul had no idea what it was doing. The great empire was paralyzed. As always, the newspapers were full of false news, they were trying to present the situation as much better than it was.

As he struggled with these dark thoughts, which had caused him a severe headache, he did not know that he would receive the most painful news of his life from the friends he would meet that evening.

As he went to the mansion the following day, his headache persisted despite the medications he'd taken. He wasn't at all in the mood to deal with the man that day, but he had no choice. The sultan's need to talk, to unburden himself, had become maddening, he never shut up. His conversations with the doctor had become an essential part of his daily routine, like the cold baths, walking for half an hour in the hall, prayers, cigarettes, and his two cups of coffee.

A night of love in Istanbul—Woman, have you no husband?

THE DOCTOR'S MIND WAS elsewhere that day, he was pensive, he only half listened to the man's constant chatter. The crafty sultan noticed the doctor's lack of interest and tried to catch his attention with a slight smile. "I'm going to tell you something today that's going to leave you completely surprised. It's a secret that no one knows." The doctor couldn't help feeling excited and curious. The sultan glanced around to make sure the chamberlains were not in the room, then leaned toward the doctor with a strange glint in his eyes and almost whispered, "What I'm going to tell you now doesn't have anything to do with politics. It involves a sultan and an empress, but it's a love story rather than a political story." A mischievous smile spread across his face, he knew he had the doctor's attention.

And he had, the doctor was waiting impatiently. The sultan lit another cigarette, and began speaking like a grandfather telling his grandchild a fairy tale. "In Paris I'd sensed that something was going on between my uncle and Eugénie, but I didn't know how far things had gone. A year after our trip, Eugénie came to Istanbul, and she came without her husband. She arrived on the yacht *Aigle* with her retinue. When my uncle received news that Eugénie was coming, he went all out for her. He had Beylerbeyi Palace readied for the empress. He had new tableware brought from Paris, he ordered hundreds of yards of expensive cloth, he had the palace chefs prepare beef tongue from Bulgaria, veal from Thrace, and tasty Bosphorus fish. The people of Istanbul were infected by the sultan's excitement, and they decorated the entire city for the empress. It was normal for royal families to visit each other, but this visit became the subject of gossip.

"The first interesting incident occurred at the reception at Dolmabahçe Palace. According to the traditions of European palaces, my uncle took Eugénie on his arm as they entered the palace. But his mother, Pertevniyal Hanım, separated them, and said, 'Woman, have you no husband?' It was a strange incident.

"Then one day my uncle went to Beylerbeyi Palace secretly, without his entourage, and returned in the morning looking tired and worn out. There are those who swear they saw this with their own eyes, but I don't know what to say. The people of Istanbul began talking about the sultan's love affair."

The possibility that these rumors were true excited the doctor, because what he knew, and the sultan didn't, was that Eugénie had visited Istanbul that year,

forty-two years after her initial visit, that she'd visited
Beylerbeyi Palace to refresh her memories and to meet
the late sultan's son.

Now the sultan was talking about a meeting that
was held after their return from Europe. The grand vizier, the ministers, and the shaykh al-Islam were present; they talked about the trip to Europe, about how
much more advanced Europe was, and that the empire needed to pull itself together and follow the European example. After what they'd seen, no one could
deny this. They were very impressed that in Europe,
men and women worked together. They couldn't get
the illuminated buildings, trains, and factories out of
their minds. At one point Ömer Faiz Efendi turned to
the shaykh al-Islam and said, "Sir, we're even going to
have to learn about Islam from the Europeans," then
explained that, "They behave in accordance with the
proper Islam we were taught, but we've become cor-
rupted, we have to start from the beginning again
and learn from them." He'd said this half in jest, but a
cloud of melancholy descended on the gathering.

The doctor sensed that the sultan was telling him
this to illustrate the disastrous state of the empire he'd
inherited.

Had he sensed something? Even though he had no
contact with the outside world he seemed to know, it
was as if he felt he had to hurry to say what he wanted
to say because time was running out and he needed
to justify himself. The doctor didn't know if he was
angry at the man or if he felt sorry for him, because

somehow he couldn't give him his full attention. Despite this, he was getting the distinct impression that the sultan who'd been known as a Pan-Islamist was in fact an admirer of European civilization. What a strange situation this was. He'd even gone so far as to say that we needed to learn about Islam from Europe.

After he left the mansion the doctor decided to walk along the shore a bit to clear his mind. The officers and guards in the garden were becoming increasingly uneasy. Small groups of officers were standing about whispering; they stopped talking and saluted when he passed, then continued talking. It was the end of October, the weather was cooler, and there was a stiff breeze from the sea.

The doctor went out the garden gate and started walking toward the Alatini factory. When he reached the shore he saw a beautiful two-masted white steamer at anchor, it must have been about sixty meters long. It was called the *Loreley*. It looked German-made. *So this must be a German observation ship. What is it doing in Thessaloniki in wartime?*

A surprising order in the middle of the night

ONLY GOD KNOWS WHY they chose to convey the order from the sultan to the former sultan in the middle of the night. Perhaps it was due to the complicated rules of military bureaucracy, or perhaps it was due to the confusion—stupefaction according to the doctor's diagnosis—into which the general command had descended. Whatever the reason, officers came to the mansion after everyone was in bed and asked that the former sultan be summoned. The doctor was glad that he had been called as well because he was anxious about his patient.

The chamberlains summoned the sultan, and he entered the hall in a solemn manner. With the aid of his cane he walked to the middle of the room. He exhibited no panic or fear. The doctor remembered how he'd bragged about his calm in the face of grave danger. This meant that he felt he was once again in danger.

The high-ranking officers greeted him as "Your Illustrious Highness." Abdülhamid said, "What's going on? What emergency brings you here in the middle of the night?"

At that moment the doctor realized that the old man's calm was the result of his helplessness in the face of death. After seeing him every day for three and a half years, he knew the sultan well enough to realize that, faced with the certainty of death, and knowing there was nothing to do, he had adopted the calm, dignified manner of an emperor. The doctor paid attention to every detail so as not to miss a second of this historic event.

The commander of the Vardar Army addressed the sultan in a respectful tone, "Your Illustrious Highness, we have received orders to bring you to Istanbul."

The doctor saw that Abdülhamid was shaken by this.

"What? To Istanbul? Why? Whatever you're going to do to me you can do here."

"It is an imperial decree," said the pasha.

"What's the reason for this decree? I've been settled in this mansion for three and a half years. My family is here. I have no intention of going to Istanbul."

"But it would be dangerous for you to stay here."

"How is it dangerous?"

The officers glanced at each other uneasily.

"I go calmly about my life surrounded by a division of soldiers. What danger could I possibly be in?"

Then the doctor understood the situation. They were going to tell the former sultan that the empire had lost the Balkans, that the Greek and Bulgarian armies were marching toward Thessaloniki, that the Bulgarian army had surrounded Edirne, and that the railway line between Thessaloniki and Istanbul had been cut. After living three and a half years in a dream world, unaware of what was going on, this was going to be a heavy blow. The doctor thought about what he would do if the man fainted.

The old man didn't faint, but his eyes opened wide in astonishment, his face went white, and his hands were trembling. "What are you saying? How could this be?"

The pashas said nothing.

"I worked hard to make the Third Army an elite force. I provided for everything. What happened to our army? Aren't they fighting the enemy?"

An elderly pasha with a chest full of medals said, "We're at war, sir. We're fighting, but we're facing more than one army."

"You mean you're losing. Which armies are these? I defeated the Greek army in thirty hours. Why can't you?"

"At that time the Balkan states were divided, Your Illustrious Highness."

"And they aren't now?"

"Unfortunately."

"Which armies are headed here?"

"The Greek and Bulgarian armies. There are the Serbs too, but mostly the first two."

"How could this be? When did these countries stop fighting each other? There's no chance they could agree about anything. Then this is...this is due to inept politics—" He stopped speaking suddenly but everyone knew what he wanted to say. During his long years in power he had always applied the principal of "divide and rule," he wanted to point out the incompetence of the new government and the brother who had succeeded him, but he preferred to be cautious and remain silent.

He gripped the handle of his cane with both hands and in the tone of a haughty emperor said, "I'm not going anywhere. I'm going to stay in Thessaloniki."

"But the enemy is about to enter the city. We can already hear cannon fire."

"From which front?"

"Karaferye."

"Then why can't I hear it? I don't hear any cannon fire."

The doctor was going to say, "Because you're hard of hearing," but he contained himself.

"Even if that's so," said the old man, "I should stay and defend this city that I inherited from my ancestors. Give me a rifle."

"Sir, how could we do that?"

"Just give me a rifle, I say, give me a rifle." His back seemed to become straighter and his voice deeper, and like a commander trying to sum up the situation he asked, "Pasha, how close are these armies?"

"A few days away."

"Which army is closest?"

"The Greek army is closest, sir."

"Who's the commander in Thessaloniki at the moment?"

"Hasan Tahsin Pasha, sir."

"Ha, the Albanian. Tell him to come talk to me. Since there are two armies, we should resist the first army, then when the other arrives we can get the Greek and Bulgarian armies to fight each other."

The doctor saw the change in the man he knew so well, the gravitas in his stance and his voice, and thought to himself, *So this is what an emperor is like. This is a different man. That whining invalid is gone.*

The pashas were overwhelmed by the threat of the approaching enemy, the three main battle groups had lost contact with one another, and they'd lost all confidence. They knew that this man who was talking to them as if he were sultan had many years of experience and that all he wanted was to apply the right military strategy. If the city held out for a few days they could have the two enemy armies facing each other, but it was not within their authority to make this decision. Only the minister of war or Hasan Tahsin Pasha could make this decision, but they were unable to communicate with Istanbul. All communications had been cut. They'd been left to face their destiny alone.

Meanwhile, the sultan started shouting, "No one should think of saving themselves by surrendering Thessaloniki. If Thessaloniki, falls Istanbul will fall."

He banged his cane on the floor three times. "I'm saying this here. Remember it. If Thessaloniki falls, Istanbul will fall!"

There was a long silence. The pashas squirmed under Abdülhamid's piercing gaze. Then they pulled themselves together and realized that the sultan who was rebuking them had no authority. Even if what he said made sense, he was a former sultan, he was under house arrest, and they'd been ordered to send him to Istanbul.

"Sir," they said, "our orders are to send you to Istanbul. This is an imperial decree."

But no matter how they tried, they could not get past the sultan's obstinacy. The pashas left, and to his complete surprise, his son-in-law and Abdülaziz's son-in-law entered the room. Both of them bowed and kissed Sultan Hamid's hand, and he embraced the unexpected guests.

"This is a surprise, I wasn't expecting you," he said. "If the rail line to Istanbul is cut, how did you get here?"

"We came by sea, Your Illustrious Highness," said one of them. "This region is dangerous, as you know, it's a war zone. We asked Emperor Wilhelm for assistance in getting you safely back to Istanbul. Out of friendship for you he sent the yacht *Loreley*. We came to get you."

Just then the doctor saw a brief glint in the former sultan's eyes. It was only a momentary flash. He knew the man well enough to realize that he suddenly had hope there might be a chance to return to power. He was certain the man thought that his brother might be deposed for his incompetence, and that he might be invited to take back the throne so the government could benefit from his experience. It could happen. Everything depended on God's discretion.

Preparations to withdraw from Thessaloniki

THE DOCTOR'S FRIENDS WERE sitting in the Olympos, the atmosphere was palpably melancholy, they sat slumped forward, calmly sipping their drinks, talking about the bad news in low voices. There were no musicians on the stage, the party was over. All of the taverns, restaurants, shops, and even homes were shrouded in silence and the darkness of mourning. As if a black cloth covered the once cheerful city. The streets, avenues, and squares were empty. People closed themselves in their homes as the cannon fire drew closer. The soldiers and officers didn't know what to do, they didn't know how they were going to receive orders from above.

"I don't understand," Major Saffet was saying. "I don't understand what's going on. What are we doing here? Why aren't we with the units that are fighting, why are we sitting on our thumbs here as if we don't know what's coming?"

"Nobody understands," said Nihat. "I don't think anything like this has ever happened before."

"Hold on. The doctor is going to come from the meeting at the White Tower. He'll tell us what's going on."

"What's going on at the White Tower?"

"The city's leadership has gathered. The governor and the military commander, Jewish, Greek, and Turkish businessmen, factory and hotel owners. The local elites."

"It's as if they put sleeping medication in the drinking water, or the entire population was bitten by tsetse flies. Everyone seems half asleep."

"What can we do, brother? We follow orders. In the army you can't act on your own initiative."

"I wonder if they've decided to give Thessaloniki up."

"Who could even countenance such treachery?"

"I don't know, but this silence is going to drive all of us crazy."

"Did you see the *Loreley*? They say it's here to get Abdülhamid."

"Why is a German ship coming for him? Don't we have any ships left?"

"The Greek navy controls the seas, Ottoman ships can't get through, the Bulgarians have taken Bük Station, which means the main road has been cut. We're under siege from the land and the sea."

"How the hell did it come to this? I can't even take it all in, sometimes I think I'm dreaming. According to an officer who returned from leave before the road was closed, Istanbul is completely preoccupied with the struggle between the liberals and the committee. It's as if the committee wants the enemy to win in order to undermine the liberal government. The commander in chief Nazım Pasha has lost contact with some of the armies. There are contradictory reports. There's a lot of confusion. Both the Eastern Army and the Western Army are retreating in the face of the enemy."

"Politics is finishing the empire off. These internal conflicts...If only they hated the enemy as much as they hate each other. You can even see it here, can we agree with all of the officers? The liberal officers are hostile to us."

The officers' conversation was punctuated by deep silences, during which they gazed into the distance or at the tablecloth.

They were waiting for the news the doctor would bring. He knew what was happening in the mansion, and he'd been at the meeting in the White Tower.

However, what the doctor told them when he arrived caused them even more distress, indeed it made them lose hope. The unthinkable was happening, they were going to surrender Thessaloniki. Representatives of the Jewish community, which made up more than half of the population, were against the destruction of the city. Naturally the Greek community thought the same thing, and were pressuring the commander to surrender to the Greek army. According to what had been said at the meeting, the Ottoman fleet couldn't even set sail, the land forces were in a state of confusion, and Edirne was on the point of falling. The officers didn't even know what to say. Thessaloniki had become a helpless island, besieged on all sides. The Greek army could enter the city at any moment.

The conversation turned to Abdülhamid. Had the *Loreley* really come to get him?

The doctor gave them some more surprising news. He told them about how the former sultan had resisted returning to Istanbul, and how he'd said, "Give me a rifle. It's my right to defend my ancestral lands, you can't stop me." His son-in-law came from the palace to convince him. The commander of the Vardar Army was there as well. They were all very respectful to him, as if he were still sultan. And the man began behaving as if he were a powerful emperor.

"But the real issue is even more important," said the doctor. "I still hate his tyranny and his regime of fear, but I have to give him his due. Don't be angry with me. He's an old man who's been isolated in the mansion without any idea of what was going on, when he first heard the news it was a heavy blow, at first he was almost in panic. Indeed he was on the point of collapse. But he pulled himself together within a few minutes, asked about the military situation, then told the pasha the correct military strategy as if he was giving an order. 'I'm not asking you to resist indefinitely, I want you to hold the Greek army off until the Bulgarians and the Serbs get here. They'll start fighting over who's going to take the city, and we can take advantage of this.'"

Saffet said, "By God, that's right. That's the only possible plan. That was his tactic for years. Getting the hunters to go after each other prolongs the prey's life."

"So, what did the pasha say to this?"

"He said he was going to carry out the sultan's orders, and those orders were to transport him to Istanbul, anything else was beyond his authority."

The officers were dismayed. What they were all thinking but couldn't admit to one another was that the army that had carried out 1908 Revolution had been overcome by arrogance. After this great victory, the general command thought the world had been laid at their feet, that they were above everyone and everything, and with the imprudence of youth had neglected military discipline and training. They didn't even think about military uniforms and rations. The communications network had broken down, the relationship between officers and men had been damaged, and political goals had taken precedence over military goals. They couldn't recover from the intoxication of victory and perform their duties as soldiers. It was clear that they enjoyed politics. Perhaps it was the ancient imperial city of Istanbul that did this to people. After all, it was a continuation of Byzantium.

The three officers remembered what the young captain had said at the congress. Unfortunately he'd been right.

That evening as he made his way home, the doctor couldn't decide if he'd seen contempt in the eyes of the

Greek waiter who'd always served them so graciously, or whether his miserable mood created this impression. He decided he would never step foot in that place again. Then he laughed bitterly when he realized he didn't have a choice in the matter. He supposed he would be heading back to Istanbul.

Sometimes strange ideas popped into the doctor's mind. *We conquered so many lands and peoples, we dominated them by force, now we say we've lost them but they were never ours to begin with. We don't speak the same language and we don't have the same religion.*

When he got home he tried to console himself by taking out his little notebook to record the historical event he'd witnessed. He had been so overwhelmed by events that he hadn't been able to write love letters for some time. But if he returned to Istanbul, the first thing he would do was to search for Melahat Hanım.

The miracle of Istanbul

ISTANBUL AND THESSALONIKI HAD different smells. There was sea there too, but the currents of the Bosphorus, the winds, and the local fish gave this city its own seductive smell. Now the sultan drew in this smell through his wide nostrils. To be back in Istanbul after so long. In the city of the world's desire. The *Loreley* passed his ancestors' palace and entered the Bosphorus to the deafening cheers of the crowds that had gathered on both shores. "Long live the sultan! Long live the sultan!" What a sweet echo this was, what a heartfelt welcome. They were welcoming the sultan they'd bundled onto a train in the middle of the night three and a half years earlier to be locked up and insulted like a common criminal. The people trusted him, they believed he would save this empire that had been beset by disaster and attacked by enemy armies, they knew that he would save them from his incompetent brother and those revolutionary rogues. The white steamer was flying the imperial flag, and a cannon salute was fired as it approached the palace. The German captain and his crew stood at attention. A band began to play the "Hamidiye March," which had been composed for him by Necip Pasha.

The palace quay was lined with dignitaries. Precious carpets had been spread on the ground, and the grand vizier, ministers, members of parliament, the shaykh al-Islam, the Greek patriarch, the chief rabbi, the Armenian patriarch, and ambassadors were waiting for God's shadow on earth. They clasped their hands and bowed their heads, because no one could look directly into the emperor's eyes. As he took his first step in Istanbul he felt he was finally in his rightful place after so much suffering. He thanked his Creator for allowing him to see this day.

The dignitaries parted for him as he made his way proudly toward the palace. The crowds gathered on the shore waved flags and wept tears of excitement. Their father had finally returned.

As the crowd parted, he could see Kaiser Wilhelm, dressed in white and looking like a Teutonic knight, approaching him with his arms open. *So the kaiser is here*, he thought. *What happiness after the misery of exile.*

He heard his chamberlain Şöhrettin Ağa's voice in the distance. What was he doing there? The voice keeps calling to him. It kept getting louder, almost drowning out the band. The sultan was angry. "How dare you interrupt the march!"

"Please pull yourself together. You're safe, my sultan, please pull yourself together."

The sound of the band began to fade.

He could smell senna, and he heard Şöhrettin say, "Look, I've brought senna tea, it will calm your nerves. Please drink it my sultan."

Leaving the mansion—Farewell Thessaloniki

WHEN ABDÜLHAMID II STEPPED foot outside the Alatini mansion for the first time in three and a half years, he stopped and leaned on his cane for a moment. He breathed in the fresh, cool autumn air. He took a long look at the garden, the trees, the officers and the soldiers, and the landau carriages that waited at the bottom of the marble steps. As if he wanted to say farewell to everything and everyone. He was leaving Thessaloniki, but he hadn't seen anything of the city. He'd been brought here in a carriage in the middle of the night, and now a carriage was going to take him to the steamship.

Thessaloniki was silent, it had been waiting for this moment. As the *Loreley* sailed away, there was a long blast from its whistle, as if it was bidding farewell not just to the city but to five hundred years of Ottoman rule.

The *Loreley* was sitting offshore, as graceful as a swan, and the ship's captain and guards had come ashore to meet him. The sight of them standing so respectfully in dress uniforms reinforced the sense of hope that had been rising within him.

The governor of Thessaloniki, the commanders of the Third and Vardar Armies, the German consul, and the city's leading citizens had come to bid him farewell. The doctor stood slightly to the rear, watching this farewell ceremony with mixed emotions.

As the captain read Kaiser Wilhelm's message welcoming him aboard, the sultan felt a kind of happiness he hadn't felt since he was deposed. He gave a proud salute to thank His Imperial Highness.

The sultan and his retinue of about thirty people boarded the launches that would take them to the *Loreley*. Everything aboard the ship was perfect, they had taken pains with his food, and had provided places for him to pray and to rest; the German discipline he so admired was evident in every detail. The starboard side of the boat was set aside for the sultan, and the port side for the family. The sultan ate his first dinner aboard with the captain. Once again, he thanked the kaiser.

The only thing that distressed him was the captain's reminder that they would be sailing among hostile ships, that His Majesty should keep mostly to his cabin and not go on deck without informing him and that his family should avoid revealing their presence on the ship at checkpoints. This meant his life of imprisonment had not yet ended, and he wondered what was awaiting him in Istanbul.

The only thing that cheered him slightly was his son's excitement and delight at being aboard a ship for the first time.

When the steamer got underway, the boy shouted, "We're going, we're going, we're sliding across the water." This delighted the sultan, but a moment later he murmured, "Who knows where we're going, my dear boy."

That night he was thankful for the precautions his brother the sultan and the government in Istanbul had taken to keep him from falling into enemy hands. Because if he was captured, he would most likely be killed. They'd taken a big risk putting him on a German ship. If Abdülhamid had changed his mind and informed his old friend Wilhelm that he wished to go to Germany, the *Loreley* would change course for Hamburg and the sultan could live as a free man. Or politicians loyal to him could launch a struggle in his name. But what if the throne was waiting for him in Istanbul, what if fortune was going to smile on him once again?

He looked up at the mahogany ceiling, thought about Mithat Pasha and pictured him in the dungeon in Yemen.

"Yes, pasha," he said, "I would rather your life hadn't ended that way, but you put pressure on me and tried to run the state. You were intelligent but you couldn't curb your passions. Any monarch in my place would have made the same decision."

Then he realized why he'd thought of the pasha now, and said, "Besides, don't think I didn't know how loyal you were to the English."

By chance the weather was good, there was no wind and the sea was calm, and they had a comfortable journey. They signaled whenever they saw a Greek warship, and the sultan and his family had to hide in their cabins. According to the ship's manifest, the *Loreley* had brought Red Cross supplies from Istanbul to Thessaloniki, and now it was returning. Since the ship belonged to the German embassy, everyone had to accept this explanation. As they were passing a Greek checkpoint before entering the Dardanelles, they saw the battleship *Averof* approaching. The captain immediately ordered the sultan and his family to retire to their cabins. They waited with bated breath as they passed close enough to be boarded. But now there were no more obstacles between them and Istanbul.

As they crossed the Sea of Marmara, the sultan grew increasingly excited. On the last night he called Lieutenant Salif Efendi and tried to get him to talk, but all he would say was, "Soon they'll have meetings with the great powers." This wasn't enough to calm the former sultan, who was swinging from hope to despair, from fear to courage, and from melancholy to cheer. Then he had one of his nights of terror, when he saw traps, danger, and treachery everywhere, and became convinced he would be done away with the moment he reached Istanbul. They would put him in a rowboat and then sink it. What could be easier than sending this rowboat into the path of another ship? It could easily be passed off as an accident, it would be enough to tell his brother the sultan how sorry they were. When he became certain this was the plan, he called Şerif Pasha to his cabin and told him he would not get off the boat if they arrived at night. They had to arrive in Istanbul in the daytime, he would not get off the ship in the dark. Şerif Pasha informed Istanbul of the sultan's decision.

The restless sultan sat by the porthole all night. With the first light of morning he relaxed a bit, but by noon the uncertainty about his fate began to oppress him again.

The *Loreley* stopped near Leander's Tower, and soon a launch sped toward it. Was it carrying representatives of the government or members of the dynasty, were they coming to greet him?

When the launch was close enough for him to see that it was carrying the commander of the Istanbul Guards and his aide, the sultan realized that he was going to spend the rest of his life in captivity, and that fortune had not smiled on him.

The commander who climbed onto the deck was deaf, and his aide had to repeat everything that was said.

"By imperial decree I have been ordered to bring you to Beylerbeyi Palace," said the commander.

Abdülhamid resisted going to this palace he'd always hated, where as a child he'd watched his mother waste away from tuberculosis, and from the damp and the ice-cold wind. "Bring me to Çirağan Palace, please bring me to Çirağan Palace. Convey my greetings to my brother and ask him to reconsider this order." The pasha gave him a mocking smile and said, "Oh, that's too bad. Çirağan no longer exists. It burned to the ground. Only owls live there now."

The pasha's words were an alarm bell for the former sultan, he knew now that Istanbul, the empire, and the dynasty had changed forever, that this new world cared nothing about him, and that personal ambitions had blinded them to the powder keg they were sitting on. So the wonderful palace that his grandfather and father had commissioned Balyan to build, and that he had hung with a private collection of paintings that included works by Rembrandt and Aivazovsky, was gone, and the commander of the Istanbul Guard was telling him this with a defiant smile.

The steam launch brought the sultan to Beylerbeyi Palace, where stern officers and a squadron of soldiers awaited him on the quay. As soon as he saw the columns of that ill-omened palace, Sultan Hamid felt as if he'd received a blow to the stomach. He could feel the stiff muscles of the tiger that had been asleep for so long he'd almost forgotten it existed, the beast was beginning to wake. He'd thought he'd escaped the tiger when he was deposed, that as a forgotten former sultan anchored in a calm harbor he was out of danger. But unfortunately that magnificent, tyrannical creature was awake.

As Sultan Hamid approached the marble palace, he shivered as he intuited that this was where he would dismount from the tiger, then for a moment he thought he saw the shadow of a thin Circassian girl. Whether you're a shah or a sultan, you can never be free from the pain of being orphaned.

"We're finally going to meet, mother," he whispered, "we're finally going to meet."

Historical Figures in *On the Back of the Tiger*

SULTAN ABDÜLHAMID II

He ascended to the throne during the Ottoman Empire's most difficult period. His profile as sultan was different from that of his predecessors. He was not much interested in poetry and calligraphy, and engaged in fine carpentry and wood carving. He was known for his interest in books, opera, and music. After thirty-three years on the throne, he was deposed and exiled to Thessaloniki in 1909. In 1912 he was brought to Beylerbeyi Palace in Istanbul. He died on February 10, 1918. Large crowds attended his funeral and he was buried in his grandfather Mahmud II's tomb.

His Wives

Müşfika Hanım

She was with Abdülhamid II when he died. When the imperial family was exiled, she remained in Istanbul. Before she died she wrote to Prime Minister Adnan Menderes, asking that the allowance granted her by the İnönü government be increased. Müşfika Hanım died on July 17, 1961, and was buried in the tomb of Yahya Efendi.

Saliha Naciye Hanım

She was prince Mehmed Abid Efendi's mother. She and her son remained with Abdülhamid II during his exile, and later moved to Beylerbeyi Palace with the sultan. After the sultan's death she lived in her mansion in Erenköy. She passed away a month before the imperial family was exiled and was buried in Mahmud II's tomb.

Fatma Pesend Hanım

She accompanied Sultan Abdülhamid when he was exiled to Thessaloniki, but she returned to Istanbul a year later to live in her waterfront mansion in Vaniköy. She was ill when the imperial family was exiled, and died eight months later on November 5, 1925. She was buried in the Karacaahmet Cemetery.

Sazkâr Hanım

She was Refia Sultan's mother. She and her daughter went into exile with Abdülhamid II, but they returned to Istanbul a year later. She and another wife of the sultan, Peyveste Hanım, moved into a mansion in Şişli. When the imperial family was exiled in 1924, she and her daughter moved to Beirut. She died in 1945 and was buried in the Sultan Selim Mosque in Damascus.

Peyveste Hanım

She was the mother of Prince Abdürrahim Hayri Efendi. She and her son joined Abdülhamid II in exile, but they returned to Istanbul a year later. She lived in Istanbul until the imperial family was exiled, after which she lived in Paris with her son until she died in 1944. She was buried in the Muslim Cemetery.

His Daughters

Ayşe Sultan

She joined her father, Abdülhamid II, in exile. A year later she returned to Istanbul, and in 1924 was exiled with the rest of the imperial family. She lived in Paris for twenty-eight years and died on August 10, 1960. She was buried in the tomb of Yahya Efendi. Before her death, her memoirs, titled *My Father Sultan Abdülhamid*, were published and became an important source concerning the life of the imperial family.

Şadiye Sultan

She joined her father, Abdülhamid II, in exile. After her return to Istanbul, she went to France in 1924 when the imperial family was exiled. She returned to her homeland in 1953. She moved into an apartment in Cihangir and lived there until her death at the age of ninety on November 20, 1977. She was buried in the tomb of Mahmud II.

Refia Sultan

She joined her father, Abdülhamid II, when he was exiled to Thessaloniki. She returned to Istanbul with her siblings after nearly a year in exile. She went to France in 1924 when the imperial family was exiled, and later moved to Beirut. She died in 1938 at the age of forty-seven. She was buried in the Sultan Selim Mosque in Damascus.

His Sons

Mehmed Abid Efendi

Abdülhamid II's youngest son. He was four years old when his father was exiled to Thessaloniki. When he returned to Istanbul he continued to live with his father in Beylerbeyi Palace. Then he received a military education and became an officer. He was exiled with the rest of the imperial family in 1924. He died in Beirut on December 8, 1973. He was buried in the Sultan Selim Mosque in Damascus.

Abdürrahim Hayri Efendi

He was with his father, Abdülhamid II, during his exile in Thessaloniki. After nearly a year he returned to Istanbul. He was exiled with the rest of the imperial family in 1924, and went to Vienna. Later he lived in various places such as Cairo and Rome. On January 1, 1952, he killed himself in a hotel in Paris with an overdose of morphine.

Mehmed Abdülkadir Efendi

He was not among the princes who accompanied his father, Abdülhamid, in exile in Thessaloniki. He was known in Ottoman history as the Socialist Prince. He opposed his father's political views and kept his distance from him. When the imperial family was exiled in 1924, he went to Bulgaria. On the journey there, his infant child died. This was the first death in the imperial family after it was exiled. Later he made his living playing the violin in Budapest. When he returned to Sofia on account of World War II, the King of Bulgaria, who had known his grandfather, gave him a job with the municipality. He died on March 16, 1944.

The Dynasty

Murad V

He became an admirer of Europe during his trip there with his uncle Sultan Abdülaziz. He established particularly close ties with the British Empire. After Sultan Abdülaziz was murdered, his mental health deteriorated. He ruled for ninety-three days.

Mehmed V Reşad

He ascended to the throne after Abdülhamid was deposed. Due to his age and inexperience, he left the administration to officers from the Committee of Union and Progress. His nine-year reign ended when he died of heart failure in 1918.

Others

Doctor Atıf Hüseyin

He was given responsibility for the medical needs of Sultan Abdülhamid and his family during their exile. Not much is known about his life. He kept a diary about Abdülhamid throughout his years in exile. These twelve notebooks constitute an important resource about this period. After Abdülhamid returned to Istanbul, Atıf Hüseyin continued to supervise his medical care until his death. He never married. He died at a young age.

Ali Fethi (Okyar)

He was a prominent figure in the Committee for Union and Progress. He was given responsibility for moving Abdülhamid and his family to Thessaloniki, and became the first commander of the unit that guarded them there. He served as a member of parliament and the speaker of parliament in the newly founded republic; from 1923 to 1924 he served as the speaker of the Grand National Assembly of Turkey, and in 1924 he was elected as deputy prime minister. He was respected for his moderate and rational personality. Atatürk personally gave him the surname "Okyar." He died in his home in Nişantaşı, Istanbul, on May 7, 1943, and was buried in the Zincirliküyü Cemetery.

Queen Victoria

Her reign of sixty-three years was longer than that of any previous monarch of the United Kingdom. She married her first cousin Prince Albert. They had nine children. The most significant event of her reign was the Crimean War (1854–1856) in which the United Kingdom joined forces with France and the Ottoman Empire against Russia. Many of Europe's monarchs were related to Queen Victoria. She died on February 4, 1901.

Arthur Conan Doyle

Arthur Conan Doyle was an English writer best known for his stories about the fictional detective Sherlock Holmes. Abdülhamid II admired these stories. After his second marriage Conan Doyle came to Istanbul for his honeymoon, and asked for an audience with Abdülhamid II. The meeting never took place, but the sultan granted him the Order of the Mecidiye.

Pasteur Efendi

Abdülhamid II followed Pasteur's work closely. He sent Ottoman scientists to learn about bacteriology from him. He donated ten thousand franks to Pasteur's institute, and awarded him the Order of the Mecidiye.

Zarifi the money changer

He was a well-known figure in the Galata stock exchange. During Sultan Abdülhamid's time he helped the Ottoman dynasty pay its debts. Sultan Abdülhamid also consulted him about business matters.

Musurus Pasha

Constantine Musurus, an Ottoman Greek, served as the Ottoman ambassador in London for thirty-five years. A distinguished diplomat, Musurus also translated Dante's *Divine Comedy* into Greek. His granddaughter Anna de Noailles became a famous poet in France, and Marcel Proust described her as "possessing the spirit of kindness and a high sense of morality." Countess Anna de Noailles holds a significant place in the history of French literature.

Empress Eugénie

In 1867, Sultan Abdülaziz and his nephews were invited to Paris by Napoleon III. This was the first visit by an Ottoman sultan to a foreign country. Napoleon III's wife greeted these visitors. It is said that Sultan Abdülaziz was quite taken by Eugénie, and when she visited Istanbul a year later he went to great lengths to welcome her.

Napoleon III

Napoleon III served as the president of France from 1848 to 1852; afterward he staged a coup, overthrew the republic, and proclaimed himself emperor, ruling until 1870. He was overthrown and exiled in 1870 when the Third French Republic was proclaimed. He died on May 5, 1871.